MURDER

THROUGH THE WINDOW

MURDER
THROUGH THE WINDOW

FRANCIS EVERTON

COACHWHIP PUBLICATIONS

Greenville, Ohio

Murder Through the Window, by Francis Everton
© 2026 Coachwhip Publications edition

First published 1930
Also published as *Murder at Plenders*
Francis William Stokes, 1883-1956
CoachwhipBooks.com

ISBN 1-61646-632-4
ISBN-13 978-1-61646-632-9

1

CHERRY HAY

A trout rose from the reed-fringed upper pool—a slash of dappled silver shot the sunlight—rippled rings broke reflected heaven blue—there was a cool, pleasant plop—then summery silence. Below the weir and through the trees, the middle pool, over which dragon-flies hovered and darted like jewels escaping from show-case velvet, lay stagnant and still beneath its covering sheet of sage green weed. Below yet another little weir a third pool lay like a mirror amidst the shady trees, and lower still, Cherry Hay, in its sheltered garden.

From this bottom pool, the water dropped ten clear feet through a tangle of climbing roses to fill the quiet garden with the gentle music of its soothing splash. The clear tinkling stream slipped slowly on, now through close-packed clumps of aromatic yellow musk, now between some stepping stones, then beneath the low arch of a little bridge and so to Plenders Priory lake a couple of miles beyond it.

The old house stood sideways to the garden; purple honey-scented buddleias clung precariously against its mellow red brick walls; a gravel path, then an unkempt sloping lawn, separated it from the stream. And across the stream, where tall mullein, a few straggling delphiniums, some vigorous but obviously uncared-for bush roses, and other garden flowers pushed valiantly through a tangled

net of choking grass and weeds to vie with the kingfisher
when he came flaunting his colors from underneath the
bridge, the garden sloped again to face the house.

A sleek starling practiced unheard music on one of the
quaint old chimney stacks. Rooks flapped lazily round
neighboring trees. And down-stream, down the valley,
among more distant trees, the gray stone of Plenders Priory stable buildings could just be seen. Wooded slopes and
sweet green spaces ringed the garden and the house.

Cherry Hay—ancient and added to—old red walls
creeper-clad—by blending her sounds and her scents—by
some subtle trick of color and contour and line—nature
had contrived a perfect place of quiet peace.

A smile flickered across Bernard Corrie's tired face. He removed his spectacles from the bridge of his long thin nose
and wiped them with deliberation.

"Paradise—perfection—peace in our time, O Lord," he
murmured softly to himself.

The fair slim girl at his side looked up at him with an
affectionate smile.

"Oh, Daddy, it's a dream," she said; "don't talk, or else
I'll wake."

2
PLENDERS PRIORY

Alighting from the dirty little local train which had brought him with so many halts and hesitations from Blatchford, George Annesley, disgusted, peered into the gloom of Millingham's cavernous station.

It was the late afternoon of a certain Wednesday in January, and the feeble lamps along the station platform seemed only to succeed in showing how dark the remoter corners of the station were. Smoke drifted across the panels of evening gray at the open station ends. Rain beat a steady tattoo on the smoke-grimed glass and corrugated iron roof. For the hundredth time Annesley wished himself back in Berlin.

On the Monday of the same week George had received a telegram from a London firm of solicitors informing him that he was heir to the Plenders Priory estates, and from the moment when he received the elevating message, a succession of depressions had swept over him, to culminate in the tedious journey from Blatchford to Millingham and that final depression of Millingham's filthy station.

On receiving the wire, he had spent a period of unhappy hesitation, for him quite unwonted, now deciding that he would wire, then he would not, to his uncle, Sir Victor Grahame of Scotland Yard, asking for the cancellation of the arrangement which, some nine months earlier, had sent him to Germany.

Deciding at length to leave the matter in abeyance until he could see his uncle, Annesley, feeling that he had made a mess of things, had caught the night boat.

The crossing had been a rough one and quite indisputably he had made a mess of the journey: the depressions and upheavals had been more than merely maritime. Then, still feeling feeble after his efforts to retain some small fragments of his own inside, George had held that devastating interview with the solicitor who had sent him the wire.

Quite naturally he had been making assessments and calculations. At the age of twelve he had spent an unforgettable month at Plenders Priory. Vaguely he remembered the long, twisting drive through the forest trees, remembered the massed rhododendrons that flanked it on either side, remembered the lake, the great stable buildings, the wide extent of the estate, and he had come to the conclusion that it could not, by any contraction of the imagination, be worth less than—well, it was a figure involving quite a number of noughts and even some commas.

But after five minutes with the London solicitor, the noughts began to hold a new significance, and the commas dwindled to one comma, which moved steadily left, curled up its tail and became remarkably like a decimal dot. For a time George simply could not understand it. It dazed him. But ultimately he began to realize that the legacy which had brought him post-haste from duty in Berlin, consisted almost entirely of death duties, and that he had become the unfortunate possessor of his predecessor's overdraft.

"You see—er—there have been an unfortunate succession of deaths in the family since old Colonel Annesley's time," the solicitor told him. "Three in four years, in fact," he added, gazing pensively out of the window at a chimney pot.

Annesley had nodded his complete agreement with the statement: his relationship with old Colonel Annesley had been so nebulous and remote, and there had been so many intervening possible heirs, that never once had he contemplated ownership of the Priory.

The solicitor withdrew his gaze from the window.

"Your cousin's predecessor was fortunate enough to sell the section of the estate lying east of the Blatchford to Millingham road. Your cousin himself raised money by mortgaging his mining royalties and by selling most of the saleable timber, but you—well, frankly, I'm afraid you are going to find things somewhat difficult. The death duties due when your cousin took the place have not yet been met. They will give you time, of course—yes, in the circumstances they'll give you time, but all the same, I'm afraid you'll find that cash will be hard to come by. Your cousin—well, your cousin seems to have got things into rather a mess."

"How do you mean, a mess?" George had asked him on a note of annoyance. It seemed that he was not the only Annesley addicted to the making of messes.

"Well, it's less than a year since he went to Plenders Priory," the solicitor explained. "He sacked the agent, who, in my opinion did very creditably, and he quarreled with those few tenants he had. The Priory itself is falling to bits. Cherry Hay, the house where the agent used to live, has been empty for more than six months. I believe there are a few cottages, but the tenants live on each other—and rabbits—and pay no rent."

"It all sounds very unprofitable." George laughed weakly, still weary from his journey. "I think I can't do better than go back to—" He had been going to add "Berlin" forgetting that he had already decided to relinquish his unfruitful mission.

"It seems to me that now you're here you'd better run down and have a look at the place," the solicitor had answered. "It's yours, you know, even if you're not very enthusiastic. Possibly—just possibly—we might be able to let it. Selling is out of the question—it's far and away too big, but with luck we might let. There's a caretaker at the Priory—the old butler from the colonel's time I think— I'll send him a wire."

This devastating conversation had taken place on the Tuesday, but after a night's needed rest, matters had taken a more optimistic aspect. The decimal dot began to look just a little more like a misplaced comma.

On the Wednesday morning, George had caught the northern express leaving St. Pancras at eleven, and all the way to Blatchford his hopes had increased steadily. He had attempted to recall the circumstances of his visit to the Priory as a boy. Yes, it must have been after his father had died, but why the dickens had he gone to the Priory? He gave it up. It was time-fogged. But he did vaguely remember the Priory and the lake, and he remembered the big stables very well. They were enormous, surely, or had time played tricks with his childish memories? Things began to come back to him. Quite definitely he had feared the stables. There had been a groom who had chased him with a stick, though why, he could not remember, and one day he had heard old Colonel Annesley saying dreadful never-to-be-forgotten things to one of the men in the stable yard—strings of words, all of them swears, and hardly any of them d— or even b—. Yes, that had frightened him. The stables began to take more definite shape. Big, ponderous double doors under a pointed arch of stone with a Latin inscription above it. Trees! Yes, there had been big trees near by, and a big square yard and a bright green copper roof and ivy on one of the walls.

All the way to Blatchford, Annesley had mused, endeavoring to recall the past, and with each revival he had become more assured, more satisfied, that even an accumulation of death duties at the rate of three lots in four years could not entirely impoverish the place as he pictured it. That solicitor! Well, he looked liverish, and the last Annesley had been an admitted numskull. The liverish solicitor had said so himself, and George had heard it from other sources. He would show them what a little energy could do.

Then after an hour's wait at Blatchford, he had boarded the dirty little train that served the branch line to Millingham, and with every mile and every pit bank passed, his spirits had sunk again, until now at last he stood, surely at the very lowest ebb of human hope, on the arrival platform of Millingham's filthy station.

He spent the night at the one hotel in the town, and in the morning, after an early breakfast, caught the Blatchford bus which the hall porter told him would pass the Priory gates. The weather had improved. The road switchbacked through pleasant semi-forest country; now between woods of silver birch and oak; now between open fields, the hedgerows browned with tall entangled bracken stalks and bare of trees, the earth light and sandy, with here and there a clump of gorse, as though even now, should the farmer forget for a space to plow, the forest would reclaim it. The collieries that had depressed him so the night before must all have lain adjacent to the railway line, for from the road neither smoking bank nor head-stock could be seen.

Twenty minutes brought him to his destination, and alighting, he faced his debt-laden legacy. It looked solid and real. True, the iron gates set back from the road behind a giant oak and a crescent of uncut grass, were red-brown with rust, but the curve of the gray stone wall was most convincingly complete.

Unwinding the piece of chain that held the gates loosely together, he stood for a moment at the top of the drive. For a good half-mile it lay straight ahead between converging banks of shining leaves with forest trees on either hand behind, and every rhododendron bush waved gently in the breeze to show its varying greens in the watery rays of the wintry sun. A rabbit—white tail bobbing—loped leisurely from wood to wood a hundred yards ahead. Magpies fluttered. And Annesley thought to himself, "My magpies, my rabbit, my park gates, my waving rhododendron shrubs and forest trees," and the spirit of possession descending on him, he hurried forward to match facts against his memory.

There, at the end of that straight stretch, there should be a double bend and a down-hill curve. Correct; ten minutes proved it. Next, a gate, and the wood should be left behind, the drive twisting and turning down the valley between clumps of trees and open rolling park. Fact and memory tallied again, but the one bred the other so quickly it was hard to say which was which. There, that was the tree he used to climb; on that grassy slope he used to lie and count the larks, some so high that their song was lost in space and they hovered, unheard—voiceless as hawks.

A pleasant tang was in the morning air, and Annesley hurried on. After a couple of miles the valley opened out, and there before him, on his right, exactly as he had pictured them, were the stable buildings with their copper-green roofs shining between the satin gray stems of the surrounding beeches, on his left, the Priory, between the two, the lake, and on the lake, a swan.

As he stood, memories thriving, he wondered who, long years ago, had planned the place. Before the old colonel had bought it a poet of world renown had lived at Plenders Priory, and it seemed to Annesley that he who had designed and built had been a poet too, for a sudden realization of its beauty sprang within him, and he understood how exactly right it was—so exact and right that had one mullioned window been misplaced, or had the angle of the high-pitched roof been other than it was, or had the stable roof been red instead of copper-green, or had one single stone been changed, the beauty would have been destroyed, just as one wrong note in a symphony will ruin a hundred played in tune.

After pausing for a moment to absorb the scene, he followed the drive to the left, and soon he was standing before Plenders Priory entrance. Smoke was coming from one of the chimneys. In one window there were curtains of Nottingham lace and a vase of bright red berries, but all the rest were bare and unadorned.

He knocked loudly on the heavy door which was opened by the caretaker, to whom the solicitor had wired—a man of sixty years or so—a man so Jenkyn-like in appearance that Annesley half expected happy phrases divorcing certain cigarettes from all sore throats.

"You'll be the next gentleman, sir," the old butler said with the solemnity of a judge.

"I be"—Annesley laughed—"and you be—"

"My name is James, sir."

"But what's your surname, James?"

"My surname's James, sir."

"Then what's your Christian name, James?"

"My Christian name's James, sir. James James, sir."

Annesley's eyes twinkled. "One twin as it were, eh, James?" he laughed.

But James was ponderous and solemn.

"Yes, sir," he answered without the flicker of a smile. "You see my father's name was James, sir, and my mother's maiden name was James—not cousins, sir, I've no holding with this in-breeding, sir—that was how it was. They wanted to keep the family all James as you might say, sir."

Annesley laughed again, a jolly laugh that echoed pleasantly in the empty hall. "Well, James, mind you don't run to seed and go cubed instead of squared."

But James's elementary mathematics had been neglected, for he merely "hoped he would do" and that Annesley would "keep him on." They spent a good hour together wandering from one stone-floored, wood-paneled room to the next—all of them gigantic; no wonder the solicitor had been so dismally skeptical about a let.

After lunch—bread and cheese was the best that James could find him—Annesley made his way down to Cherry Hay which lay tucked away in a little valley of its own nearly two miles beyond the Priory, and he walked up past the ponds to the boundary of the Cherry Hay land which ran alongside Little Plenders' Golf Links. Standing on a little hill he could just see the club house, and beyond it, spoiling an otherwise perfect sylvan view, a colliery pit bank with its aerial—God, what a word for it!—ropeway. One by one the tall latticed steel towers carrying the ropeway had been submerged, until the end tower, carrying the wheel round which the buckets turned, alone stood clear of rubbish. The wind was blowing from the bank, and as Annesley rested and watched, the buckets on the ropeway came creeping along the pitbank top to trip on the trigger and empty their contents below, and as each bucket tilted up, the faint thud of falling debris could just be heard. Thud! Something had fallen to bury that which had fallen before—to bury it completely and hide it for ever from human eyes.

Yes, undeniably the colliery spoilt the place, not that it mattered very much to Annesley, but it did definitely spoil Cherry Hay having the colliery so close. Thinking of the colliery made him think of Germany. The company he had been with there had owned collieries, and steel works too. And thinking of Germany made him think of his uncle, Sir Victor Grahame. It was not going to be a very pleasant interview. But unpleasant interviews had to be faced, and Annesley was not so readily depressed to-day. He had spent it in lovely country, his own country too in spite of his debts, and not in an evil-smelling ship's cabin; and so, following directions given by James James, whistling softly to himself, he made his way across the golf links and caught a slow train from Little Plenders into Blatchford, where he caught an express that carried him back to London.

As he sat in the express he thought what a quiet day it had been. He might have been right off the map. From the time he left the bus in the morning—apart from James James—he had not seen a single soul until he stood on the platform at Little Plenders—not a single soul. Yes, he had though—and Annesley smiled gently to himself as he remembered the picture—there had been a big man in one of the bunkers on the golf course, a big man with a red face who had flogged away angrily, muttered a curse, and then picked up.

3
THE LOST RESEARCH

"Scotland Yard please."

Annesley, smiling happily to himself as he stuck his feet out against the metaled bottoms of the opposite up-turned seats, settled himself as comfortably as he could in the none too luxurious taxi. Quite inexplicably it had given him pleasure to ask for Scotland Yard. The driver had looked at him—or Annesley perhaps had only imagined that he looked at him, but it came to the same thing—with a sudden flicker of interest as one who thinks to himself "one of them sleuths," and as Annesley was a sleuth of sorts, but only of sorts, to ask for Scotland Yard and be looked at with a sudden flicker of interest, gave him defi-nite feelings of pleasure. Indeed it was quite extraordi-nary what a number of ordinary everyday things did give Annesley definite feelings of pleasure. But then, he was feeling very well. In the whole of London there could have been few people feeling so well as Annesley did as he sat smiling in his taxi. He was almost too well.

Looking at him, no one could have guessed that he had failed in a mission entrusted to him and that he was now on his way to explain his failure to his uncle, Sir Victor Grahame, of the "Special Investigations Department" at Scotland Yard.

That artists are temperamental and untidy is an accepted fact. That scientists, men and women with fractional, fifth-place decimal minds who spend their whole grown lives in manipulating such easily mislaid articles as riders and molecules, are often equally untidy is also a fact—but it is not so generally accepted. If, for example, Romney, say, had lost one of his portraits no one would have thought very much of it. No one would have censured him. His friends might have said, "Did you hear that poor old Romney's gone and mislaid one of his old masters? Perhaps he lost it in America," and that would have been the worst they would have said. But when in the summer of the year—a folder containing all the experimental results, figures, considered conclusions and notes, on future work, the whole caboodle in fact, concerning certain research on the subject of "The Erosion of Special Alloy Steels when subjected to high velocity gases at high temperature"—a research which had cost a tax-tired nation nobody knows quite how many thousands of pounds—when this folder of papers disappeared from that Mecca of precision and accurate tidiness, the British Physical Laboratory at Hendon, the nation, the press, and more particularly the *Daily Flail,* which happened to be short of a stunt at the time, were scathing and astonished. It was most unfortunate and untoward.

The *Daily Flail* surpassed itself. It gave its readers the total acreage of the great laboratories at Hendon and worked out for them the estimated salaries paid to the staff at a rate per square yard, and spacious as the great laboratories were it came to quite a considerable figure. When compared with the amount of completed useful research per square yard it was a truly gigantic figure. The *Daily Flail* went into the whole matter very thoroughly. It explained to its intelligent readers that "The Erosion of Special Alloy Steels, etc., etc." was a subject vital to the perfection of the gas turbine, that British engineers, German engineers, American engineers, and engineers of other nationalities were all feverishly at work on the perfection of the gas turbine; that the gas turbine when perfected would enable a Rolls-Royce to carry a complete spare engine in one of the side lamps say, and that, fitted with a gas turbine, an Austin Seven would immediately become an Austin Seventy; that the country first perfecting and protecting the gas turbine would lead the world in industry for more than a generation; that the lost research papers contained the very essence of the problem and that Dr. Beresford, the head of the metallurgical department concerned, was to all intents and purposes a government official. They would not have been at all surprised to learn that the doctor was receiving a salary of three thousand pounds—and perhaps more. They wanted to know whether he was or whether he was not responsible, and what the government intended to do in the matter. They were astonished that Dr. Beresford, a man of science, could have been so culpably careless. Mrs. Beresford, on the other hand, was not in the least astonished. Every morning for years she had collected spent matches from the edge of the bath, various window ledges, and other odd unexpected places throughout their house at Hendon, and on those rare occasions when she brushed her husband's clothes she had emptied out his pockets. She could have told the *Daily Flail* things. But the *Daily Flail* knew nothing about Mrs. Beresford's difficulties with the household matches, though it published her picture on the back page—"Wife of Dr. Beresford who is held responsible for the loss of National Papers." They published Dr. Beresford's photograph too, and the photographs of some of the staff (female, of course) playing tennis on the lawns attached to the laboratories. In addition, they described the jolly, sociable, staff teas held there in the summer months and clearly implied that while the staff, male and female, stole time from their well-paid work in order to research pleasantly on the lawns with their gastric juices, thieves had burst into the building and had stolen the fruits of their other researches.

It was all very profitable and satisfactory for the *Daily Flail,* but it was most annoying for Dr. Beresford. The police, for instance, gave him endless trouble.

As luck would have it, the date on which the papers disappeared could not be placed more exactly than as lying within a period of three months. The erosion research had been completed in February, the results had been carefully written up and the doctor had signed them, as his practice was, at the end of April. They had been filed away pending the completion of a further section of the work, and when the papers were wanted for reference towards the end of July, they were nowhere to be found.

Tidy and clean as the British Laboratories at Hendon are, never have they been turned out and spring cleaned as they were that July, and never was any cleaning, spring or otherwise, completed with less result to show for it. All the rough notes, in fact a complete rough copy, was there in its proper place, but the fairly typed-out final copy had completely disappeared.

That was all troublesome enough, but it was as nothing to the troubles caused by the police when they took the matter in hand. Not only did they insist on searching the laboratories all over again, but they searched Dr. Beresford's private residence and the private residences of those members of the staff who had been even remotely concerned in the matter. They asked for—and it caused the distracted doctor endless further bother—a complete list of those who had visited the laboratories during the suspected period. The ordinary business and casual visitors were easily dealt with; their names, addresses and occupations were all set down in the Visitors' Book, but the various delegations from scientific bodies were more difficult to deal with. There was one delegation of German scientists, and one particular German in the delegation, a certain Herr Doktor Meissner, closely connected with a German steel company and a recognized authority on steel alloys, who, as one-by-one other sources of recovery dried up and failed, came to be particularly suspected.

So far as the British authorities knew, the Herr Doktor had led a blameless life, but, on the other hand, it was difficult to believe that the papers had been taken by an ordinary thief, difficult to believe that these particularly important papers had been taken by chance from among all those useless and entirely unimportant papers that surrounded it, and having spent many thousands on the original research, and more than a thousand again on the searches made by the police to recover the original research, it was decided to spend yet more, and the matter was handed over to Sir Victor Grahame.

Quite obviously it was not a matter on which a friendly foreign government could be approached, and as Sir Victor's nephew, George Annesley, was an engineer of sorts, had metallurgical knowledge of sorts, and a knowledge of the German language scarcely surpassed by the natives, he was despatched to Berlin. All the available ropes were pulled, and for a period of nine months Annesley had worked hard in the laboratories of the Aktiengesellschaft Stahlguswerke und Kohlenstoff with which Herr Doktor Meissner was connected, and had kept both his eyes and his ears well open. He had been provided with introductions enabling him to become personally acquainted with the Herr Doktor, and he did become acquainted with him, well acquainted, almost intimate, but he learnt exactly nothing concerning the efforts of German engineers to perfect the gas turbine, and he learnt no more concerning the whereabouts of the missing papers.

He had reported his lack of success at intervals to his uncle; he had asked to be withdrawn, but his uncle had always replied telling him to "hang on for yet a few weeks longer," and now here he was feeling excessively bright and well in a London taxi on his way to tell his uncle of his legacy and of his decision to have done with Germany—even if it meant severing his connection with the Special Investigations Department of Scotland Yard.

As the taxi sped along the Embankment, George indulged healthily in abdominal exercises, and the hidden rotary muscular flexes that went on beneath his vest could only have been excelled in their easy rapid regularity by a gas turbine. The editor of the *Daily Flail* and Sir Arbuthnot Lane would have been exceedingly gratified could they have beheld them.

George, however, was not thinking of the *Daily Flail*. He was thinking affectionately of his uncle. Sir Victor Grahame did abdominal exercises too, but they were of the kind current before the *Daily Flail* was thought of, and they certainly produced more obvious results.

Yes, undeniably, Sir Victor was fatter than he should have been, and if prosperous farmers still exist, then he looked like a prosperous farmer, so much like a prosperous farmer indeed, that when nephew and uncle met, after Annesley had said, "Well, uncle," and Sir Victor had replied, "Well, George, my boy," Annesley always felt an almost irresistible desire to ask him how the crops did.

The taxi drew up at Entrance E, and entering the ugly building, Annesley was shown to his uncle's room at once.

"Well, uncle."

"Well, George, my boy."

Sir Victor, badly dressed in a smooth gray suit of the kind that suffers easily from sedentary shininess, got up from his desk and stood with his back to the empty fireplace. His trousers were bagged at the knees. There were little tufts of sandy hair above his ears, little tufts that somehow suggested that were you but to show Sir Victor a turnip, they would turn forthwith into mutton-chop whiskers, and his face, though he rarely faced the weather, looked weatherbeaten like a sailor's. Gray eyes twinkled kindly from it, and Annesley could almost imagine a sniff of stable-yard scents—could almost hear the clucking of expectant hens triumphant.

"It was good of you to come so promptly, boy. You must have left at once when you got my letter," Sir Victor continued after a moment's pause, during which he looked his sturdy nephew affectionately up and down. Annesley finessed.

"I had a dashed rough crossing."

Sir Victor took a letter from a drawer in his desk. "You know, George, I remembered your mentioning this chap Corrie and so I thought I'd better see you at once. Wasn't he with you in Birmingham? Here's Dr. Beresford's letter. You'd better look it through before we discuss it."

Annesley, hiding the surprise he felt, held out his hand for the letter. It ran:—

"Dear Sir Victor Grahame,—I am enclosing for your careful attention the copy of a paper recently published in the *Journal of the Iron and Steel Institute*. It is by a man named Bernard Corrie who I find is an associate member of that body. You will see that the subject is 'Special Steel Alloys and their Anti-Erosive Properties.' Without going into too much detail I would tell you that the paper appears to me to be, in the main, a clever and well set out summary of other workers' results. There is one very remarkable feature about it, however. At the end of it the author makes a number of detailed suggestions regarding the lines on which, in his opinion, future researches should be carried out, and his suggestions for this future work are almost identical with the researches dealt with in the missing papers. In fact, to be perfectly frank with you, had we followed the author's line of reasoning we should have saved ourselves endless expense and trouble. In several cases where we took a tortuous route, he has got there direct.

"Bernard Corrie—I have been making a few discreet inquiries—is quite unknown in the metallurgical world, and I can only conclude that either:

"(*a*) He is in possession of, or has had some access to the missing papers, or

"(*b*) By some almost uncanny stroke of luck he has hit on what it took myself and my excellent staff years to find out at the B.P.L.

"It is my considered opinion that (*b*) may be deleted, and I think that your department might with advantage investigate and explore the matter further.

"Yours faithfully,

"James Dawson Beresford."

Having read it, Annesley handed it back to his uncle. "How people like Beresford do dote on (a)s and (b)s in little brackets, don't they? Well, you can take my word for it, uncle, there's nothing doing. It's merely Dr. Beresford's inherent inability to accept the fact that any one can jump to a conclusion without an expensive staff. I've lost touch with Corrie a little while I've been away, of course, but he's just the sort to surprise you by writing a paper on a subject he knows nothing whatever about, and then, after having told him, if you dare, that he's a conceited piratical ass you find that he's gone and put his long fingers plump on the pertinent spot. It wouldn't be the first time he's done it by any means. Why, when we shared rooms together he wrote an article in the *Financial Times*. Lord, how I ragged him! It was entitled 'What is Wrong with our Banking System' or something big-businessy of that sort, and when I asked him what the dickens he could know about finance beyond knowing where to pawn his watch, he told me he'd been making a careful study of Economics *for three months*—Economics—*three months*—and he didn't even see how funny it was. And then I'm hanged if there wasn't a leading article about it and correspondence by the column. He'd cribbed bits from books he'd read and twisted them round till they read like his own. Quite likely he did think himself that they really were his own. And then he'd tacked on some bright original suggestion. I'd back him against a bellyful of Beresfords any blinking day."

"Yes, that may be. That may be. That's all very well. But did you know that he had a job at the Patent Office?"

"I did, and I'm quite sure that it has nothing whatever to do with his interest in the subject of erosion and gas turbines. I know as a fact that he got the job by the merest accident. His sister got it for him. The manager at the bank where she works knew some one in the Patent Office and between the two of them they knew sufficient people to work it. Corrie was shell-shocked, you know."

"Well, and what has that got to do with it?"

"The doctor said he had to have a steady regular job. He was in a queer way. Miss Corrie tackled all the government departments, the Disabled Officers' Association, and every one else she could think of. I remember her telling her brother of the hopes she had about it and I was actually staying the week-end with them—it would be about a year before I went to Berlin—when she came home one Saturday and told us that she'd finally fixed it up."

"Yes, and it would be just about at that time that the papers disappeared from the B.P.L."

Annesley shook his fair, well-brushed head. He never on any account anointed it with oil, always it was tidy and shone as if he had. "It must be a pure coincidence then," he suggested. "And it's not very extraordinary either when you come to think of it. I should like to bet you that he's seen something or other that's interested him about erosion or gas turbines at the Patent Office, that he's bought a dozen books or so, mugged them up as though he were swotting for some exam, written his wretched paper at the peak of his enthusiasm, and that by now he's probably forgotten all he ever knew about it."

"Yes, and it's quite an ordinary coincidence too, I suppose," Sir Victor interjected dryly, "that his uncle owns a big block of shares in the Magnet Motor Cycle Company."

This time it was Annesley's turn to remark, "Well, and what has that got to do with it?"

Sir Victor crossed to the window and pulled down one of the blinds which was crooked. He let it run up with a rush.

"Well, they might be interested in the development of small gas turbines, might they not?" He smiled, turning to his nephew. "You know, George, you're far too ready to ignore Dr. Beresford's letter. He knows what he's talking about. Corrie may be cute and clever, all you say he is, but on the other hand it may, as Beresford says, have been

almost impossible for him to have jumped to those conclusions without seeing the lost papers. No, I'm very far
from satisfied even if you are, my boy. Come now, tell me
all you know about him."

For half an hour Annesley sketched the life and charac-
ter of Bernard Corrie, B.Sc., as he knew it, whilst his fat
uncle padded about the well-carpeted room.

"And you still count him your friend, in spite of all
you've told me?"

"Yes, and so would you, uncle, if you knew him. You
know you can't behave as other people behave if all your
inside arrangements are different. Before the war not a
single insurance company would look at him. How he ever
got to the front I can't think. And he's been shell-shocked
since. But on his good days he's the best chap going."

"That may be. That well may be. But it's got to be
looked into all the same, my boy."

At this juncture Annesley told his uncle of Blenders
Priory and how it was he had so promptly obeyed the
instructions to return home which were contained in the
letter he had never received, and Sir Victor looked thoughtful on receiving the information.

"Well, it cuts both ways," he said after a moment; "(a),
as Dr. Beresford would say, you are intimate with Corrie,
and if there is anything to find out you're half-way there
already, but (b), you are sadly biased, possibly have natural scruples about spying on a friend, and you have in
addition, other interests."

Uncle and nephew discussed (a) and (b) at length before Annesley finally decided to take the job on. He argued
to himself that if he did not, some one else would. That
if Corrie had had anything to do with the papers disap-
pearing from Hendon, which he did not believe for a moment, Sir Victor Grahame would find him out—and then
there was Corrie's sister, Marion. Also there was the fact

that Annesley had enjoyed telling the man at the wheel of
his taxi to drive him to Scotland Yard. To own Plenders
Priory, to have some hope of clearing the estate of debt,
that was something—something to look forward to in the
future, but to work for his fat, pleasant uncle, to be on the
perpetual edge of some possible excitement, to belong to
Scotland Yard—that was everything—everything Annesley
most desired for the present. And to continue on the lines
of Dr. Beresford who had caused the trouble, the upshot
of it all was that uncle and nephew agreed:—

(*a*) That Annesley should continue in his uncle's service after giving him the most solemn assurances that his
friendship with the Corries should not be allowed to stand
in the way of duty—a promise which, later, cost Annesley
many unhappy hours.

(*b*) That Annesley should become a temporary factory
inspector with a view to future opportunities of nosing
round the. works of the Magnet Motor Cycle Company
which were situate in Derby.

(*c*) That Annesley should renew his intimacy with the
Corries and that for the time being at any rate, he should
tell them neither of his legacy nor his connection with
Scotland Yard.

Sir Victor rang up the Home Office for an appointment there and then in order to arrange it. Now, when
Sir Victor sat down to a good dinner—and he did quite
often—he worked his way slowly and steadily through all
the courses, but he could bolt a bread-and-cheese lunch of
surprising proportions in the fewest possible gulps. That
was why he was so fat. And when Sir Victor took up a case
he never, never let it drop until he got to the end of it—a
quite definite end either one way or the other—nothing
ever petered out in indecision. At times too, he could get
through a quite amazing amount of work in the shortest
possible time, and that was why he was the head of his

department.

Apparently this was one of Sir Victor's bread-and-cheese efforts, for having finished his telephone conversation he hurried—if hurried is a word that can be used in connection with his portly movements—across to the Home Office to complete the final detail arrangements.

An engineer already, Annesley found little difficulty in acquiring such additional knowledge regarding the Factory Acts and their proper application to the engineering industry as would enable him to function as an assistant factory inspector sufficiently efficient for the purposes Sir Victor Grahame had in mind. He was attached to a southeast London area (so that he could lodge near the Corries) and Mr. Humber, the chief inspector of the district, who, having been told that Annesley had high connections, immediately, by some unknown process of logic, expected him to turn out a dud, was amazed at his new assistant's persistent application.

For nine months in Berlin, Annesley had lingered down a lane that led nowhere, now for three months he worked harder than he had ever worked before. In the intervals he had occasional further depressing interviews with his solicitor about the impossibility of either letting Plenders Priory or meeting the ever more pressing demands of the Income Tax authorities, and in addition he renewed his broken friendship with the Corries.

The Corries lived in a gloomy little house in Blackheath, and Annesley found himself forced into several professional misstatements in his efforts at a natural explanation of the reasons that had led him to forego his alleged lucrative employment in Berlin for the lesser prospects of an assistant factory inspector. Corrie thought he was an ass and told him so in just those words and many more. And Annesley thought that Corrie had grown more touchy and inflammable than ever. Indeed, it seemed to him that those good days when Corrie was "the best fellow going" were now so scarce and far apart that they lost their soothing effect on the intervening highly irritant spaces.

But he stuck to it. For one thing it was his job to stick to it, and he kept on telling himself, as he had told his uncle, that people who had queer insides and had suffered from shell-shock had to have allowances made for them. And for another thing—there was Corrie's sister Marion.

Quite definitely, in fact, had he but known it, he was dangerously definite about it, Annesley had not fallen in love with Marion Corrie. Afterwards he liked to think to himself that not only had he not fallen in love with her, but that he so definitely had not fallen in love with her that she could never by any possible chance have suspected him of—well, of having been less definite. He was always glad of that. For, one week-end—it was after he had been living in rooms in Blackheath for about three months—he learnt—reverting again to the lucid methods of Dr. Beresford:—

(*a*) That Corrie's wife, who he thought had been dead for years and years, had only died a year ago.

(*b*) That Corrie and his wife had not got on well together, and that there was something rather unusual, even mysterious, about the manner of her death.

(*c*) That in all the circumstances Marion Corrie could be dashed hard and unsympathetic with her brother.

And finally and most importantly,

(*d*) That Corrie's daughter, Elizabeth, whom previously he had never met (she had always happened to be away at school when he visited the Corries before he went to Berlin, and since his return had been staying with relatives) was—well, he was pleased to think that he had not fallen in love with Marion in such a decidedly definite manner.

4
BERNARD CORRIE, B.SC.

A morning spent along with grumpy Mr. Humber, the chief inspector of his district in some smutty East London factory, a long afternoon spent in getting pat those of the factory acts and regulations considered the most essential, and a short evening spent whenever possible with the Corries—six weeks of such days and Annesley, more assured than ever that Corrie had never seen the missing papers, felt himself ready to travel north and investigate the activities of the Magnet Motor Cycle Company at Derby.

The Corries were all very sorry when he went. Marion, Corrie's sister, was twenty-seven, twelve years younger than her brother; Elizabeth, his pretty daughter, just nineteen; and for much the same reasons both youthful aunt and grown-up niece were sorry. Marion was sorry because of that same lack of definiteness in their relationship, which, when he came to know Elizabeth, had gladdened Annesley's heart so; and Elizabeth was sorry because she thought him the kindest, jolliest, most considerate and best tempered man of her acquaintance, and because of those altogether indescribable urges that compel birds to build nests at spring-time. In addition Annesley had helped them more than they guessed to lessen those permanent feelings of tension, which, like wireless electric waves, permeate the family life of any nervous dyspeptic, and Bernard Corrie was not only a nervous dyspeptic but he was a nervous dyspeptic previously completely spoiled and subsequently shell-shocked. He could be amazingly difficult. Annesley thought him worse than ever he was, but he knew not one half of what Elizabeth knew about it, and Elizabeth in turn only knew a fraction of what Marion knew. It all came back on poor Marion. Her brother could be distressing.

Indeed you would have to see Bernard Corrie and know him to believe him possible. You must imagine him though at the age of thirty-nine, the weakly son of once well-to-do parents; petted and spoilt from the day of his birth; never sent to school but taught at home, first by a governess, and then by his various tutors; having little idea of games and less of how to lose them, a combination of inabilities that, coupled with his excitable, conceited disposition, bred countless shameful scenes; tall, he was six foot two; thin, when Corrie stripped anatomy was taught; red-haired with a thin spot in the middle; having the eyes that go with red hair, rather red about the rims, a trifle watery in windy weather despite protection afforded by pince-nez perkily perched on the bridge of his long, thin nose. You must try to imagine his neck with its Adam's apple agitating freely above an artistic bow—he never wore a simple tie. You must imagine him, one minute dancing an ungainly jig to the gramophone in the little drawing-room at 17 Walkden Road, Blackheath, and the next, smashing the ruddy record with at least one entirely original swear for every note imprinted on it because he had slightly scratched a finger on the blasted perforating needle; one minute rhapsodizing in the little back garden over some small spot of perfectly ordinary pale-blue sky that winked weakly through a bank of cloud, the next, swearing and shouting at his neighbor's children because they had ventured to peep through the hedge. You must imagine him as one of those strange beings who really like poetry and chamber music; as interested in sex and unashamed to talk about it; as alternating between wild enthusiasm about some person or some project and dark despair of almost suicide-suggesting depths; as constantly fussing about his health; wondering if his kidneys had floated into his stomach with flatulent results, or whether he might not have, perchance, carbuncles on the brain; indeed, as one so constantly consulting his doctor about fantastic imagined ailments that now he was greeted with, "Well, Mr. Corrie, what is it to-day? A distorted diaphragm or incipient undulation of the left uvula?" You must imagine all these things, and yet, if you are to picture him correctly, you must imagine too, that at times, as Annesley told his uncle, he could be one of the very best on earth. Loyal to his friends, conceited, fond of children, blasphemous, sloppy of mouth, doting on animals, loud, vile tempered, firm of chin, amative, bawdily inclined in conversation, enraptured by music, rheumatic, keen brained, a nervous vortex of human faults, ailments and aspirations that wore down every member of his household excepting Mrs. Glegg—George Annesley's altogether queer acquaintance—Bernard Corrie.

When Bernard was a baby Mrs. Glegg had been his nurse, and her husband having lately died she had returned to what remained of the Corrie family as their elderly maid of all work. It was she who opened the front door to Annesley when he came to stay for the week-end just before he went to the Midlands.

He had caught a bus from Blackheath Station which dropped him at the end of Walkden Road. As he swung along he noticed how the lilac buds were swelling in some of the small front gardens. It was spring, but no spring disorders disturbed the well-regulated flow of Annesley's blood. He never caught cold in the winter either. Apart

from twice being sick when at sea, that was when he went
to Berlin and came back again, he had never been ill in
his life. Even his teeth were all quite perfect. Inside the
Corries' garden gate there was a sheet of newspaper that
had blown there from the road. It looked jaundiced and
tired and Annesley crumpled it up into a ball, then, after
a moment's hesitation, he threw it back into the road again
where other papers lay. Yes, Walkden Road was that kind
of road—there were papers blowing about at times. It was
very nearly "not quite." You might have been surprised,
but certainly not astonished, had you met one of the
inhabitants going home with a naked jug of beer or an
obvious paper of fish and chips.

The little front garden of No. 17 looked cared for,
however, even neat, in spite of the fact that in the narrow
border below the sitting-room window there was an odd
glove and a new pair of scissors. Thinking to himself that
the untidy Elizabeth had left them there and that Marion
would be vexed did she know it, he picked them up. He
was just a little late. The Corries, on Saturdays, dined at
one o'clock, and when Mrs. Glegg opened the door to him
he hoped he had not kept them waiting.

She assured him with a good-natured smile that he had
not. She liked Mr. Annesley—a real gentleman and always
pleasant.

As he put his suitcase down in the narrow passage hall
and the glove and scissors on the table, he heard angry
noises coming from the dining-room, and by the time he
reached the door they had grown louder and angrier still.

The dinner table was ready set. A cold joint, a yesterday's remainder, was in its proper place. Mats waited for
the vegetable dishes which Mrs. Glegg might bring in at
any moment. A trifle in a glass dish, and a bowl of bananas
and apples were on the table too, so that the second course
could be brought into action immediately the first had

been despatched, for the Corries had planned an excursion
to Epping Forest with a theater to follow in the evening,
as a sort of farewell celebration for their week-end guest.
Funds for such frivolities being none too forthcoming, it
was quite an event, and Marion, the organizer, had the
program arranged as though it were a Cook's conducted
tour. She knew the number of the best bus take them to
their destination, she had a large scale to show them where
to walk for the bus that would bring them back, she knew
the inn at which they would take their tea, and the restaurant in town where they would take their supper. It was
no casual expedition. The theater tickets were in her purse
and her purse was in her overall pocket. She had allowed
for and thought of everything—everything, even to having the trifle and fruit ready on the table to save delay
between the courses.

When Annesley entered the room she was half leaning,
half sitting, with her back against the window-sill, one
hand stuck deep into the pocket of her overall, a time-table
held in the other, her well-defined chin defiantly tilted, a
neat, efficient little figure framed by the window behind
her. Elizabeth, with troubled eyes, stood with her hands
on the back of one of the cheap rush-bottomed chairs. On
another, at the table, dangerously adjacent to the appetiz-
ing trifle, her father sat. He was thumping the table with
one of his fists.

"I tell you again it's six hundred and four from Strat-
ford Broadway that we want," he shouted, making the
trifle shake like a jelly. "Hallo! Annesley, here you are at
last."

Elizabeth gave him a smile.

Marion merely nodded. "It isn't, it's a hundred and
ninety-six; six hundred and four only goes as far as Ley-
ton," she said in a manner that implied that not only did
she run 17 Walkden Road and plan everything for it that

had to be planned, but that also, secretly, as a spare-time job, she ran the whole of London's buses.

"It's six hundred and four! Damn and blast it, Marion, why won't you sometimes let some one else be right?" Bernard shouted, speaking apparently to Mrs. Glegg away in the kitchen or even the next-door neighbor.

"It's a hundred and ninety-six," calmly.

"It's six hundred and four," excitedly, a vein down the middle of his forehead beginning to show, the plates on the table leaping like lambs when he struck it.

"It's a hundred and ninety-six."

"It's six hundred and four." All Walkden Road might have heard it.

It was absurd. They were like children. There was no stopping them. Annesley was surprised at Marion, who, as a rule, never opposed her excitable brother. He wondered what was the matter with her—but they went on and on, and every time Corrie shouted, "It's—six—hundred—and—four—I—tell—you," he thumped the table in the blanks, and again when he finished the statement, and at every repetition he thumped with wilder, heavier thumps until by accident at last his fist came down on the edge of the trifle dish and like a flash he was covered with sponge cake and custard. It shot all over the place in the most surprising manner. A lump of it landed on the mantelpiece. A piece of angelica stuck like some sleek caterpillar against the wall. Custard frothed about Corrie's red hair like a successful shampoo in the making, covered his face and his glasses—dripped from his chin. A particularly nice piece of sponge cake nested coyly in one ear—no American movie comedy star was ever more covered with glory or less appreciative of the part he played.

"Curse it all, *now* you—see what you've—made me— well, do," he yelled, and pushing Annesley roughly to one side he dashed out of the room and upstairs.

"Dear me. I'm very sorry," Marion remarked weakly, taking off her overall.

"Well, that's our picnic pickled anyhow, if I know anything," Elizabeth remarked ruefully.

Annesley felt awkward. Dash the fellow, he was always upsetting things.

Mrs. Glegg swabbed up the mess and the three sat down to what remained of their dinner. In the middle of it Marion ran upstairs to see what she could do for her brother. She found him propped up in bed reading. His trifle-bespattered suit lay in a heap on the floor.

"Do you want any dinner sent up," she asked him, "or have you had enough?"

"No, clear out!"

"You might have sponged these first, I think, even if you did have to sling them on the floor. What had I better do with them now, I wonder?" she asked herself aloud, holding them up.

"Burn them—and blast you—go!"

Marion, however, did what she could with them in the bathroom and went downstairs again to finish her dinner. She refused to set out for the picnic. "You two go, and I'll try and persuade Bernard to come to the theater. If he wouldn't be so cocksure of himself life would be a little easier. Here are your tickets. I'll keep the other two. And look, you'd better take this with you," she added, holding out the time-table. "The bus routes are here. I've marked it here on page—on page—on—oh, I say—" Her lips began to tremble. She laughed suddenly. "It's six hundred and four after all!"

They all laughed. They pretended, even to themselves, that they were laughing at Marion, but really they laughed at Corrie with his custard-covered red hair looking like an inverted poached egg. Elizabeth laughed till the tears ran. Mrs. Glegg in the kitchen began to wonder what had set them off so, and Corrie, in bed upstairs, felt sure they were laughing at him. It was just like them. If they felt as ill as he did they wouldn't laugh. He blasted Annesley's vigorous health.

Ultimately Elizabeth and Annesley gave up the picnic and set off for Kew Gardens by themselves where they dissipated the admiration they felt for each other on the unheeding flowers. Then after supper they proceeded to the theater, where to their surprise, and secret disappointment, they found Bernard and Marion already in their places. It was a crook play, and a good one too, but though he sat next Elizabeth, Annesley had no enjoyment in it. He hardly attempted to follow it. The time had come when he would have to do what he hated doing. Marion had no enjoyment in it either. For her it had been a day of bitter disappointment. She had fallen in love with Annesley years ago, the very first moment she saw him in fact, and now she felt him slipping away. He had pressed her to come for the picnic, but too obviously he had been content to go with Elizabeth and leave her. It was not quite fair of Marion. She had been emphatic. But that made it no easier for her when she knew all the time that had he but asked her just once more, she would have yielded and gone with the others. Bernard had spoilt her one holiday in the week just as he had spoilt countless other holidays, and now in the theater, counting from right to left they sat, Marion, Bernard, Elizabeth and George—she could not even see him.

After the end of the first act Elizabeth could not see him either, for he went out, and he did not come back.

He got his hat and coat out of the cloak-room, and he wrote a note and gave it to the program girl with instructions where his party sat. She was to go and give it to them in the middle of the coming act. It ran:—

"Dear Corrie,—I am so sorry but I have just
met a friend and he wants me to go elsewhere
with him. I shall be back at your house soon
after eleven. It sounds most awfully rude, but
you'll understand when I see you and explain.
It's too long-winded for this note.

"George."

Corrie, when he got it, did think it rude and said so in
his usual emphatic way. But Corrie was in his highest spirits. He had scored over Marion who had told him about
the bus. He was the only member of the party to enjoy the
play.

Annesley, meantime, took a taxi all the way back to
Walkden Road. He did not bother to try the front door
of number 17—he knew that it was locked and that Mrs.
Glegg was away for the week-end. He went round to the
back where he climbed onto the outbuilding roof and got
in through the bathroom window which he knew was unlatched. The latch was broken. He had broken it himself.
He was quite convinced, absolutely convinced, that Corrie had nothing to do with the Hendon papers, but he
had promised his uncle that he would search the house
for them, and when the promise was made he had argued
that if he did not do it himself some one else equally com-
petent probably would. Now, however, alone like a thief
in the house, it seemed altogether different. He hated it.
And when in glancing through some papers in a drawer in
Corrie's bedroom, he learnt that Corrie's wife, whom he
always thought dead for many years, had died little more
than a year ago, he hated it more than ever.

When he had finished his search he unlocked the front
door and waited for the theater party, first preparing a
proper explanation for his sudden departure from the theater and then reading.

They were late coming home. Corrie, still bubbling over with good spirits, had taken the reluctant Marion and Elizabeth each by an arm when they got out of the theater, and had marched them both the full length of Piccadilly in a fine drizzle of rain to look for a "nice little place" he knew where they could get some sandwiches and coffee. They passed several perfectly respectable cafés where satisfactory sandwiches could have been secured at a reasonable price, but he was in such good spirits that he barely noticed Marion's protests, her reminder about the waiting Annesley, or her statement that sandwiches were prepared and ready at home—no, he *would* find his "nice little place." They tramped the full length of Piccadilly and wearily back again nearly to the Circus before he admitted that his "nice little place" must have moved. Then, having dragged them a tired two miles, he hailed a passing taxi to carry them a couple of hundred yards or so, to the Café Royal where he spent more than they could afford on unwanted food and drink.

When they did at length get him back to Walkden Road they found Annesley asleep in an arm-chair with the cat on his knee. He told them how, tired of waiting, he had been fortunate enough to find the bathroom window unlatched and he gave them the convincing and complicated story he had concocted to account for his flight from the theater.

Once in bed he slept like a—well, he slept like a sleeper—he heard nothing. He heard neither Corrie when he yelled in his sleep, as he nearly always did after any excitement, nor poor Marion when she went downstairs to get him a hot-water bottle. Elizabeth heard them both, though she pretended to herself that she was not quite sure. She felt most comfortably certain, however, that even if she did really hear the noises she knew she heard, Marion would not allow her to do anything. Marion was rather like that. If there was anything unpleasant to do Marion did it. She was selfish about unselfishness.

And on the Monday morning following a tired Sunday, Annesley went north to Little Plenders.

5

THE PRIORY IS LET

Little Plenders, that is to say the old village, for the new colliery village down by the railway line hardly counts, sits on the top of the steep little ridge of hills that runs along the northern boundary of the Little Plenders golf links. It is a village complete with school and institute, with green and pond, and with an old inn—the French Horn—all of them ordinary and calling for no remark. No one would say, "Little Plenders—let me see, Little Plenders—oh, dear me now, oh yes—now I remember, you mean the little place on the hill with the fine old church in the valley, or the nice big green, or the quaint old inn." The church is not particularly old, the green is little and not very green, and the only quaint thing about the French Horn is old Mrs. Girling the landlady.

Annesley thought her the quaintest old soul he had ever seen, but she suited him. The French Horn suited him. And Little Plenders suited him. It lay ten miles north-west of Blatchford and as many miles north-east of Derby, where the Magnet Motor Cycles were made, and from the garden at the back of the French Horn you could look right across the golf links towards Cherry Hay, whose chimneys just showed through the trees, and beyond Cherry Hay to the wilder country between the Priory and the Millingham-Blatchford road.

Geographically, remembering that even in a third-hand Morris such as the one placed at his disposal as a factory inspector, ten miles can be comfortably covered in thirty minutes, it was admirably placed for Annesley's purpose. The office of the district inspector was at Blatchford, the Magnet works at Derby were not more than a dozen miles from Blatchford; Blatchford, as stated before, was only ten miles from Little Plenders; at Little Plenders there was the French Horn kept by Mrs. Girling, and from the bottom of the garden behind the French Horn, George could gaze over the tenth hole of the Little Plenders golf course, which was a nice bogey five, dog-legged, with the green tucked into the hillside below him, and away to his unproductive acres. So he took a private sitting-room— the only sitting-room—at the French Horn. He took it because he wanted to lodge in Little Plenders overlooking Cherry Hay, and in the whole of Little Plenders there was nowhere else to lodge. And certainly Mrs. Girling, who came from Suffolk and finished all her sentences on a note an octave higher than the average of the rest, looked after him as no one else could have looked after him. She was getting on in life was Mrs. Girling. "More's seen this face than will see it," as she put it pithily; and it was a pity too, for it was a fine old face to see.

Sometimes in the evenings colliers walked up from the new village to sit and drink in the French Horn, and it was from chance remarks of theirs that George first heard of Mr. Henry Primrose, the recently appointed—and he gathered none too popular—manager of Plenders Pit. The next time George heard him mentioned was in the club house on the golf links where most of the members seemed to have something or other to do with the coal that lay buried beneath them. It had been George's first appearance at the club, and having had a round with a kindly member who had taken pity on him, he had sat down alone for tea at one of the little tables. At a neighboring table two other men were taking tea and talking coal.

"Well, I'm sorry for you. That's the worst of these big combines—you never know whom you may get. What did you tell me his name was?"

"Henry Primrose."

"Where did you say he came from?"

"Lancashire somewhere—he was at one of their other pits."

"What's he like to look at?"

"He's like—well, the tale's going round that at the Notts, and Derby Managers' dinner the other night, the waiter went right round the table saying, 'Beef or pork, sir?' but when he got to Primrose he just said, '*Pork* for *you,* sir,' without a question mark at all—that's what he's like."

That was on the second Saturday after Annesley left London.

On the Monday following he went over to Blatchford to look round the works of the Little Giant Motor Cycle Co. It was the Magnet works at Derby that he was really interested in, but he went first to the Little Giant works at Blatchford, arguing to himself that there he would be able to ask all manner of questions without raising suspicion, and that his first visit would help him to know what to look for on his second.

His new district manager, a Mr. Haydock, had been advised that Annesley was there for a special purpose and that he was to allow him to go where he wanted and give him such help as he could. He had been told enough to arouse his curiosity and not enough to satisfy it.

"You know, they'll think it rather odd—I was over the Little Giant works myself only last week."

"Will it matter?"

"They'll think it rather odd."

"Perhaps you could give me a letter of introduction, saying that I am taking over the Blatchford area, or something of that sort, and that you'd like me just to have a look round," Annesley suggested.

Mr. Haydock seemed to think it was rather difficult. "It's not my business, of course—I don't even know what you're here for; if I did, I might perhaps be able to advise you—but it seems to me that it would be better if you waited, say another week or two." The sentence was full of little pauses and each little pause was packed tight with question marks, but Annesley got his note and gave no information for it. It was addressed to the managing director, Mr. Lobley.

The Little Giant works lie about a mile out of Blatchford, and they consist of so many bays set end on to the line that from the train the long outline of the roof looks like the edge of a saw, and the name "Little Giant—Little Giant—Little Giant—Little Giant Motor Cycles" repeats itself so often that passengers have been known to suffer from a sort of induced syncopation, finding themselves only able to stammer, "Here's my—here's my—here's my—here's my ticket" when they gave it up. But all Blatchford was proud of the Little Giant works, and no one was prouder than Mr. Lobley, the founder of the company and its managing director.

Now Norman Lobley was a self-made man. He had worked at a bench and was proud of it—now that he had left it. He had manufactured bicycles and motor cycles—all of them guaranteed to stick together—at such a rate and so successfully that he was a reputed millionaire, and at the same time he had manufactured a certain number of aitches—some of them not so safely attached. He had no idea of it himself, but the fortune which, in his own opinion, had been born in his brain and bred by hard work, had been largely a matter of luck. Plenty of people in

Blatchford, for instance, had as many brains and worked as hard as Lobley did, but no one had made as much money. It was just a matter of output, and the output of the Little Giant Company had become so enormous that the quite expensive and stupid mistakes Lobley sometimes made had no obvious effect on the profits; errors costing thousands that would have swamped a smaller concern, merely altered the cost of a Little Giant machine by an inconsiderable fraction of a penny and came to be looked on as "the bold forward policy" of the company's managing director, who, after making one fortune out of his manu-facturing, made another on the quiet when he persuaded his shareholders that it was to their advantage to sell the place, lock, stock and barrel, to the New All-British Steel Trust, which, like a number of British things, belonged to Britain's Uncle Sam, and owned Plenders Pit in addition to numerous other collieries and works.

Important man that he was, Lobley gave George quite a lot of his time. George, who had forgotten that the higher you go the more rarefied the atmosphere becomes, and that to an extent the same rule applies to the amount of work done by workers, was rather surprised. Lobley, who had a habit of looking away from you when he spoke, sat with one leg thrown carelessly over the arm of his desk-chair, and with his pallid, rather common, handsome face tilted most of the time to the ceiling, talked for nearly half an hour. He almost seemed to be showing off.

"We never hide anything here, Mr.—er"—here he glanced at Annesley's card—"er—Annesley. 'Open confes-sion is good for the soul' is a little slogan I am always driving into my staff. I will not have things 'idden—things hushed up. The days of secrecy are dead."

Annesley said, "Yes, quite."

'I say to my customers, 'Come and 'ave a look round. We welcome you here. *We've* no slipshod work to hide.'

And I say to my competitors, 'Look round our works by all means, learn how we do it, copy us if you can.' Some of them have accepted my invitation. But they can't do it, Mr. Annesley—no one can copy our magnificent organization and production efficiency."

Annesley spent the day there and he found it all quite true—nothing was hidden. He went everywhere and saw everything he asked to see. He was compelled to agree with Lobley too on the subject of efficiency; indeed the momentum of the place—one great stove had not been cold for seven years—was such that he doubted whether it could stop turning out motor bicycles even if it tried to.

It was all quite different when, a week later, he visited the suspected Magnet works at Derby. There he had no friendly chat with the managing director. He did not even see the works manager. He was handed over to a foreman who, without saying a word, managed to indicate that in his opinion the whole idea of factory inspection was idiotic, and that it was quite impossible for a factory inspector to be anything else but a fussy old woman. There was quite a to-do when Annesley wanted to go into the laboratory— which, unlike the laboratories he had seen at the Little Giant works, was little more than a name, and he came away with the impression that there might be something in Sir Victor Grahame's suspicions after all.

Then two surprising things happened.

He had gone out towards the Cherry Hay end of the links one evening with a mashie and a dozen balls to prac- tice short approaches. For an hour he approached balls over bunkers with a precision he could never hope to equal in match play. Then, just as he had decided to walk back along the tenth hole and up the steep little hill to the French Horn, he noticed a big man and another man mak- ing their way across the field that lay between the links

and the Cherry Hay ponds towards the house. Out of curiosity he followed, to come up with them talking together
in the yard behind the house itself. As he opened the gate
from the lane by the ponds into the yard he heard the
shorter of the two men say:—

"I don't know, you know, Primrose. It's handy for us,
but I'm not at all sure—not at all sure—that these old out-
buildings could be made suitable for Taverner. Who does
it belong to, by the way?"

Annesley introduced himself. He wondered who Taverner was and why the outbuildings would not suit him. He
hoped for a tenant.

"Good-evening. I saw you cross the field from the golf
links. Are you interested in the house? I'm wanting to let it."

The light was none too good, and it was only as he
finished his sentence that he recognized the shorter of the
two men as Norman Lobley. The other man then was Primrose. He thought of the waiter at the colliery managers'
dinner. Even if Lobley had not mentioned him by name he
would have guessed who he was, for never was human more
hog-like. He thought too of the big man who had slashed
away so angrily at the ball in the bunker the first time he
crossed the links on his way to Little Plenders Station, and
the aggressive manner in which the big man before him
glared down at him, somehow connected the two.

"Mr. Lobley, isn't it?" Annesley said.

"Yes, you know I was just thinking to myself that I
ought to know you, but I can't—"

"I was over your works the other week, Mr. Lobley—
factory inspector."

"Ah, yes, of course, of course, but did you say—"

Annesley laughed pleasantly.

"Yes, it is rather an unusual combination, I suppose—
landowner and factory inspector—though I don't quite
know why it should be. I'm wanting to let."

"We're wanting to buy," Primrose grunted.

After further conversation they agreed to meet at the club house the following evening and it was there that the first surprising thing happened. Annesley had brought some plans with him and he had told them of the Priory after hearing with some pleasure that, in addition to their friend, Mr. Taverner, who, it appeared, was no other than *the* Professor Taverner, they both wanted houses too. Annesley stuck to his determination not to sell. Cherry Hay—there was something about the name and the house and the ponds that attracted him. As far as he could see, never so long as he lived would he be able to afford to live at Plenders Priory—but Cherry Hay—he might. Now he would rather not sell Cherry Hay.

Lobley suggested a lease.

"What's the block of buildings here, Mr. Annesley?" Henry Primrose asked, pointing to the map with a finger like a sausage with a nail on it.

"Those are the stables." Annesley explained their size and, roughly, their arrangement.

Lobley coughed.

"That sounds just what we want, eh, Primrose? I ought to explain, perhaps, Mr. Annesley, that Primrose and I are financing Taverner on some research"—Annesley almost felt his ears move—"on the low temperature carbonization of coal which, as you perhaps know, is very much to the fore just now. I take it that you wouldn't object to our making any small structural alterations to the stable buildings if we undertook to reinstate." He looked at Primrose as one who wondered whether he might not have said too much.

Apparently he had.

"Bit premature. We haven't even seen the place," the big man growled.

"Oh, that's all right, my dear Primrose. Mr. Annesley, I am sure, understands that we are only discussing the matter in quite a preliminary way."

Annesley, of course, assented. But as the conversation proceeded, his hopes of letting the Priory at a figure beyond his wildest flights of imagination rose steadily. They were interested when he told them how big and secluded the Priory was. They were more interested still when he suggested that perhaps by making some small interior alterations it might be cut up into three separate commodious and quite convenient houses for Taverner and themselves as well. A lease was suggested.

Lobley murmured, "It's just the very thing. Near your colliery, and I can be at the works in twenty minutes."

"I keep on reminding you we haven't even seen the place," Henry Primrose protested as Lobley's enthusiasm increased.

"No, but subject to its being what Mr. Annesley says it is—and we've got the plans—it's just the very thing. Look here, Mr. Annesley, you'll excuse us if we go into private committee. No, no, my dear fellow, don't move, pray; we'll go into the smoke-room and we'll be back in ten minutes."

Lobley had got some magazines with him and Annesley picked one of them up whilst he waited for them to return. It was a copy of the *Motor Cycle*. He turned over a few pages. Another paper fell out on to the floor. He picked it up. It was "The Anti-Erosive Properties of Certain Steel Alloys by Bernard Corrie, B.Sc."

Annesley put it very carefully back again on the table.

Lobley and Primrose returning, they arranged to pick him up at the French Horn and motor him over to the Priory the following evening, and when Annesley got back to the French Horn the second surprising thing happened.

There was a letter for him from Bernard Corrie. In it Corrie told him that his uncle and his cousin had both been killed in a motor accident, that his uncle had died intestate, and that therefore, much to his surprise, he found himself a man of wealth. Among other possessions that Corrie itemized in his letter was that big block of shares in the Magnet Motor Cycle Co. that had so interested Sir Victor Grahame.

Sir Victor Grahame was intensely interested when a week later his nephew came to see him.

"And you say you've let the Priory to them for three years?"

"Yes. Patterson—he's the solicitor—came and fixed the whole thing up in less time than I thought it possible for a lawyer to do anything. There are still some papers to sign, I believe, but apart from that, everything's agreed and settled."

"Figure satisfactory?" Sir Victor Grahame asked, looking down at his watch chain which hung clear of the curve as a well-behaved tangent should.

Annesley told him the figure and his uncle apparently thought it very satisfactory. He whistled softly. "You lucky young devil!"

"Uncle, what do you think of this for an idea?"

"Not much if it's yours. What is it?"

"Suppose I try to let Cherry Hay to the Corries! Then we shall have the whole bunch of suspects happily segregated on my estate!"

"But, my dear boy, you'll get brain fever."

"Well, what do you think of it?"

Sir Victor thought a great deal of it and said so, and a few days later George wrote to Corrie from the French Horn.

6
CHERRY HAY IS SOLD

At the tender age of four months little Bernard Corrie hurled his bottle out of his cot, through the nursery window—closed of course—on to the head of a policeman chatting with the cook in the area below. As the broken glass showered about, the dear little fellow yelled. "Curse the blinking teat; why the blazes can't they get me one with a bigger blasted hole in it!" It sounded just like any ordinary inarticulate bellow, but that was really the opinion the sweet little fellow attempted to express, and when his mother came to find out what the matter was, the sun shone on the red down that covered his ugly head, and he smiled at her in a fashion so angelic that she had not the heart to smack him, which was quite a thousand pities.

Yes, right from the very beginning of things Bernard was unfortunate. He was unfortunate in the matter of not getting the smacks he deserved; he grew up with the firm conviction that he only had to bellow sufficiently loudly to get exactly what he wanted, and that conduct, however outrageous, could always be atoned for by apologies alone. He was unfortunate too in attracting to himself the most virulent Bolshevik members of every known type of germ: croup, scarlet fever, mumps, measles, ordinary and German; he had them all, and more besides. Indeed he spent so much of his early youth in bed that he became thin and

long like forced rhubarb, and when he did grow up he was
unfortunate again in his marriage.

For, at the age of nineteen, Corrie had put his finger
to his nose and twiddled them at Fate by falling in love
with one Bobby, a chorus girl. Bobby had owned a flat in
Fulham and it was there that Corrie fell.

To do her justice, Bobby never had thoughts of marriage. Corrie was one of a number—not a countless number, but just a number—and when, on learning that he was
to be a father in seven months' time, he had rushed her to a
registrar's office, she was too astonished to protest in time.

Then Fate took a lash and nearly flayed Corrie alive.
For seventeen weary years she gave him no month of respite. In very little time she taught him how quickly passion flowers fade, and when the war came, she sent him,
one of the few who had welcomed the scourge, back home
again, a shattered wreck, within the year. Then she played
ducks and drakes with the family finances, and their in-
vestments, which Corrie's father had talked of as "securi-
ties," dwindled down through every stage of insecurity to
become mere forlorn hopes on the liability sides of official
receiver's statements, until, when Corrie came out of a
nursing home towards the end of the war, his father had
died of his worries, his mother's health was undermined,
and the family income had shrunk to less than two hundred a year.

But Fate had forgotten Marion, and she was to be
reckoned with. Possessed of abounding energy and good
health, more than a little attractive with her cool brown
eyes and crisp short hair—it was before the days of the
universal shingle, and short hair on a woman was striking
then—Marion took the situation in hand. She found a job
for herself at a bank in the city. On the family doctor's
advice she refused to treat her brother as a permanent
invalid. She was told that with time and care his nerves

would recover, but that he must have quiet, steady employment, and she worried the authorities until they grew
sick of her importunity and gave him a job in the Patent
Office in self-defense. She persuaded Bernard's old nurse,
Mrs. Glegg, to come back to them, and in spite of their
straitened circumstances, she saw to it that her niece, Elizabeth, was sent away to school. All these things, single-
handed, did Marion manage, and like many successful
managers, she grew a little hard in the process.

Bernard, at times, thought her very hard. His disordered nerves played the queerest pranks. For months on
end he could not bend his back—another time it was his
sight—then he would see red stars. And always Marion
would say, "It's only your nerves you know, Bernard, after
all," as though disordered nerves could have been turned
into well-ordered nerves if only he had had a little more
determination. Always she seemed to be encouraging him
to go to work when he felt too ill for work. If it was one
of his good days Corrie would merely mutter, "Oh, you
well people," but if it was one of his bad days and Marion
ventured on such remarks a certain vein down the middle
of his forehead would stand out angrily and then there
would be hell to pay. Marion and Elizabeth learnt to look
for it, that vein, and "Bernard's in good vein" became a
family saying.

Marion was undoubtedly good for Corrie though. He
did steadily get better. There were times of setback—
months when he could not sleep, terrible times when he
walked in his sleep if he did. Twice he woke to find himself
out in the street in his pyjamas, and for a time Marion had
to lock his door on the outside after he had gone to bed.
And Corrie hated that and feared it, for it reminded him
of the time in the nursing home—and of what might have
happened had he grown worse instead of better. There was
a man in the same ward who—

Then just as things were really beginning to improve, Fate played her trump card, and Bobby, who had left him as soon as she could after Elizabeth was born, turned up again. Not the gay Bobby Corrie had married, but a rather bedraggled Bobby—a broken Bobby seeking sanctuary to die in.

It was school time and Elizabeth, who had been kept in ignorance, was away for her last term when the doctor pronounced the case a hopeless one, and Corrie could not quell a feeling of intense relief.

"Now Elizabeth need never know," he thought.

Then, when Corrie, just a little bent under his bludgeonings, with a few gray hairs at either temple, had reached the age of thirty-nine, and Elizabeth, slim, vivacious, entrancing, the apple of both her father's eyes, had reached the age of nineteen, Fate exchanged her lash for a dice box and scattered a shower of sixes. Marion got a double rise and was taken on to the permanent staff at the bank. Corrie himself gained quite unexpected promotion at the Patent Office. His mother, who had reached that stage of ill health when life becomes a mere hesitation at the door of death, died peacefully in her sleep.

There was a definite improvement in the relationship between the family income and the family expenditure, and a few months later, about the time when George Annesley gave up his job in Berlin and took rooms in Blackheath, economic ends were meeting. Then, after Annesley had gone north to take up his duties as a factory inspector, Fate flung them a final six, and a ten-ton lorry coming too quickly round a bend in the road away in a Derbyshire village, killed a certain widower who had been careless enough to make no will, and his only son at one fell hoot. The widower turned out to be no other than Corrie's Uncle Amos Smith about whom he had heard his mother speak when in reminiscent mood, and Corrie, who had never so much as set eyes on him—there had been a

family coolness—was next of kin and came in for something over a hundred thousand pounds.

George Annesley was the first person Corrie wrote
to when their good fortune came, and the Corries were
just recovering from the shock of it all when his answer
reached them. They were having breakfast in the little
back room—a room that looked dismal and dreary in spite
of the bright May morning, a room in which the furnish-
ings were faded and half the light obscured by the wing
containing "kitchen with bathroom over," that jutted out
at the back of the house.

Corrie was seated at one end of the little table, with his
back to the window. It was the best position for reading
the paper, and Corrie always had the best position, and at
breakfast time he read the paper—when he had time. To-
day he had plenty of time. It was his first day of freedom,
for, to Marion's secret alarm and expressed disgust, he had
given up his job at the Patent Office.

She sat at the other end of the table—dark, alert, and
efficient. She had been down before seven o'clock. She
had cooked the breakfast and she would catch the train to
the city at 8.45 where she would give further proof of her
efficiency at the bank.

For three years she had caught the train that went out
of Blackheath Station for the city at 8.45; and she had
not had to run for it once. This morning it never even
occurred to her that her capable niece, Elizabeth, who had
nothing to do all day, might have been the proper person
to get up and cook the bacon. It never occurred to Elizabeth either. Marion did things. Gradually in the course
of years it had grown to seem proper that Marion should
do the things that had to be done, so that now, had Elizabeth suggested getting up, it would almost have seemed as
though she were robbing her youthful aunt of her prerog-
atives and rights.

But Elizabeth must not be censured too much in the matter. She would have got up willingly, really and truly willingly, had Marion suggested it. She was very fond indeed of her Aunt Marion. They were more like sisters than aunt and niece. Marion, rather short, steady, capable—so steady and capable that somehow one forgot how truly pretty she was. Elizabeth—bright, blue-eyed, fair-haired, gay—so gay and joyous that her prettiness fairly jumped at you—especially if you happened to be a man.

Elizabeth sat facing the fireplace. She had just come down. Corrie helped himself to bacon and picked up the morning paper. Annesley's letter lay underneath it and he flung the paper on the floor and opened the letter instead. Aloud, he wondered what on earth Annesley had got to write about. He stretched out a hand for the cruet and propped the letter up against it, eating his bacon as he read. His plate wobbled—it was still on the top of Marion's and Elizabeth's empty plates—he pushed them with an angry clatter from underneath his own. He adjusted his glasses with a muttered curse and he mumbled, "Well, I'm blest!"

Elizabeth coughed.

Marion laughed.

"We're no good at all—worms—female worms—but with perfectly healthy empty stomachs. Could we please have any bacon rind Your Highness happens not to be wanting?"

Corrie was contrite. "Oh, I say—here, you serve it, Elizabeth." He pushed the dish towards his daughter, rumpling up the tablecloth. "But listen to this—listen to this! Shiver my timbers and douse my lights! Old George has come in for the Plenders estates in Nottinghamshire!—wants us to go and have a look. Cherry Hay—Plenders Priory—what the devil!—suggests we should all of us go and live there—wants us to go and look."

He tossed the letter to his sister and devoured his bacon as though he had never even heard of indigestion. But Marion, reading it, frowned. "Will you go?" she asked.

"Go? Of course I shall go! We shall all three go. You can quite easily get Saturday morning off and I'll wire him this morning."

Marion felt disturbed. For the past three weeks she had feared it and now the crisis had come, as crises have a way of coming, before she was prepared. Remembering the doctor's advice, "steady, easy employment, Miss Corrie— enough to keep him from thinking of himself, but not too trying—steady and regular—that's what he wants," she had tried to dissuade him from throwing up his job. There had been more than one bitter scene; she had even enlisted the doctor's aid, but Bernard had been adamant. They could all of them say what they damn well liked but he was not going to work in the Patent or any other office. Marion could stick to her bank if she felt steady occupation essential to health and happiness, but he—he would write a book—he would retire to the country and build himself a workshop where he would invent things—he would—there was no end to what he would not do.

The future unfurled itself like a banner of achieved ambition. But for Marion the future looked more like some endless, hectic, scenic railway whose every upward sweep predicted a double dip, a scenic railway on which she would ride, a mere attendant, unpaid, unthrilled, to journey's end. No, could she but keep him in London, she would stick to her bank where her work was her rest—on that she was determined. But should he retire to the country—what then? No one could manage him as she managed him. Could she fairly leave him to Elizabeth and Mrs. Glegg?

"Why can't you go and have a look by yourself—or take Elizabeth?" she said, looking up slowly.

Elizabeth pounced on the letter.

"Here, what's it all about? Let the little one have a look."

Suddenly excited Corrie pushed back his chair, the vein down the middle of his forehead swelling out.

"But—dash it all—you *shall* come, Marion! Here's a chance to get away from all this—this filthy hole—and you and your bank shan't stand in the way! Damn the bank! We'll buy the blasted bank!"

He was shouting.

Without the least warning he was plunging them into a scene, and Marion, having visions of other scenes and the nights that followed them, attempted to soothe him.

"All right, Bernard, all right. You wire and I'll see what I can do, but don't go and get excited, old thing, or you'll spend the week-end in bed. Now I must go for my train. You look after him, Elizabeth, and don't forget to make your bed to-day."

She left them.

They spent most of the morning in looking up trains and wiring to Annesley. The afternoon Bernard spent in looking into the housekeeping. When Marion got home at six o'clock, she found him dusting an already dusted draw-ing-room, and she knew it meant trouble. The little scene at breakfast had upset his nerves, and when his nerves were upset, or when his back ached, or when any of his other aches were active, he flew to a duster as other men fly to tobacco or drink. The trouble began soon after he went to bed. He fell asleep in ten minutes and woke again in another ten with a strident yell that rent the night.

It woke the two little boys who lived next door—they said, "It's poor Mr. Corrie having one of his nightmares," and turned over and went to sleep again. It woke Marion too, but she did not go to sleep again. She spent half the night filling hot-water bottles.

But Bernard got his way—as he always did—and they all three caught an early train for Blatchford, where George Annesley met them in a Morris—in a Morris that it was difficult to believe had ever been "this" or even "last year's model."

It got them safely to the Priory, however, and, quizzing the noble owner about the rust on his gates, they rattled down the drive between the rhododendron bushes, Marion's heart sinking as she saw the beauty of it all.

Elizabeth, who sat next to George at the wheel, mistook the stables for the Priory. "My God!" she whispered, awestruck, when told of her mistake, and when at last they got to Cherry Hay, she suggested to Marion brightly, "This will be one of the hen-houses then, dear."

They extracted themselves from the car. George was enjoying himself. It was jolly. It would be jolly to have them at Cherry Hay. Corrie—queer, but clever—Marion, she seemed very quiet—and Elizabeth—Elizabeth's eyes were shining.

They looked over the house and they admired the garden, Corrie going into ecstasies over both.

Marion—feeling uncomfortably like a spoil-sport—thought the rooms looked rather dark. "It is a pity," she said, "that the dining-room and the drawing-room both face nearly north." The water supply was criticized as well. It came from a spring away towards the Priory, and was pumped into a tank in the roof by a thing called a ram, and at every plunge of the plunger there was a noise in the pipes through the house. "Plunk—plunk—plunk—" persistently, gently pulsating, wherever you went.

George explained the action of the ram.

"I hadn't noticed the noise before, Marion. It's air in the pipes I fancy. I'll have it put right."

"Don't fuss, Marion, don't fuss—for heaven's sake don't fuss so—it's soothing compared with Blackheath trams and

Blackheath cats. Why, I don't suppose we'll hear it at all when once the furniture's in."

One would have imagined that nothing could ever have disturbed Corrie's pleasant equanimity, but out in the garden he had a sudden pain in his right side.

"It's that confounded rheumatism," he muttered.

George commiserated.

"I'm very rarely free from pain, laddie; but we carry on somehow, don't we, Elizabeth?" Corrie groaned, holding on to his daughter as one who makes a fight not to show that he is bravely bearing well-nigh unbearable pain.

Annesley suggested that he should go back into the house and rest, or sit still for a time in the car.

"No, no, I tell you. Damn it, don't fuss! You take Marion and show her your bally puddles that you've been telling us so much about. Go—go—I tell you!"

Marion made a move and beckoned George to follow.

"Poor old Bernard's worse, I'm afraid, isn't he?" Annesley said as soon as they were out of earshot.

"No, I don't think so. Really I think he's much better. It's fifty parts nerves. He imagines things, you know."

"Poor old Bernard. He's been through a lot."

"Yes, he's been through a lot."

They walked up to the end of the third pond and over to the Cherry Hay boundary where it ran along by the golf course. They stood for a moment watching the aerial ropeway above the top of the colliery tip. It was working. The rubbish dropping from the buckets made little black smudges against the bright May sky; a slight breeze blowing towards them brought with it the faint sound of the impact when the contents of the bucket fell.

Marion asked him how it worked. She liked to know how things worked, and he told her as they made their way slowly back to the house. In the yard at the back of the house she hesitated, put a hand on his arm, and halted. He turned to face her inquiringly.

"George, don't press him to come. It's very beautiful, but for him, the very last place on earth. Why, what will he find to do all day? Nothing—nothing but think of his aches, and he doesn't need helping in that."

"But he wants to come—don't you want to come?"

"Me? Oh, I don't matter."

Their eyes met. There was a desolating pause, and she knew that she had lost him. Never had lover a better chance. These two had never spoken a word of love. He had never kissed her, she had nothing to go on, but they both had known for all that. Surely there had been something, something indefinable, some delicate adjustment of wave-length—now they seemed all out of tune—the distant music had faded away.

In silence they walked back to the house where they found Corrie and Elizabeth standing on the little bridge that carried the drive across the garden stream. As they came up Corrie took off his spectacles and wiped them. A smile lit his tired face.

"Paradise—perfection—peace in our time, oh, Lord!" he murmured.

Elizabeth looked up at him affectionately. "Daddy, it's a dream. Don't talk or else I'll wake!"

Annesley left his car in one of the old sheds at the back of the house, and together they made their way past the ponds, across the golf links and up the short hill to Little Plenders and the French Horn, where, by taxing the house to capacity, he had managed to secure accommodation for his guests. And after dinner, after the two girls had retired for the night, George and Bernard, George remembering his conversation with Marion and feeling guilty, Bernard saying to himself, "Blast the women," discussed the

suggestion that the Corries should come and live at
Cherry Hay. George wanted to let for he had visions of
Cherry Hay for himself; Bernard insisted on buying, he
had fallen in love with the place—and after a time, Annesley, remembering his debts and not forgetting Elizabeth,
gave way and they settled the sale.

"That's that, then," George said. "Never mind the papers, it's a deal. Come in to-morrow if you like." He held
out his steady muscular hand and Bernard took it with his
lean and rather shaky one.

"You shall have the check in a day or two," he replied,
delighted. He was a bally landowner.

But he did not admit the fact until they were well on
their way back to London next afternoon. A man and a
rather attractive girl joined their carriage at Kettering,
and Corrie took the opportunity. He began to talk in an
unhushed voice about the Priory and Cherry Hay. To an
outsider it was not quite clear which it was he had bought;
in fact, apparently, he had bought them both.

Marion looked out of the window.

And next day—Monday—she gave a month's notice at
the bank.

7

"THE BEST LAID PLANS—"

Moralists may preach example's inspiration, may urge you, "Hitch your wagon to a star," and, without a doubt, both morally and physically, it is most pleasantly uplifting, this looking down on lower things. However, fortunately for most of us, you do not have to climb even such a moderate mountain as, say Snowdon, to obtain a pleasing view. Indeed, morally, you have no need to climb at all—a modicum of self-conceit, a dash of imagination, and you can look down from your own little self-created summit on that poor fool Jones and that well-meaning ass Smith in the murk of the valley below you, and—the Lord be praised for it!—it takes nothing from your pleasure either, when you remember that, really, all the time, Smith and Jones are perched on their own little private pinnacles from which they peer down at you. Physically it is much the same; the view from Everest may be amazing, but, after all, from Snowdon, you can see right to the very edge of your own vision—and there is quite a good view over the low stone wall at the bottom of the garden behind the French Horn at Little Plenders.

As he sat there late one evening in early September George Annesley, his pipe firmly held between his strong white teeth, thought he had seen no other view just like it, but then quite a lot of it belonged to him—and possession improves a view.

Not only did the greater part of what George saw belong to him, but in a sense he had peopled it himself. In the mellow evening light he could just see the curve of the wooded hill that hid the Priory, and at the Priory there lived Lobley, Primrose, and Professor Taverner, *the* Professor Taverner, and they lived there because it had pleased him to imagine that they might be concerned in the theft of certain papers and because he permitted them to. They paid him fat, satisfactory rents for the privilege. Nearer, through trees, he could see the chimneys of Cherry Hay, and at Cherry Hay lived Corrie. He had sold Cherry Hay to Corrie because his fat uncle at Scotland Yard thought fit to imagine that Corrie might have had something to do with the missing papers. He had planted them there—at least he thought he had—just as a gardener plants plants— the lobelias there, the primroses there, and the coreopsis there—so. He felt god-like. Like a god he had willed it, and they, after the manner of stupid human beings, had gone and made a mess of it all against his will.

It had certainly been an inspiration though, to assemble the suspects together. He quite forgot that so far as the Priory was concerned the suggestion came from Lobley and Primrose first. But no matter, it was a good plan. Lobley & Co. were interested in the subject of erosion or they would not have had Corrie's paper. They were up to something. And if they were up to something, then clearly, with Corrie, the innocent author of the paper (so Annesley thought), as their nearest neighbor, something must come of it. And if Corrie was not innocent then the plan was equally good. As a factory inspector, he had the right to go into the Magnet works at Derby, of which, so a letter in his pocket told him, Corrie had been made a director on his uncle's death, just whenever he liked, and as a friend

he had the privilege of going to stay with them at Cherry
Hay. Not a very god-like, or even friendly thing to do
perhaps! But then, as Annesley sat on the little stone wall
smoking his pipe, he had not one real suspicion of Corrie.
On the contrary he thought of himself as clearing his queer
friend who, at times, could be one of the best. Had he not
sold him Cherry Hay, where, in spite of what Marion said,
a quiet country life would do him a world of good, at a
ridiculously low price? Corrie's handicap was twenty-two,
and he had enabled Corrie to live in a beautiful old house
within a few hundred yards of a first-class golf course.
There was both scope and opportunity for almost unlimited improvement, and what more could a god provide for
a man! By the time the Priory lot had run through their
leases he would have satisfied the tax collector's more
urgent demands, and then he would marry Elizabeth, if
she would have him, and live at the Priory with her.

He would be very happy, he would do his utmost to
make Elizabeth happy, Corrie would be happy because
of his recovery, and Marion—well, Marion, he supposed,
would be happy for the same reason. That was how he
thought of it. Put into print it may look a little extrav-
agant and stupid, but it must be remembered that these
were George's private unuttered thoughts, and the private
thoughts of quite a number of modest clever people would
look a little out of drawing if they strayed and got into
print. No, Annesley's best friend could not have accused
him of attempting the god-like—neither could his worst
enemy for that matter. Neither was he stupid. In fact, he
was clever enough already to have doubts, very disturbing
doubts, about the wisdom of what he had done.

The Corries had moved into Cherry Hay in early July
and Lobley and his friends got into the Priory about a
month later. Annesley, on his uncle's advice, had given
out that he had been recalled for a time to the south-east

London district, so that, undisturbed, the guilty and the innocent might settle in. During his absence he had received letters from Corrie himself, from Marion, and also from Elizabeth, and it was these letters that had given rise to his first vague feelings of doubt. Astonishingly, they none of them seemed happy—not even Elizabeth.

Bernard wrote and told him that he was feeling worse—much worse—and that Marion only made him worse still by constantly badgering him to go and see a nerve specialist or go back to London and rot in steady employment among the specifications at the Patent Office. Apparently she had been sufficiently lacking in good taste to discuss the matter with their neighbors at the Priory and they were pestering him too. From Corrie's letters it was evident that Cherry Hay and Plenders Priory had passed rapidly through the stage of formal calls to the stage of friendly "dropping in;" they were nearest neighbors, and in Bernard's letters Norman Lobley's niece who kept house for him began by being "Miss Lobley, a regular peach," then she became "Miss Lobley," and then in his last letter she was referred to more than once as simply "Joyce." Somehow Annesley suspected that Bernard had fallen in love with her, not merely because she had changed in the course of a few weeks from "Miss Lobley" to "Joyce;" there was nothing in that by itself, but in later letters from both Marion and Elizabeth she was still "Miss Lobley" to them. Too, she was a "peach," Marion's letter implied it as well, and it was just like Bernard to prefer a peach to honest apples.

It seemed that Corrie had been coopted on to the board of the Magnet company after Annesley had gone north and before they—the Corries—had left Blackheath. By reason of his early incursion into the field of economics he had known what to look for in a balance sheet, and not liking what he saw in the Magnet balance sheet, Corrie had been to their annual meeting, where he had spent a pleasingly unpleasant hour. There had been references to it—"Scene at Company Meeting"—in the press, and cuttings were enclosed in one of Bernard's letters. He was the largest shareholder, and whatever the demerits of the Magnet directors in the matter of directing those operations necessary to the profitable manufacture of motor bicycles, they evidently thought they knew how to deal with Corrie; like phagocytes with a juicy germ they made up their minds quietly to absorb him. They did absorb him quite successfully, but he refused to be quiet. Instead, he set out to learn all he could about motor cycles and the processes necessary to their proper manufacture. Annesley gathered, that as soon as he had got to Cherry Hay, he had gone to the absurd length of making an arrangement with a firm of motor engineers in Millingham, who had bought for him every known make of motor cycle, including one of Norman Lobley's "Little Giants," so that he might watch a fitter pull them to bits and compare them one with the other, component by component; he had ordered a big six-cylinder car to enable him to dash in to Millingham or Derby. As his enthusiasm swept to its peak, his co-directors, not knowing him, must have become quite needlessly alarmed. Annesley, however, could have told them of past enthusiasms. Already, so he gathered, the first violence of the explosion was subsiding and Bernard, exhausted, was spending every third day or so in bed, and was even dividing the other two between his new-found activities and golf with Elizabeth and Joyce.

From Marion's one letter Annesley had learnt a surprising piece of information. James James, who had been taken on by the Primroses when they went into the main section of the Priory, had left, and gone as general factotum to Cherry Hay. It seemed that Mr. Primrose had not suited him, but Annesley, when he read it, wondered if Mr. Corrie would suit the quiet James James any better and began to think of other possible reasons for the transfer. It seemed to him at right through Marion's letter there was a quite uncalled for note of bitterness. Bernard, she told him, had taken to shouting and walking in his sleep again and had become more difficult to humor than she had ever previously known him—in two short months he had lost two long years' improvement. Professor Taverner, whose brother, it appeared, was a doctor at a large London asylum, agreed with her that he was in a condition, which, if matters were allowed to drift, could only end in mental collapse, but whereas, when they first got to Cherry Hay, Bernard had always been running to the doctor about nothing, now that there was real need for medical advice, nothing would persuade him to see one. Between keen desire to get him to a specialist and natural anxiety not to make him worse by over-fussing, poor Marion seemed to be having a difficult time, and she certainly implied that the whole of the trouble was traceable to George. Indeed her letter was one complicated variation on the single theme, "Why did you do it?" which came through every sentence like some over-emphasized water mark. Even when she wrote of the golf Bernard and Elizabeth were playing, she managed to imply that Bernard only played because Miss Lobley did, that Miss Lobley was the worst type of minx, and that that was George's fault as well.

And Elizabeth's letters had not been reassuring. George felt the last, a long one, which had reached him only the day before in London, when he put his hand in his pocket for the matches, and having re-lit his pipe, he read it again as he sat on the wall.

> "Dear George" (it ran)—"When on earth are you coming back again to Little Plenders? I cannot understand this place. Since we got here everything seems to be going to bits.

The house is a dear old house—excepting for the wretched water pipes that make it thump like a giant's heart—the golf is A1, the garden's a dream, there are bunnies in the woods and trout in the stream, the weather's been wonderful, our neighbors at the Priory are as neighborly as can be—and yet we're all as jumpy as performing fleas afflicted with St. Vitus's dance!

"You know you never told the Prioryites that we had right of way down their drive and round by the stables, though how the dickens they fancied we got here this poor C3 brain can't conceive. Anyhow, your gross neglect nearly landed us into a nice old mess. Daddy and I were walking up through the rhododendrons towards the gates to catch the bus for Millingham, when Mr. Lobley and his *beautiful* (she got Daddy middle peg first ball and I believe she has a leg break, so you beware!) niece met us in their car. They pulled up and Mr. Lobley asked us who we were and what we did—and they both seemed almost too astonished when we told them we lived at Cherry Hay. Just at first Mr. Lobley was quite rude about it; he was sure there must be some mistake, and I don't know what might have happened, had the niece been less bewitching. It got Daddy on the wrong leg right away, so to speak, and before he could get going in his usual form, Mr. Lobley had learnt that he was talking with *the* Bernard Corrie who had written a paper on something or other, and in less than no time they were purring together like twin engines, and what with that, and Miss

Lobley's spell-binding beauty poor Daddy was so above himself that he'd have got into the wrong bus and gone to Blatchford if I hadn't been there to stop him.

"Mr. Lobley, as you, great secret one, probably know already, is managing director of the Giants, and—talk about a magnet and a silver churn—Daddy's got a regular pash on him. He, Daddy, will have told you about being made a director of the Magnet Company, and for a few weeks we lived in such a complicated state of high ignition and compound compression that I thought we should all blow up. Even Mrs. Glegg has learnt the difference between a bookcase and a crank case and asked Marion the other day if she knew what had become of the master's piston ring, meaning his napkin ring all the time, and James James regularly refers to common or garden manure as 'exhaust material!' We've lost some of our revs though these last few weeks and—oh, but I forgot to tell you of that, we did very nearly have a real explosion—a regular backyard backfire.

"Daddy had got hold of a Little Giant machine, and having pulled it to bits in one of the sheds at the back, was trying to stick it together. The poor dear, having just dropped a valve or something down one of the sparking plugs, was feeling all—you know—when Mr. Primrose—Daddy didn't know who he was, of course, at the time—and it's too silly that a thing like that should have a name like that, because instead of reminding one of some sweet, shady hedge bank, he reminds one of a pit bank—came marching through the yard like a pig in plus fours with his golf bag over his shoulder, and this time (this sentence has run to seed) it was Daddy's turn to ask about the right of way and there weren't any mermaids by to put him off his stroke. I wasn't there but I understand he was right at the very top of his form, and began by telling Mr. Primrose that he ought to be buried under his pit bank, and ended up by hurling a Little Giant piston straight at his face, but fortunately it wasn't straight enough and landed in a bed of nettles up the lane, which stung me all over when, later on, I went to hunt it out. It quite upset poor Daddy though, and he had to retire to bed, and then it seems he should have known all the time that the Priory people *had* a right of way to the golf links and the colliery, and there was another hectic hour before Marion could persuade him to go and apologize. As luck would have it though, when he did go, the Lobleys were having tea with the Primroses (Mrs. P. is like a cabbage—purple pickling sort) and the rift has been healed, or rather I should say welded, so that now you can't even see where the crack was—we're getting that thick!

"Professor Taverner *is* rather an old dear though. He's got a head like a peg top and a mouth like the mouth of a tortoise, just a line, a real geometry one, all of it length and none of it breadth.

"That all sounds agreeable and affable, and I can hear you asking, 'What about the afflicted acrobatic fleas?' but it's Daddy and Marion.

I don't know what's come over them both. Daddy can't sleep and he's gone all jumpy like he used to be a year or two ago, and Marion is going about with a face like a last year's lemon. She hates being here. She won't play golf herself, Daddy only plays because of Joyce Lobley, Marion is always running her down and Daddy gets dippier and dippier over her, and I'm dashed if I see why the poor dear shouldn't dip if he wants to—after all it's his own dip. And I—well, I feel as unpopular and out of place as a sparrow hatched by mistake in a cuckoo's nest—Daddy only wants me to play golf because it makes it easier for him to get games with the lovely alluring Lobley girl; if I do, he hates me to see her showing him how to hold his clubs (she's awfully good), which she does as often as she can, and Marion hates me not to play because she knows that Daddy will hit a ball right into the very deepest rough and never find either it, or himself, or anything else ever again if I don't.

"What a screed! But when your lordship condescends to travel north again one of us will be very pleased indeed to see you.

"Yours,

"Elizabeth."

Half amused, half angry, George thrust the letter into his pocket again. For a time he stood looking over the valley towards Cherry Hay and the hills that lay beyond it. Whilst he read, a transformation scene had set; the soft but definite contours of the many, wooded, sunlit slopes had changed to vague indefinite differences of shade where faintly detailed banks of gray ran into unetched banks of blue, and blues into deeper blues, that crossed and merged and swept to the dark horizon above the fading evening landscape. The country that half an hour ago lay mapped out below him had slipped into shadows like a stage—the lights are switched off one by one—the footlights go— perhaps a servant brings a candle on, or a burglar swings his lantern. The sun had set. In a window at Cherry Hay a yellow light flickered in and out as a bough of a near-by tree was rocked to and fro by the breeze.

Annesley turned to go indoors. As he made his way up the garden path the pit bank on his left looked like a dead black wall, topped with a glow of sunset red against which the ropeway skips stood out like wicked little beads, little black beads that day by day and year by year dropped dirt, now just an ugly smudge on the doomed green grass be- low, next hour a mound, a little grave, a heap, a hillock, a mountain—a mountain of ash and corroding filth which, like a cancer, ever creeping, threatened to fill and defile the fair valley.

George, as he made his way to his supper, had no such thoughts as those however. To-morrow he would go down to Cherry Hay and the Priory and have a good nose round. He would have a look inside the stables too or else he was a Dutchman. As he closed the door behind him, a little breeze that seemed to hold the sigh of many trees blew across the valley from Cherry Hay, and could he but have known it, every tree was whispering, "Fool—oh, fool—by my leaves what a fool!"

8
THE MYSTERIOUS DISC

If, instead of picking up mere scraps of news from letters, George Annesley could have extended his god-like propensities to embrace a knowledge of all the hidden things that had happened at Cherry Hay during his absence, he would no longer have doubted the wisdom of his efforts. He would have been absolutely certain that so far as the Corries were concerned he had been their evil genius. In other words, Marion was right again, as she nearly always was.

To an outsider it must have appeared that the Corries had hove to at last in a harbor of calm contentment. They had exchanged their ugly little rented house in Blackheath for the beauties of their own Cherry Hay, the clanging of trams for country sounds, the hurried catching of crowded trains for the leisurely catching of mottled trout, one endless unsuccessful effort to make ends meet for a settled affluence, and one would have imagined that many months must pass before contentment turned to boredom.

But the Corries were not content. The calm they had hove into was about as real as the calm of a yeasted lump of dough, in which unseen, unheard microscopic multitudinous upheavals slowly but cumulatively alter the face of things.

Elizabeth, the bright and gay, grew jealous. She did not know it and would not have admitted it.

"Don't be so absurd," would have been her comment.
But all the same she was jealous.

Somehow, in some indefinable way, the fact that her
father had fallen in love with Joyce Lobley spoilt her own
love for George Annesley. It seemed to sink the standard.
And to add to her unhappiness she received no single line
from Annesley. As a matter of fact he did write to her once
and then he forgot to post it; an omission that for Elizabeth took some of the gilt off the gingerbread.

But Bernard's gingerbread was gilded until it glittered
again, and he bathed in the rays with the thrill of some
slum child sent to an Alpine sun school. Since his first
flounderings in the sea of inexperience had washed him
ashore on a wave with the unsuitable "Bobby," his romantic life had been but a mud-flat of petty affairs and repres-
sion. Now the long-delayed returning tide carried him out
of his depth again. Joyce, her mysterious beauty, his sudden release from drudgery, his altogether unexpected escape from financial insecurity, the beauty of his surround-
ings, all was propitious for his love. Wind, moon, and tide
combined urged on the flood, into which he plunged with
the confident strokes of an experienced, but long-denied
performer.

His ardor, however, did not increase the general happiness. At his most equable, he was one of those who think
home a sink down which they may swill their outer life's
unlovely leavings. Always, as far back as Elizabeth's memory carried her, any trivial mischance might set a spark to
war-frayed nerves and blaze into a scene. Now it seemed
almost as though the peaks of his happiness with Joyce
demanded balancing depths at home, and any sore-headed
bear could have given him lessons in manners.

As Marion told George in her letter, whilst at Blackheath he had seen his doctor about something or other
nearly every month in the year, now he met every direct

and indirect suggestion that he should run up to town for a few nights and take the opportunity of seeing so and so with, not blank refusal, but vehement refusal deserving many blanks.

As a matter of fact he was utterly afraid to see any doctor, and this was the root cause of nearly all the trouble that befell them could they but have known it. The excitement of his legacy, his move to Cherry Hay, his altered habits of life, all had been bad for him, and before a month had passed Bernard knew for certain, knew by certain indescribable whirrings in his head, that Marion was right. By that time though, he had met Joyce Lobley. Cherry Hay in sunshine—Joyce—a nursing home, so-called—could any one blame him? You, who have put off that visit to the dentist for so many, many months—can you blame him?

To Bernard, the first sure sign of relapse was that when he closed his eyes at night he saw things—terrible hair-raising things—Primrose, perhaps, equipped with tusks instead of teeth; tusks with naked eyeballs on the ends below empty bloody sockets—things more terrifying still and doubly terrifying by reason of their uncontrolled persistence—things that made him, afraid to close his eyes, lie staring at the night for hours whilst the beat of his heart raced the beat of the water that pulsed in the pipes. Then he began to see things when his eyes were open too, and he knew that his brain was going. Fear increased insomnia and lack of sleep increased his fears—a vicious circle—he dare confide in no one—already they had noticed it—the mad-house waited him—and Marion's suggestions, Taverner's hints, every private half-heard conversation became for him a menace.

Even before he was shell-shocked Bernard had been liable to wake with a yell at the moment of falling asleep. The doctor had assured Marion that it was nothing to worry about, "Quite a common symptom of nervous cases. It occurs just as the brain loses control and sleep comes creeping in. Some people jerk in much the same way. It will vary with his general state of health, but you need not worry." And Marion had not worried. It took a lot to worry Marron. But now, accustomed to it as she was, she did feel some alarm, so sudden and strident, so alive and white with terror was the yell that shot through the house like a flame each night. To the uninitiated it was blood curdling, and they lost two maids the first month.

He was just at the height of his motor bicycle enthusiasm when he first began to imagine that his nerves were breaking down again, and it was just about then that he got his new six-cylinder car. He drove it out to Cherry Hay from Millingham himself.

Warm machine oil—there can be no stink like it for turning a tender stomach, and Bernard, who in his desire for motor cycle knowledge had stood it for a whole afternoon and evening, felt sick when he started for home. But although he had not driven since he drove in France he got on famously. The car was a beauty, indeed the dash was so wide and spacious that as you sat at the wheel you could hardly see what time it was by the clock away on the left, and its broad polished acres fairly bristled with switches and knobs—he knew what some of them were there for. He had never owned anything that pleased him so much before.

The sky was overcast with cloud and it was approaching dusk when at eight o'clock he left the garage. The car took the hill between the woods on the Blatchford road like a live thing; thirty—"Don't go more than thirty for a week or two, Mr. Corrie"—thirty-five—he barely touched the accelerator—forty—forty-five—it was splendid. Among other gadgets there was a traffic indicator worked by a little knob on the dash and Bernard pushed the knob to the right as he prepared to enter the sweep in front of the Priory gates. He glanced at the mirror over his head just to make sure there was nothing behind. It was an unnecessary precaution; already he had lit his rear red arrow. It was unfortunate too, for in gazing at the past he neglected the future, took the bend too quickly caught the accelerator with his foot when he hurriedly applied the brake, and to his horror, though he tugged at the hand-brake as well, slipped slowly into the iron gates across the top of the Priory drive.

He felt suddenly dizzy. For a few minutes he sat perfectly still. The damage, however, was not as serious as he expected. The peak of one beautiful shining wing was nearly doubled under until it touched the wheel, the other was slightly buckled, the radiator was not even scratched, and after a time, his elation gone, he was able to proceed slowly down the drive between the rhododendrons.

This time he proceeded cautiously in third gear. He put his headlights on. They were powerful and satisfactory, lighting the shrubs like the wall of a tunnel, and all went well until he reached the end of the wood, where a rabbit made a dash to cross, changed its mind, and, hypnotized by the headlights, behaved generally like the chosen hen member of a poultry suicide club. Bernard, yelling. "Curse the vermin!" made a lunge at the brake but made the same mistake again and the big car lurched forward instead of losing speed; there was one soft bump when the front wheel went over the fluffy warm body and another pitifully less pronounced, when the back wheel did the same. Now, when Corrie shouted, "Curse the vermin" (he had shouted it quite loudly though there was no one within miles to hear him) it was not because he thought of rabbits as vermin, but because he hated to think that he had killed one, for the president and officials of the R.S.P.C.A. combined could not have outdone Corrie in the matter of loving animals. He walked back and picked the little creature up. It was still quite warm and limp and he stroked the white fur on its underneath.

"Poor little bunny, you shall be buried and not torn to pieces, anyhow," he murmured gently, as he forced his way through the rhododendron bushes. Then close to the wall at the edge of the wood he scratched a hole in the leaf mold and placed the rabbit in it. He was straightening out the leaves again above the little grave when his hand struck something hard. He picked it up and took it back with him to the car to examine it more closely. It was a bright little metal disc, six inches or so in diameter, dished on one side like a concave mirror. Round the periphery there was a band of a dark red substance which Corrie guessed to be an insulating material and embedded in this were about twenty of the tiniest sparking plugs he had ever seen. They were complete with contact points and terminal screws of the same bright untarnishable metal as the plate itself.

Wondering what on earth it could be and what useful purpose it could have served, Corrie got back again into the car, putting the mysterious article in the capacious cubby-hole on the dash, and made another attempt to finish his journey.

He got into third gear again and all went famously so long as the road ran straight or bore to the left, but when he took a right-hand turn it brought the off-side tire scraping against the damaged mudguard. However, he did manage to attain a fair speed, and he reached the point where the drive bends sharply back to the right round by the stable buildings without further mishap. At this point the drive drops towards the lake as well, and pull as he might at the hand wheel, the tire jammed against the damaged mudguard so that he could not swing the car round, and to avoid his previous errors with the foot-brake, this time he grabbed at the hand-brake instead. Unfortunately, however, he changed his grip on the steering wheel and accidentally knocked the hand-control lever down to the open position.

It seemed to Corrie that whenever he put the brakes on the blasted car careered forward at greater speed. Now it made straight for the big stable door. He gave vent to one gasping cry. He lunged with his foot on the foot-brake and he tugged at the hand-brake lever, but the front wheels bumped gently against the big double doors, and as though he had touched some spring, one of them sprang wide open and Joyce Lobley, bare-headed, stood before him, the light from his lamps lighting her hair like a halo.

Then dizziness overcame Corrie again. He collapsed across the hand-wheel. He thought to himself, "What an ass she will think me! What an angel she looks!" And closing his eyes he nearly fainted.

Joyce had been over to the new laboratory in the fables with a message from her uncle for Professor Taverner. Only two minutes earlier she had passed the gray pointed arch into the stable courtyard. There had been no one about. Now, when she came back she found a big car, standing with its wheels actually touching the doors—its engine silent. The powerful headlights blinded her. She closed the heavy stable door and the Yale lock clicked behind her There was still no movement in the car. She went round to the side, and, looking in, recognized Corrie.

"What's the matter? You look ill. Is there anything the matter?" she asked, getting into the car and taking her place by his side.

"No—at least I shall be better again in two ticks. It's the beastly car. I bashed in the mudguard—an accident. Then because of that I couldn't take the corner and nearly rammed the doors. The blasted brakes seem only to make the bally thing go faster."

"Poor you! Why, you're shaking. You'd better sit still for a minute."

They sat still for five. She was soothing, understanding—yet not too sympathetic. She was just exactly right. She made him feel that it was quite an ordinary thing for a full-grown man to shake like a leaf because he had nearly had an accident.

"Would you like me to come along with you?" she asked him after a time. "I've nothing on earth to do."

"I—I don't like—it seems so dashed silly—but it would be most awfully kind if you would. Makes me feel no end of an ass though."

"But why? Any one, even Malcolm Campbell, might feel too ill to drive a car. Nothing silly about it."

Bernard made no further protest and, starting the engine, he put the lever in reverse, thinking to himself as he did so, "Now, why the dickens can't Marion be more like this sometimes." But there was nothing dainty about Bernard's driving, and letting the clutch in with a bump, he stalled the engine.

"Now the infernal machine won't move at all!" he cried querulously. "The wheel must be jammed by the mudguard, I think."

Joyce laughed quietly. Had Marion laughed in exactly the same way she would have been sneering at him. But Joyce—

"Never. It's a twenty at least, isn't it? Why you've got the brakes hard on! Here, change seats. Let me take it."

They changed places and the car behaved like a lamb. It was as though some spoilt and fretful child had finally got what it cried for. It glided back into the darkness behind them without a sound.

When they came to the sharp right bend before you go down the hill to Cherry Hay, the wheel fouled the mudguard again, and Joyce neither charged the fence, tugged at the steering wheel nor lost her head, but backed and went forward alternately, taking three bites at the job.

Corrie made appreciative noises. As they slipped down the hill through the trees he thanked her again. "And, I say—I say—would you very much mind not coming in? Is it awfully rude of me?—but, Marion, it means endless explanations—"

"You poor dear—do they tease you? It's beastly of them. But I couldn't come in anyhow—and of course I understand."

They crossed the bridge over the garden stream, and drew up by the Cherry Hay door.

"That's the garage, there, with the open doors, isn't it? You get down and I'll run the car in and go."

They shook hands. Their ridiculous little intrigue seemed to make it natural that he should hold hers for a moment.

Corrie disappeared into the house—a sick man head over heels in love.

Joyce put the car away for him as she promised, and started out on her two-mile tramp back to the Priory, a little annoyed but intensely amused by Bernard's characteristic display. She knew perfectly well that he would do anything she might ask him to do but that he had entirely overlooked the fact that she would have to walk home alone. He was more concerned that Marion and Elizabeth should learn as little as possible about his incompetent driving—in fact his one concern was Bernard Corrie and what other people thought of Bernard Corrie.

When she had gone some hundred yards or so she suddenly began to wonder whether she had had her hand-bag with her and went back to the garage to look, where to her surprise she found James James sitting in the driver's seat with the headlights on.

"You'd left the headlights on, miss. I was looking for the switch," he explained.

Joyce felt perfectly sure she had switched the headlights off, but they looked for her hand-bag together,
James James picking up the peculiar disc his master had
found and putting it back without comment. Being entirely uninterested in matters mechanical, he had no comment
to make. Indeed, it might have been a butter dish so far as
James James was concerned and he probably thought that
it was.

The hand-bag could not be found and Joyce departed.

An hour later, when Bernard (having explained to Marion that he had caught the mudguard on the gate post and
that he would go and have a look at it) came out to fetch
the queer little concave disc, it was nowhere to be found.

Quite clearly he remembered placing it in the cubby-
hole on the dash and equally clearly it was there no longer.
It was nowhere else either.

And that was one little incident that the god-like,
man-planting George Annesley knew nothing about.

9
INSOMNIA

One Saturday morning, about a week before George Annesley returned to the French Horn, the first faint flapping of the wings of disaster stirred the quiet air.

Joyce had sent a note across from the Priory to explain that she was prevented from playing golf, and Bernard, who had already burnt his boats by refusing to take Marion into Millingham because of an imaginary appointment at the club house, went off much against his will to pretend to keep it and play with Elizabeth alone. Marion, annoyed, set out on foot to the gates for the Millingham bus. It was a long walk and she could have obtained nearly everything she wanted at Little Plenders, but, having stated that she must go to Millingham, to Millingham she meant to go.

About a mile past the stables, before the big wood near the gates is reached, there is a smaller wood some twenty yards from the drive, and down a narrow glade with his back to one of the trees she saw Primrose, and standing in front of him, Joyce, and as Marion passed the big ugly man raised up the girl and kissed her mouth.

Marion saw it clearly. There could be no doubt about it. She saw the fluttering leaves printed in shadow by the sun on the girl's white frock and beautiful upturned face, she saw Primrose put his big fat hands underneath the girl's arms and lift her up. She saw the kiss and there was no mistaking who they were. Much disturbed, she hurried on.

And at night, worn out and worried, she lay awake in bed wondering what she ought to do; should she brave the storm and tell her brother? Would he believe her if she did? Or should she speak to Joyce?

And Bernard also lay awake afraid—afraid to close his eyes because of the things he knew he would see—afraid to lie awake because of the things he thought he might see, for twice recently, lying awake he had imagined a face at his window, but always when he went to the window there was nothing there.

At length, however, he did fall asleep and then a noise like a drum, repeated till it beat response from his dormant brain, disturbed him. He sat up in bed, but the recurrent plunking of the throbbing pipes, the rarer rattle of some distant badly-fitting door, an owl whose hideous hoot flashed fear through the air from an outhouse building, the usual noises of a country house at night, were the only sounds to reach his straining ears.

Then the beating of the sleep-destroying drum came once again, drew his gaze to where the window was, and fear—the sort of fear that far transcends the fear pain or death unshriven, fear that must surely feed its foul roots from those myriad mystic years of savage past that lie latent beneath their thin veneer of more enlightened later days, fear that can mock the image of God in man, crack a man's brain, find him a human soul and in a second leave him there a gibbering lunatic instead—fear—fear clutched his heart, and froze him. Against the black window, white fingers were drumming—white fingers—lustrous—that wriggled and writhed on the luminous stump of a hand. The thing, though it was minus the arm, cut off square at the wrist, with no visible means of support, moved about like a live thing against the pane, beat against it like some great moth or fluttering bird, banged and blundered, till Corrie thought the glass would break and fresh fears swamped him; then it hovered for a moment as though it floated by itself in air, beckoned, clawed, clutched, grew fainter and fainter—and vanished.

Corrie closed his eyes for a minute and opened them again. No, it had not come back. That cursed owl again—the noise in the pipes—no other sound. He got out of bed, found his dressing-gown, switched on the light, and went over to the window. It was an old-fashioned casement with three panes, the center one fixed, the others opening out-wards. The left-hand pane was open. The hand had fluttered and drummed against the middle of the right.

His first thought was that some one might have played him a trick—perhaps a stuffed glove and phosphorous paint—stuck on a pole and held against the window. Then he remembered how the fingers had moved and he prickled again with fear. It had come to that at last, then—he *was* seeing things!

Then suddenly he thought that with a ladder some one might yet have played the trick. He opened the window and leant out. Within the radius of the light he could just see the stone flags below, and across the yard the outline of one of the outhouse buildings. He called gently, "Hallo! Who's that?" He repeated the call, but receiving no reply, crawled back into bed where he thought of how he wanted Joyce and dwelt morbidly on the dark horrors of lunacy.

Lunacy! What would madness feel like? What caused it? Heredity? Could one become mad as the result of shell-shock and disordered nerves? He remembered something about pressure on the brain—a small clot of blood. But his brain felt remarkably clear. He ran through the names of all the people he knew and he could remember them all without hesitation—even the names of quite unimportant junior people in the various departments at the Patent Office. He repeated one or two of his favorite poems. Yes, his brain was quite remarkably clear—his hearing too. He could hear the ducks up by the ponds and very faintly, noises at the colliery away beyond the golf links. The noise in the water pipes seemed to shake the house—like a pulse at high fever. He could hear them throbbing in the bathroom across the landing, and the fancy came to him that if he went and turned the taps on blood would gush—blood—hot and cold. That was the damned silly sort of thing he was always thinking of. People like Annesley never thought things like that—bovine—stupid. Perhaps that really his trouble all the time—he was a genius. He certainly felt extraordinarily alive and clever at the moment; his brain was working by itself. He would never go to sleep again. His thoughts dwelt on Joyce—supposing he did marry Joyce! . . . All these years, what a lot he had missed! He found paper and pencil and wrote some verses. Day had dawned when he finished them and about six o'clock he dressed, crept downstairs and went out of doors.

He walked towards the Priory and at the stables, hearing a humming noise, he climbed down the little grassy slope between the building and the drive and tried to peer in through the frosted glass.

"Hallo, Mr. Corrie, you're early afoot."

Corrie started. It was not very comfortable to be caught peering into some one else's window even if it was only a stable window. He turned round quickly. The quick movement brought a dizziness—suddenly his head was splitting. Professor Taverner, wearing a cloth cap, was standing on the drive just above him.

"Oh, it's you, professor. Yes, I've been for an early walk. I suffer a lot from insomnia, you know. I wondered what the noise was."

Standing up above him, the professor's head, Bernard thought, looked more like a peg-top than ever. A peg-top with a cap on and a line where the mouth ought to be. The line extended as Corrie mounted the little bank again to the path, the exertion making him feel as though his head would burst.

"You look ill. If I were you I should go home," the professor said, and walked away towards the Priory without another word.

Corrie made slowly for Cherry Hay, feeling too ill to worry about Taverner's rude and abrupt departure.

Marion, too, had had a bad night, but she got up at seven as usual.

As a rule Bernard was the last member of the household to come down to breakfast and, surprised to see his bedroom door open, she went in. She was just picking up his pyjamas—his untidiness always exasperated her—when she noticed a sheet of paper on the table at the side of the bed, and thinking that it might be some message she picked it up and read it.

Words such as "urge," "lust" and "desire," anything in fact that suggested, however vaguely, that love was more than comradeship and kissing and that babies were not an entirely feminine product, reacted on Marion much as the shape of the human figure reacted on our great-grandmothers. Her lips curled. She pictured Primrose—a married man—kissing Joyce in the wood. It was all of a piece—such words led to such things. She crumpled the offending verses into a ball, and thrusting it into her overall pocket, made her way downstairs.

"Marion! Marion! Is that you, Marion? I want you here in the dining-room!" It was Bernard, shouting angrily.

He was standing by the fireplace, and held out an Income Tax demand note towards her in a trembling hand.

"You said you'd put it away last night before you to
bed, and here it is this morning for all the maids to see
and read."

'All the maids' amused Marion. There were two—Mrs.
Glegg and a little girl called Katie and, of course, James
James.

"Oh, I'm sorry, I forgot," she said. "But I don't suppose
for a moment they'd understand it even if they did read it,
and they haven't been down long either."

"But if I hadn't got up what might have happened—I
ask you? It's a blasted and damnable shame that I should
have to get up when I'm ill to see to things of this sort.
I can barely stand and yet I simply dare not stop in bed
because of this sort of thing. Oh yes, you may smile! You
don't care a damn—not a damn—you don't care a damn, I
tell you!"

Marion stood silent and helpless. He waved his arms—
went on and on—swamping—nauseating—like the un-
healthy-looking endless snake that comes creeping out of
a chemical pill from a Christmas cracker when you put a
match to it. She remembered the thousand and one things
she cleared up after him every day, she remembered his
pyjamas, the verses left by the side of the bed, and temptation overcame her. Straightening the crumpled sheet of
paper out, she held it between finger and thumb with little
finger scornfully extended and handed it to him.

"And this. This doesn't matter, I suppose. It doesn't
matter if 'the maids' do read this."

He grabbed at her wrist and held it so tight that she
winced with the pain.

"I don't think much of your verses, but 'the maids'
might like them. And Joyce would. I saw her kissing Mr.
Primrose in the wood beyond the Priory only yesterday."

The words were out before she knew she had said them.

He went as white as a sheet.

"I could kill you for telling me that—it's a lie!"

He hurried out of the room nearly knocking Katie down as she brought the breakfast in.

They spent a wretched day hardly speaking to each other. Elizabeth could not understand it—everything so beautiful and every one so beastly.

In the afternoon Bernard wandered up by the ponds where he stood looking down at the water, his thoughts on the morning's quarrel. He had been an ass and would have to apologize and make it up. It was amazing though. They seemed to have not the faintest glimmerings of his unhappiness. Here he was at forty—life practically at an end—at any rate there was nothing but suffering ahead. Or could he hope to capture Joyce and make yet another start with some one to help and understand him? He moved round to the narrow path that ran along the top of the weir above the middle pond, where he stood looking down, his thoughts as dark as the shadows in the water.

He thought of suicide. Only the day before he had read in the papers that there were fifteen thousand a year in England alone. If it were not for Joyce— He wondered how long it would be before they found him. They would all be damnably sorry then. Marion would go back to London after the funeral. Black would suit her, but not Elizabeth. The hearse would pass quite close to the Priory, or would they carry the coffin across the golf links to Little Plenders? He screwed the coffin lid down and he chose the final hymn, then, having had little lunch, he went in and insisted on having two eggs for his tea.

In the evening he was quite jolly. They played three-handed bridge, and he even urged Marion to cheer up.

And that night, slipping into sleep at once, he dreamed a dream.

He was alone, walking through country that was strange to him. The ground he trod was of trampled earth, and

giant cedars, in twos and threes and little groups, blocked
out his view, and yet he knew that both hard, bare earth
and funereal trees continued countless miles all round
him. It was neither daylight nor dark but the air about
him seemed to hold some soft translucent haze as though
sunset's afterglow had been entrapped and held entangled
by the whispering trees.

And now about him he beheld silent figures flitting
through the shady light, heard the tread of hurried feet,
and, urged by a whispering voice within, he hurried too,
until, in an open space, towering so high that the top was
lost to view, he came upon a church.

Steps ringed the great building on every side and up
the steps the quiet figures crowded to the open doors. A
drone as of prayers and sounds of song could be heard
within, and thinking to himself, "Now I shall know all
truth. The testing time has come," he entered, queerly
elated, with the throng.

A gallery ran along three walls and he was in the fore-
most row. He was on his knees, and round about him,
close packed, heads bowed, hundreds swayed and mumbled fervent prayers, and up towards the distant unseen
roof, tier on tier, till the hazy light there hid them, countless other crowded galleries prayed. And facing him across
the church, like some great spread fan of living loveliness,
a choir of a thousand haloed angels sang. And at the point
from which it seemed the fan of living grace sprang out,
in bright relief, a jewel set midst lesser stones, one more
divinely lovely than the rest knelt at an altar of gold in
prayer, her sweet head bent, her white hands clasped in
silent supplication.

Then, as though one spirit only swayed each soul,
with one accord, the praying and the singing ceased. The
kneeling angel stood and pointed towards the lucent mists

that hid the roof, and, through the shining air with silver wings wide-spread, a great bird swooped in slow smooth spirals down past the watching galleries and placed a roll of parchment on the marble pavement at her feet.

Along with countless thousands Corrie rose, craned forth his neck, felt heartbeats hurry, for he knew that now the knowledge man has craved since man began would be proclaimed; that the meaning of the universe, man's little lot on earth, the great hereafter, love, and the seed of life itself would be defined; that now the very kernel of the core of doubt would be destroyed. With eager hands the haloed angel first unwound, then quickly scanned, the sacred scroll.

Then she jumped on the altar and, reading from the scroll, she sang in a second-rate music hall voice whilst the angels swayed from side to side in time with the tune and joined in the chorus behind her. And when Corrie heard the song he blushed till he thought his head would burst, for it made oblique but unmistakable references to certain essential biological processes that are banned by the censor from all but Bible and text-book. The serried crowds roared their unabashed delight. And to Corrie it was horrible. He sprang to his feet aghast. He nearly choked. He would not stand it, and he had just made up his mind to jump over the edge of the gallery and stop it all, when the figure standing next to him seemed to guess what he meant to do, for he turned and gripped him tightly by the arm.

"I was only just in time!" he said.

Corrie stared. It was Taverner. He looked over the edge of the gallery and there was the moon reflected in water. He looked down at his feet, which were numb with cold— they were bare in his unlaced shoes. He had got his pyjamas on with his overcoat on top. He looked at Taverner again. It *was* Taverner. They were standing side by side at the edge of the upper pond.

Then, just as he began to wake to the fact that he had walked up by the ponds in his sleep, that Taverner was real, and the mismanaged message from heaven a myth, he saw a bit of his dream enacted again in the field beyond the water. There was mist, soft, fleecy patches floating white in the moon on the grass, and through the mist he saw shadowy figures moving, then a bird, with six-foot wings wide-spread, which rose, circled, and swept silently into the night.

"Look! Look!" he cried. "It's the bird again." Then he remembered his dream, which struck him as funny, and laughed a foolish laugh.

Taverner held him by the arm, spoke sternly, as one striving to stay hysterics. "Come now, I'll see you home. Do you know that it's gone two o'clock?"

Corrie gazed at him stupidly. "But you—didn't you see it—the bird? It was after I left the church and woke."

"No, my dear fellow, there was nothing. You're only half-awake now."

"But I was awake. I knew exactly where I was and that you—but what in the name of the devil are you doing here at this time?"

Taverner laughed. "You mustn't imagine that you've made a corner in the world's bad nights, Mr. Corrie. But you'll catch your death of cold. Come along."

And on the way back to the house the professor related anecdotes about the sleep-walkers he had known. He seemed to be well up in the subject. He held Corrie by the arm. He chatted pleasantly. He could see that his companion was overwrought. The man's teeth were chattering.

"Yes, and once a friend of mine—but—but he, poor chap—"

"Well, what happened to him?" Corrie asked, intrigued by the other's hesitation.

"Oh—well, he began to see things—I'd forgotten it—but you've no need to worry about that. It was drink that did it in his case."

"What happened to him?"

"In the end—the common lot—he died. But before he died, poor chap, he went—er—he suffered mentally."

Corrie shuddered. He was on the point of telling his kindly companion that he had been seeing other things too, when they got back to Cherry Hay. The back door was standing wide open, and with the assurance that he would now be all right, he went upstairs to bed, where he overslept.

10
INVITATION AND ACCEPTANCE

Bernard's nocturnal adventure at the edge of the pond occurred a few days before Annesley came back again to Little Plenders. Professor Taverner came over and gave Marion all the details of it and she made renewed but unsuccessful efforts to persuade her difficult brother to see a doctor. At his request nothing had been said about it to Elizabeth and therefore Elizabeth had said nothing about it in the long letter which Annesley read a day or two later, as he sat on the wall at the bottom of the garden behind the French Horn.

He went to Cherry Hay next day as he had promised himself he would, and intending to call at the Priory too, instead of cutting across the links and down by the ponds, he got out the old Morris and went round on to the Blatchford road and down the main drive between the rhododendrons.

At the Priory he met Joyce Lobley for the first time and he thought her a nice simple girl and not at all the sort of girl he expected from Marion's and Elizabeth's letters. He asked her if he might go over to the stables to see the inside alterations.

Politely but quite firmly she refused.

She was very, very sorry indeed, but she had been ab-solutely forbidden ever to take any one inside the stable

doors. She knew that, as agreed, all the inside partitions
had been taken down on one side of the quadrangle in
order to make a big laboratory for Professor Taverner, but
she could not take him in.

"Professor Taverner is not there now, I suppose, Miss
Lobley?"

"No. I'm sorry, he's away."

Annesley, not wishing to appear unduly inquisitive,
went on his way. When he reached the stables, however,
curiosity overcame him and, running the car a little way
along the lane towards Cherry Hay, he got out and tried
the big double doors. They were very securely locked.
There was not even a proper key-hole to look through—
only the bright little brass disc of a Yale lock. Not only
did the big doors look unshakeable like solid blocks of
wood, but there was neither handle nor other projection
to catch hold of did you want to shake them.

No one was about. Annesley walked round by the lake
side of the building and he was just returning towards
his car on the Cherry Hay lane when, to his surprise, he
saw Corrie come striding out from behind some bushes
towards two men in overalls standing by a water butt near
the rear wall. They were drowning a half-grown tabby kitten. Apparently it had already suffered one unsuccessful
immersion and one of the two men, a big, coarse-looking
fellow with an unshaven chin, was swinging it backwards
and forwards by the tail.

It was sheer unadulterated cruelty, and Corrie's comments as he ran towards them were unadulterated too,
much to the big man's annoyance,

"'Ere, 'oo'er yer callin' names, guvner?" he jeered, and
dashed the kitten in Corrie's face directly he got within
reach.

It was two to one, but to Annesley's delight Corrie went
for them without a moment's hesitation though he had not

the ghost of a chance, and went over like a ninepin when the second man shot out his fist and caught him in the midriff. At that moment Annesley arrived on the scene of action and the striker went over like another ninepin. Then the big man, taken unawares, felt a grip like a vice at the back of his neck. It felt as though his windpipe was being forced into his stomach. It felt, too, very much like being drowned when a few seconds later he found his head in the water butt.

Annesley held him there as long as he dared, short of murder, gave him a push that sent him reeling, and escorted Corrie, who had got possession of the ill-used kitten, back to the car.

It was all over in three minutes, but for at least three weeks the big man had a round black bruise on one side of his thick neck where Annesley had stuck his thumb into it, and four long black bruises on the other side where Annesley's fingers had applied the opposing pressure. He had to have medical attention.

"You great bullock!" Bernard laughed, when, five minutes later, holding the half-drowned kitten on his long, thin knee, they were seated in the car.

George grinned. As he had always told every one, on his good days, Corrie was one of the best.

He patted one of Corrie's thin knees. "And you," he said, "are a lion-hearted stick of rhubarb."

When they got to Cherry Hay, however, Bernard, like a stick of rhubarb without any heart at all to it, wilted, and went to bed. Marion was out, and George and Elizabeth played a round of golf together.

But on the following day George had a long talk with Marion alone and, pacing the lawn by the stream, she told him of all their troubles.

"But, Marion, he really doesn't seem any worse to me."

"Oh yes, he is—much worse. I know by all sorts of little things that you would never notice. I can hear him walking about his room at night. He pretends it's the noise in the pipes, but I know it isn't. We've had men out twice to try and put them right but it seems to me that they don't know a thing about it. First it's too much air and then it's not enough water."

"But, Marion, it's my job. Of course I'll have them put right. I said I would before I sold Bernard the house. I believe there's a more up-to-date make of ram on the market, and if it's that, and there is, I'll buy it."

"Are you sure you can afford it?"

"Quite sure. And, anyhow, I'll do my best to persuade Bernard to come away with me for a short holiday."

They were standing near the little bridge and Bernard, who had just come down for the first time after his heroic display at the stables, standing on the drive above them, overheard the conversation starting from the words ". . . I'll buy it."

So now, he thought, Annesley is to be dragged into it.

Two days later he was sure of it. He received a letter from a solicitor in London offering him, on behalf of an unnamed client, nearly twice as much as he had paid for Cherry Hay. The letter came at breakfast time and he glared at Marion as though he would slay her on the spot, and put it in his pocket.

And the next time Annesley came over from the French Horn he called them both into the dining-room and went off the deep end. He used every word that isn't in the dictionary and all the bad ones that are, and nothing would persuade him that it was not a put-up arrangement between them. He told Marion that she could go back to London and he hoped she would, and he told Annesley to off and not come near the place again.

Marion said, "All right, Bernard;" and George said, "All right, old man." And they left him consuming his own fire.

George did stay away for a few days and then he came for a week's visit. Elizabeth brought him the invitation which Marion wrote. It originated in Bernard's bedroom when they were making his bed.

"Is Daddy really ill, do you think, Marion?"

"I'm getting rather worried about him."

A pause, whilst they turned the mattress.

"You really do like living here, I suppose, Elizabeth?"

"Ye-es. Yes, I like it. But I don't like Daddy as much as I did in London. I see him twice as often and he takes less than half the notice of me. In London—well, there were days, but here, you never seem to know where you are."

"I wish you'd leave more sheet to tuck in at the bottom. There, that's better. You know, I was wondering if it mightn't buck him up a bit if we asked George Annesley to stay with us for a week or so. You could walk over to Little Plenders this morning and ask him."

"But has Daddy asked him? From something he said the other day, I thought that—well, that George was just a little unpopular."

Marion smiled. "That will be all right, dear. I'll arrange it. I'll give you a note. And I've no doubt that *you* can persuade *him.*"

On the way to the French Horn, Elizabeth pondered on the conversation. It was surprising—surprising that such a silly, ordinary sentence could mean so many things according to the words you stressed. If you put the emphasis on the "you," then, quite absurdly, it meant that Marion was in love with George Annesley and knew all the time that George was in love with her—Elizabeth. It meant all manner of tragic things. She said it again, aloud, as Marion had said it, and ran into Joyce Lobley coming back from a round of golf.

It made her feel rather foolish. She could see by the flicker in the amber eyes that Joyce had heard her.

They stood talking for quite five minutes. They had nothing to talk about and few tastes in common, but they held quite an animated little conversation. What about? Well, ask any woman what she finds to talk about with another woman she dislikes. If you're a man she won't be able to explain it—if you're a woman, you won't require to ask.

But Elizabeth always talked when there was any one to talk to, and quite often when there was not. After she left Joyce, she sang. It was a lovely day. The hill beyond the golf links looked lovely. Even the colliery tip couldn't spoil it. And Elizabeth certainly did not spoil it. She looked pretty and felt it.

When she got to the French Horn, George Annesley thought her the most beautiful woman on earth.

Elizabeth stood watching him as he read Marion's note. She wondered if he would come. She endeavored to judge his intentions by his expression—but she got no farther than being glad that he had no mustache and thinking that he had rather a nice, doggy, faithful, trustful sort of look about him.

It took him just no time to read the note.

"Come along inside and have some cider," he said when he had finished it.

"But will you be able to come?"

"And buns," he added, ignoring her question.

"But can you come?"

"Let me see, either—and then the answer is 'Yes, certainly,' or—and then the answer's the same. Come along inside and have some buns and cider."

"Dear me! Sunstroke! Let me see. 'Keep the patient's head lower than the feet. On no account give meat or alcohol. Send for a doctor.' You mustn't have any cider."

"Cider's not alcohol."

"No, but it's ''ic.' No, *you* mustn't have any. You look rather queer, too, now I come to look at you. But there's no reason why I shouldn't."

"It's looking at so many figures. It always makes me feel light-headed."

"Really? This is no place for me, I'm sure."

"Oh, come along in and have some cider. Figures, not figures."

"Oh, I see, figures—not figures."

They went into his sitting-room where Mrs. Girling brought cider and biscuits to them. The table was strewn with papers; George had been going through his accounts.

"Ahem—the rent roll. The king was in his counting house." Elizabeth laughed.

"How much do you think a man might get married on, Elizabeth?"

Elizabeth's eyebrows lifted. "It depends on his tastes, his temper, and just how much she loves him," she answered.

"Well, supposing that you loved him very much?"

"Oh, then—well, it would always be less than that."

"You—do you mean—even if that was this?"

She nodded and he picked her up, and she sat on his knee in a big arm-chair. But, pictorially, it was a ghastly failure.

"Now, how the dickens do they do it?" he asked, looking up at her. "Why, your head should be down here on my shoulder."

"So it should. And your shoulder—golly! You'd either have to be eight feet high or sit from the knees. This wants looking into."

"It's practice, I expect," George said meditatively. "You see what a maidenly man you've got."

She ruffled his hair and they practiced with such concentration, and time swept by them so swiftly that Marion

and Bernard were sitting down to lunch when Elizabeth
got back to Cherry Hay again. She had intended to aston-
ish them by blurting out the fact that she was engaged to
George Annesley, but, seeing the unskilled savagery with
which her father hacked at the carcass of a chicken, she
decided that the news would keep.

11
MURDER

In the middle of Annesley's third night at Cherry Hay tragedy engulfed them. The day had been a difficult one; in the garden after breakfast Annesley had told Corrie that he was engaged to Elizabeth, and Corrie had thought it fitting to attempt the role of heavy father.

He had inquired—and it was quite natural that he should inquire—but somehow it struck George as being intensely comic—about finance, and George failing to repress a smile, Corrie had flared.

"Well, it may be amusing to you. Elizabeth will marry you whether I like it or not, but I suppose I am entitled to show a little interest!" That is a thoroughly expurgated edition of what George understood him to say—the rice of the dish, as it were—but rice so heavily "Corried," in dish so blistered with blasphemy, that George for a few brief seconds found his tongue scorched speechless.

Recovering, he thumped his blasphemous father-in-law-to-be's thin back with a disrespectful and heavy-handed joviality. "Daddy," he cried, "you've missed your vocation—you ought to have been a blast furnace manager!"

And Bernard, instead of taking the remark in good part, only glowered and walked back into the house, where, unfortunately, he collided with Marion, who asked him for money. There was a scene—a real talkie—and Katie, the maid, overheard them.

It warped the day; to escape the strain they went early to bed, and Annesley, whose bedroom was on the second floor, woke in the middle of the night, thinking he heard a call for help from the landing below him. Jumping out of bed, he ran to the switch, but the fuse must have blown, for the room remained in darkness. He opened the door and listened. He could hear a queer medley of noises; Elizabeth talking to some one—Corrie groaning—inarticulate sounds—a pause—a door banging—the water pipes plunking—then Elizabeth again, calling him loudly by name.

"George! George! Help! Quick! Help!"

It rang in the darkness.

Snatching up his dressing-gown, he pelted downstairs to plunge into unlit Bedlam; Corrie, wildly excited, waving his arms like windmills and reiterating, "I tell you I saw her outside the window," seemed to be in his proper setting; Mrs. Glegg talking like a female attendant at an asylum, telling Corrie not to get excited; Elizabeth calling, "George!" in a frightened voice; all colliding and running helter-skelter in the dark. A smash in a tube could not have produced more panic.

"For heaven's sake, shut up! What is the matter? Why on earth don't you switch the lights on?" he asked angrily.

His deep voice among the nervous excited ones had a calming effect.

"Oh, George, something terrible's happened," Elizabeth cried, finding him and clinging to him.

"None of the lights'll go up anywhere," Mrs. Glegg told him.

"I tell you I saw her outside the window. I can only repeat that I saw her outside the window! She dropped. I heard the thud."

"But who? Whom did you see outside the window?"

"Marion."

"Marion! Outside the window! Do you mean she's fallen out?"

"She seemed to hang in mid-air and then she fell. I heard the thud."

"Then why the devil—"

His sentence unfinished, Annesley pushed Elizabeth from him and ran downstairs as quickly as darkness would let him. He called back over his shoulder entreating Corrie once again to shut up and look for candles and matches. Downstairs, he hurriedly unbolted the back door, but when he had drawn the bolts he found it to be locked as well. The key had gone. He dashed to the front door, overturning a small table in the dark, only to find that the key to that was missing too.

He called up the stairs again to Corrie, who came down holding a lighted match. He had got his trousers and coat on over the top of his pyjamas, and absurdly, Annesley noticed that his braces were twisted. The match was shaking in his hand like a Bengal light in a boy's; his face was as white as a sheet, he had forgotten his glasses, and looked old and odd without them.

"I say, Corrie, both the keys are missing, front and back."

Corrie stopped suddenly on the stairs and Annesley thought he saw him jerk back his head as though the announcement amazed him.

"Wait a jiffy—I think I know where they are. I'll find them."

Corrie turned at once and disappeared, and before he returned, Elizabeth, who had gone into the kitchen while George was trying to unfasten the front door, came to him bearing a candle.

"Whatever makes your father take the keys to bed with him?" George asked her.

"The keys to bed?"

"Yes. But never mind. Come along into the kitchen with the candle and I'll get out of the window whilst he finds them."

They hurried into the kitchen, where Elizabeth, treading on a cockroach, screamed and dropped the light, and it seemed to Annesley that Fate was poking him back—he pictured a devil with pitchfork stabbing at him in the dark—keeping him inside the house he could not get out. He would never get out. For once he was angry.

"Look here, Elizabeth, for God's sake pull yourself together and give me that candle and the matches. Marion may have broken her leg—or worse—though how—and here we all are dithering about like hens."

"I'm sorry, I haven't got any matches. We could only find one box and Daddy has that."

"Well, run and fetch them. Run! Run!"

Then the kitchen window was shuttered, and not familiar with the unlit geography of the place, Annesley wasted nearly another minute before he could find it, unfasten it, and climb out into the little closed yard at the rear of the house, where he was met with a locked and keyless door again.

It was set in an eight-foot wall, but by catching hold of the top bolt and putting his foot on the latch, thoroughly roused, he managed to scale it, tearing one of his fingernails and cutting his hands, till they bled, on some glass at the top of the wall.

At long last he was in the outer yard and he ran towards the front of the house, only to fall headlong over something soft that lay in his path. For one brief second, knowing where Marion's bedroom was, it did not occur to him that it might perchance be she, but when he turned his head to see what it was that had tripped him up, he could just make out a small black mound, and, curving out from underneath, an arm, white against the ground.

As he knelt down beside it, the night was so dense that it seemed to bear down on him, and the nearness of the house, along whose eaves a gentle breeze went whispering, to dye the darkness deeper still. There was no moon. The stars were all behind thick cloud—cloud that held no soft reflected light from near-by town. It was night—black night, black and bewildering as townsmen in the country find it.

The bed clothes were on top of her—an eiderdown and blankets. A sheet shrouded her as she lay limp and white and still on the cold stone flags, one arm bent underneath her, her clever face twisted queerly round, and before his hand had found her heart—he knew.

Then Elizabeth was there with a lamp she had found. She was kneeling by his side.

"Marion, darling, speak to us—oh, Marion, my darling—my darling! George—she's—"

And Annesley could only whisper, "Yes."

They lifted her up and he carried her in, her black hair, breeze blown, brushing softly against his face as, heavy and limp, she lay in his arms.

Yes, she lay in his arms. God alone knew how many unuttered aching prayers she had prayed that thus she might rest one day—how the dear thought had made her quiet heart hurry. And by the irony of fate it was Annesley of all men who carried her in, her unhurried heart next his—quiet, steady, still, as, unwanted and dead, she lay in the longed-for embrace.

He carried her upstairs and by the light of the little hand-lamp they laid her on the bed. They folded the quiet hands. They fetched bedclothes from Corrie's room and covered her reverently with them.

"I thought her room was the one at the end of the passage," George whispered.

"She changed with Daddy—a few nights ago, I think—just for the nights—he couldn't sleep. But George—George—are you sure?"

"Yes, dear, I'm quite sure," he answered gently. "But get me a looking-glass. We must telephone for a doctor. Who's nearest?"

And when Elizabeth had fetched the hand-glass from the room in which Corrie had slept that night, Marion's own hand-glass it was, he held it to her face, but there was no soft breath to dim that last reflection. He put the glass face down on the bed and there seemed something final in the act. It was "Finis." Marion would never use her looking-glass again. Her initial—a silver M—was on the back. It had been her last birthday present from Elizabeth, who stood sobbing quietly by the bed. George went to her.

"Poor Marion, and poor you—poor little you," he soothed, caressing her pretty fair hair.

Then suddenly the electric light shot up. They must have left the switch down. It startled them. It was just as though some one had suddenly shouted in church. They turned instinctively towards the bed and his hands dropped slowly from her shoulders.

"I say, Elizabeth—look—!" he whispered.

Round the white column of the throat, quite clearly defined, was the angry red imprint of fingers; a round red mark on one side where a thumb had pressed, and on the other side four long red bruises, already turning black, where fingers had applied opposing pressure.

12
PERJURY

George Annesley staggered up the twisting Cherry Hay staircase with his limp and pitiful burden, but Corrie, instead of following him, made for the dining-room, where he sat down in the dark at the table. He felt altogether too unnerved for immediate movement; indeed, he felt that he might have fainted had he attempted it, and he wanted, if he could, to collect his scattered wits and think. If only he could think! So he sat in the dark with his head in his hands.

Already he had made up his mind for the worst—people who precipitated themselves out of upper story windows on to hard stone flags were killed. Besides he had known, how intimately he had known, an earlier similar disaster. Quite distinctly he remembered hearing the thud when Marion struck the ground, just a dull, heavy thud with silence after—the hopeless thud of a body and not the thud of a live thing—yes, he knew without the shadow of a doubt that she was dead. He needed neither Elizabeth nor Annesley to come and confirm it.

Sitting there in the dark, he felt confused, irritable, full-headed, as he imagined doomed men must feel before an imminent stroke. Try as he might he could not concentrate his thoughts. They did just as they liked with him, and whilst he wanted desperately to estimate exactly what had happened, he found himself instead, wondering whether he ought to go and have his blood-pressure tested, and wishing that he had screwed up pluck enough to play the coward and leap into one of the ponds.

Sitting there it seemed to him that that would have been a desirable ending for through all his confusion of thought, through the numb agony of the knowledge of Marion's fate, an idea more tragic still, an idea pregnant with unthinkable possibilities, came suggestively surging.

Clear as a cameo he remembered leaning out of the bedroom window, seeing the heap of bedclothes in the yard below, and then turning round to see Marion's stripped and empty bed, a white oblong, in the dark room behind him. He remembered that, and he remembered pulling down the unproductive switch, fumbling for the handle of the door, opening it, and calling out for Marion in the passage. That was all perfectly clear.

But every earlier incident was hazy; of how he came to be back in his own room where his sister was sleeping, with the door shut behind him, he could recall nothing. He did have misty memories of standing at the foot of the bed, of his first astonishment at finding himself there, and of seeing what looked like a bundle of clothes hovering in mid-air outside the window. There had been sudden convulsive movements, bare legs had appeared, something had slipped, then the bundle itself had fallen too. Vaguely he remembered thinking that this must be yet another of those disturbing hallucinations that had come to him of late and that if only he closed his eyes for a time he would open them again to find it gone. But he could remember nothing whatever about going to the window. Before he stood at the end of the bed all was a blank, and there was another blank afterwards. It was as though he had turned his head away and in doing so had missed a yard or two of film at the very crisis of a picture.

What had been done during those missing minutes? Had he had any active share in poor Marion's misadventure? That he was in the room was certain, but why had he not prevented her from falling out of the window, and if he had not prevented her, then what was it that he had done? These were the questions he asked himself as he sat alone in the dark, and recalling that other never-to-be-forgotten night, he buried his head in his hands again.

Then the light went up and Annesley and Elizabeth—Elizabeth with a face as white as a sheet—were standing on the other side of the table.

"Well?" he asked them dully, looking up at length.

Annesley, in answer, shook his head from side to side, and Corrie hid his haggard face behind his trembling hands again.

Elizabeth crossed over to the fireplace behind him, where, with a sound that was compounded of shudder and sob and sigh, she sank into the big arm-chair, and such a hush fell on them then as only comes when souls have been so stirred that human functions halt and fail, and sounds seem so spaced out in time that a century of silence lies between the two ends of the pendulum's path.

Upstairs, Annesley had slipped on his coat and his trousers, he had insisted too that Elizabeth should dress; now he sat on the corner of the dining-room table and slowly filled his pipe.

As he pushed the tobacco carefully home it seemed to him that he alone of the three correctly assessed the horror of what had befallen them. Marion dead—an accident—sudden tragedy—an inquest—a winter's grief—then spring again perhaps. But Marion dead with the angry mark of fingers round her neck! That meant not only an inquest, but a term of terror terminating in a murder trial. It meant for Corrie, at the best, shame and death; at the worst, incarceration for life—to die at last, a lunatic, in some government asylum. There would be no spring after that winter. It would be like night if the earth of a sudden had ceased to spin and no longer swung the shadows to the waiting dawn.

He lit his pipe and looked across at Corrie. "Look here, Bernard, you've got to pull yourself together and come upstairs with me. What's become of Mrs. Glegg, Elizabeth?"

"She's dressing, I think."

"Well, your father's all in. Find some brandy or whisky or something, if you can. Put a kettle on too if you can find anything to put it on. And then, no, first ring up the doctor. The police can wait till later on."

"The police!" Corrie whispered.

"Yes, old man, the police; now pull yourself together and come along upstairs with me."

The doctor—Corrie had consulted him about a good half-dozen ailments during the first three weeks after he came to Cherry Hay—lived in Millingham. As a matter of fact he had got Corrie down in his mind's eye as worth— well, as being one of those persistent patients so helpful to a doctor's practice—and so he rose more readily than usual, and started out for Cherry Hay at once, when after some moments Elizabeth succeeded in getting through to him on his bedside telephone. Having given her message she went into the kitchen, where she found Mrs. Glegg, fully dressed, reviving the kitchen fire, which still showed a few red embers—it was two o'clock—with sticks and castor sugar. She found a bottle of brandy and took it along with some glasses into the dining-room where the men had already returned.

They were standing face to face by the empty grate; her father, his air of dull indecision gone, had anger written on his face. George Annesley was looking worried.

"Ah, here you are, Elizabeth. Now you—both of you— must have some." He poured them out some brandy and helped himself as well.

"You sit down there, Elizabeth. You're sure you're warm enough?"

Elizabeth nodded.

"You've rung up for the doctor?"

She nodded again.

"And he's coming at once?"

"Yes."

"Then we've just got half an hour, say, in which to talk things over. And—and—well, we've got to face the facts. There can be no doubt about it. Marion never fell out of that window—she was pushed out."

"Or pulled out," Corrie interrupted.

"Well, tell Elizabeth about it, Corrie. Tell her what you've just been telling me. Tell us absolutely everything but don't waste time."

And in a voice that gradually gained in confidence and strength Corrie told them what he could. "I'm almost certain that I was awake when I saw her outside the window, and if I was, then I couldn't possibly have had anything to do with it," he concluded. Then he hesitated and added, "But—"

"But what?" Annesley asked him.

"But I don't blame you—either of you, Elizabeth—if you feel that you can't believe me. It sounds—well, doesn't it?"

Elizabeth rose from her chair and went to him. She put her arms round his neck. She stroked his thin disordered hair. "Why, Daddy, darling Daddy, of course we both believe you. Don't we, George?"

And of all miserable mortals on earth, at that moment, George Annesley must have been one of the most unhappy. He struck a match—made no reply.

Elizabeth uncoiled her arms.

"George!"

George busied himself with his pipe.

"It isn't what we think that matters. It's what the police are going to think," he said slowly, holding the match to the bowl of his pipe, his attention on that, his eyes kept away from the pain in Elizabeth's eyes.

"It isn't what *we* think that matters! It isn't what *we* think that matters! Oh, isn't it just?"

Annesley squared his shoulders. "Look here, both of you, we've got to look this in the face. I didn't mean it doesn't matter in that way. But, I ask you, what would any one think? Just look at the alternatives. Assuming that you did wake up in a confused state to find yourself in Marion's room, then either you were even more confused than you know and admit, and you strangled her, and pushed her out of the window in your sleep, or you did it, know you did it, and are lying about the rest; or one of the others of us in the house did it, or some unknown agent, for some unknown reason, got into the house and tried to spirit her away."

"Well, did you ever know me to tell a lie, George?" Corrie asked, so angrily that speech for once came swear-free.

"No, not exactly, your statements sometimes have elastic tendencies, but then, we all— No, I've never known you to tell an out and outer, but then, I've never known you placed in the same position."

"I'll never speak to you again, George," Elizabeth said sadly.

"That won't help your father much. Don't you see, Elizabeth, don't you see that all this about Marion being seen outside an upstairs window—why, no one will believe it."

"You don't believe it?" Elizabeth asked.

"No. Frankly, I don't—I can't."

"You think Daddy killed his own sister and then lies about it?"

"I'm sure that any one else would be certain that he killed his own sister and then lied about it. They wouldn't even have to think. And, Elizabeth, dear, don't you see that just now—now at this moment, nothing else matters?"

"But it does matter. It does matter!" Elizabeth cried, stamping her foot as she said it.

Annesley looked at the clock. "It matters for just a quarter of an hour. Then the doctor will be here and later the police. After that—well, our opinions won't count for very much. I should make friends with the doctor if I were you," he added, turning to Corrie, "for if you tell the police what you've just told us, a certificate for insanity's the only thing to help you, and that won't help you very much."

"George, you're—you're beastly," Elizabeth sobbed.

"I'm not. We've got a quarter of an hour. I'm trying to make you understand it. We've got a quarter of an hour."

There was certainly no time to waste, but Corrie took off his spectacles and wiped them deliberately on his handkerchief, which was a habit of his when wondering what to say.

"It's worse than that—much worse than you think," he said at length.

"Look here, George is right, Elizabeth," he continued after a pause. "In a sense it doesn't matter, and honestly, that was what I was trying to puzzle out when you came and found me here in the dark just now. I've got to tell you both something. I don't quite know how much you know about your mother, Elizabeth, but she ran away and left me as soon as she could after you were born. When you were seventeen—why, it was only the year before last—it was your last term at school—she came back to me. She was ill when she came—thoroughly worn out—at death's door in fact, and she died within a month of her return. Towards the last she suffered from—a sort of asthma. There were times when she used to have to stand at the window and fight for air. On the night she died I woke, just as I woke to-night, to find myself standing at the open window of our bedroom with a piece of her nightdress in my hands. She was killed on the points of the railings. Everything came out at the inquest, of course. The fact that I had been in a nursing home, what I'd been there for, her illness and the nature of it, were all explained. That we'd quarreled came out as well, but the coroner pointed out that there was absolutely no evidence, nothing to indicate that I'd pushed her, that in fact it was more probable that I'd caught hold of her nightdress in an attempt to save her, and the jury returned a verdict of accidental death without retiring. I just woke up to find myself standing there in the dark with a piece of nightdress in my hand. Honestly, I remember nothing about it. Nothing. Not nearly so much as I remember about to-night. I can only tell you that for nights I've been imagining that I saw things outside that window—you know, I put it down to my—to my nerves. I've been worried about it. A man hung there a night or two ago. Before that there was a hand. It sounds grotesque and idiotic, but I wonder now if I really saw the things I thought imaginary then. I don't expect you to believe me, but I'm telling you the truth."

Annesley got up from his chair.

"You still don't believe me?" Corrie asked.

"Yes, I do. Up to a point I do believe you, Bernard. I believe you're telling us what you believe to be the truth. But is it the truth in fact? You—well, you must surely have some doubts yourself. How could she be hanging in a bundle of bedclothes outside the window like that? You must have doubts. From your behavior upstairs just now, I feel pretty sure that you have."

Deep in thought Annesley paced the room. He drew back the curtains from one of the windows. "We shall see the doctor's car as it comes down the hill through the trees." Then, full of anxiety, he paced backwards and forwards again.

"But it won't do. It won't do. Why, they'll never believe it. If we tell them the truth, that you've been seeing things of late, that you woke up in Marion's room not knowing how you got there, and that you saw her hanging outside, mysteriously in mid-air, there's one conclusion only they can come to. They're bound to learn you've been shellshocked, that you've been in a nursing home for—well, for such cases, and they're bound again to learn what happened when your wife died. No, it won't do. We shall all have to tell some other story."

"But wouldn't that be—" Elizabeth began.

"Perjury?" Annesley interrupted her. "It certainly would, but if we all three stick to it they'll have a job to prove it."

"All four, you mean—there's Mrs. Glegg. She must have heard us talking." It was Corrie who spoke.

"It's an added risk, but we'll have to take it. Run and fetch her, Elizabeth. It's nothing to the risk you run, Corrie, if we don't."

And when Mrs. Glegg came in, Annesley explained the position, repressing all the doubts he felt himself. "The police won't believe Mr. Corrie saw Miss Marion outside the window, you see, Mrs. Glegg. They'll think he did it either in his sleep or—or when he was half-awake. He tells me you know about what happened when Mrs. Corrie died, and if we tell them he was in the room alone they'll—well, they'll shut him up."

Mrs. Glegg had put her apron on and she smoothed it out now with her rather red hands. She murmured, "Oh, dear!"

"So, if you're agreeable, Mrs. Glegg, we're going to tell them something else. Listen carefully now. You, Elizabeth, first heard noises downstairs. You got up and opened your door and then you thought you heard some one call out, and you came down to find Marion's door open, the bed empty, and the bedclothes gone. You couldn't understand it at all. Whilst you were pondering what to do, Mrs. Glegg, who had heard the door bang—you're a light sleeper, Mrs. Glegg—got up, and seeing your bedroom light on and a light in the passage below—"

"But the lights wouldn't go on," Elizabeth interrupted.

"Yes, they would. We need say nothing about that, so far as I can see. Seeing the light in the passage below, you, Mrs. Glegg, came downstairs to see if she wanted anything. You couldn't understand the empty bed either, and you, Elizabeth, knocked on Bernard's door to wake him. When you went in he was in bed—only half-awake. You told him about it and you looked in the rooms downstairs, and then you came and woke me, and we found her in the yard below the window. We'll tell the truth about the bedclothes and we've none of us noticed the mark on her neck. You didn't say anything about that to the doctor, Elizabeth?"

"No, I didn't. But isn't it rather odd—not to have noticed it, I mean? And hadn't we better tell the truth about the lights?"

"Look here, I damned well don't like any of it," Corrie said, getting up excitedly. "If there's trouble coming it's coming to me. I ought to stand the racket—besides, surely in the morning, when daylight's here, there'll be something to show how it happened."

"Oh, Daddy—Daddy, darling—just think what it might mean."

"Shut up, Corrie! Of course we must carry it through. You agree, don't you, Mrs. Glegg?"

Mrs. Glegg nodded and Annesley continued.

"No, I don't think it sounds too unreasonable that we should none of us have noticed the marks on Marion's neck. We might easily have missed it or thought it due to the fall. As for the lights—I'm not sure. Don't you think it will look as though we're trying to make out that something we didn't know about had happened in the dark?"

"But isn't that what we want to do?" Corrie asked.

"I'm certain it's better to stick to the truth about the lights," Elizabeth said decisively. "They may be able to check it."

"Right you are, then," Annesley agreed, giving way; "but remember that all we know is that Marion fell out of the window—we can't understand it. The only odd thing to us is that the bedclothes were in the yard."

"But need they be?" Corrie asked again.

"Yes. They're sure to show marks where they've been on the ground. The bottom sheet was there as well, and we can't re-make the bed. The doctor may be here at any—"

"May I come in?"

They turned to see Dr. Butterworth standing in the doorway. He was gazing at them through his spectacles. Annesley swore a string of unsaid oaths, for he knew the risk he was running and that the doctor's early appearance had doubled the odds on the risk. Without further discussion of detail what chance had the four of them now of telling four tales that tallied? Mrs. Glegg! What chance would Mrs. Glegg have against the nicely-calculated questions of a probably skilled and certainly skeptical police inspector? Mrs. Glegg! A kind-faced old darling, nearly sixty, perhaps, with the figure of the period when isthmuses were fashionable for women, good to the core of her well-covered heart, but with what brand of brain was the kindly old face equipped? One of those broad, dark, heavy faces that go best with woolen stockings and seem

somehow to have disappeared with the advent of artificial
silk, eyes wide apart under ridges of well-marked black, a
mouth that made no pretenses, a chin that seemed somehow overawed—but did that broad brow bulge or did the
nearly unnoticed chin recede, and which was the proper
index to the brain of Mrs. Glegg? On the answer to that
the success of their scheme hung suspended.

As the doctor stood in the doorway, Annesley attempted to assess her with a sideways glance and he breathed a
sigh of relief, for whilst during their discussion she had sat
unmoved, smoothing her apron, nodding her head, seem-
ing to understand that time was short, that the tragedy
of Marion's death might be but the shadow of tragedy to
come, and that Bernard, her favorite, might yet be vitally
concerned, now she was holding her apron to her fine old
eyes from which undoubted tears ran freely. So astonished
was he at the change, that, quite unwilled, his mind began
to hint the word hypocrite, but before the word had tak-
en shape he realized that the tears were real and that like
some great actress, Mrs. Glegg could curb and then release
them when the time was ripe. He felt that, after all, they
had perhaps a sporting chance.

"Now, Miss Elizabeth, dearie, you moan't greet no
more," Mrs. Glegg said huskily through her apron, and
Elizabeth, seeing afresh the picture of poor Marion lying
dead on the bed upstairs, a picture that their discussion
and their plight had veiled, began to weep as well, and
Annesley, beholding them both in tears, again felt reassured.

Dr. Butterworth was reassured as well. Annesley had
drawn back the curtains from the window so that they
should see the doctor's headlights, but their discussion
had held them absorbed. The doctor had been out to
Cherry Hay before, he knew the way, and, as the car came
down the hill through the trees, he noticed the light in the

window. But he was accustomed to seeing lights in the
windows of the houses he visited even if it was at two
o'clock in the morning. There was nothing odd in that.
He was accustomed to walking straight in if he found the
front door open. It saved a lot of valuable time. He was
accustomed, too, to finding little groups of anxious relatives talking together in low, hushed tones.

Having the largest practice in Millingham, he had at-
tended countless little Millinghamites as they battled with
birth at dawn. He had seen them, pink and immature, set
out on the journey of life; he had seen countless others,
experienced and tired, pull into the shadow of the common terminus at close of day; he had tended them in times
of stress between, and what he did not know about mourning and grief was not worth knowing. In countless stricken
houses he had grown to gauge grief exactly; he knew dull
despair and heartbreak, and he knew when relatives disguised relief and wondered what the will was.

But in spite of all this accumulated experience the doctor felt himself faced with something fresh as he paused
for a moment in the dining-room doorway. These four
people looked somehow unnatural. Though such words as
"conspiracy" and "guilt" never entered his capable head—
why should they?—he did definitely have the momentary
impression that there was something queer and unusual
about them, that there was something more than mere
surprise at his unannounced appearance. Just at the time
though, he thought very little about it. The impression
was so faint and fleeting that by the time he had moved a
pace it was gone, and there before him was the customary
waiting group. But later on, vague and fleeting as these
first impressions were, he felt it his duty to tell Inspector
Jacobs about them. Yes, Annesley would have done very
well to have kept his attention more closely on the window
from which he had thoughtfully drawn the curtains back,

so that he might see the doctor's car as it came through the trees down the hill. Or, failing that, he would have done well to have locked the front door. It was the first mistake of several.

The usual greetings and an introduction to Annesley completed, Elizabeth took the doctor upstairs where she left him alone to make his examination, and a few moments later the doctor whispered "so" to himself as he noticed the marks on the dead girl's neck. There were bruises as well—all the expected evidence of a fatal fall from an upstairs window. But in addition there were those angry markings on the white neck and one leg was grazed down the shin from knee to ankle, and the doctor said the word "so" softly again as he straightened out his thin, tall back. He stood for a moment glancing round the bedroom, which seemed in order and undisturbed, then very thoughtfully he went downstairs.

Annesley had used the respite of the doctor's absence to repeat and emphasize his instructions to Mrs. Glegg. He had questioned her as he imagined she would be questioned later on, and the answers she gave him would not have shamed a hired expert witness. He told her approvingly, "You'll do, Mrs. Glegg." And she retired to the kitchen, leaving them to prepare to face the doctor.

As they waited, Elizabeth first began to realize some of the difficulties that lay ahead. If she had these feelings now, whilst they waited for the kindly doctor, what sort of feelings would she have later on? "What shall we say to him when he comes down, Daddy?" she whispered.

"Say nothing at all. Leave it to me. Let him speak first," Annesley answered.

But when the doctor did rejoin them it was not as simple and easy as he thought it. In the first place, Dr. Butterworth seemed to have made up his mind to "let *them* speak first," for he stood disconcertingly still and silent. And then, again, the light, which hung from the center of the ceiling, shone full on his spectacles, and instead of having eyes to look at, there were two bright blank discs, and it seemed to Annesley that it placed him at an immediate and definite disadvantage.

With what grace a "so-so" golfer may perform his practice swing, and how strange that at the moment of action he should waggle but a hesitating club head and then mismanage its motions! It had seemed to Annesley that it would come natural to him to open out with some easy phrase beginning with "Well, doctor—" but now his tongue might have been some new and untried implement, and the longer he waggled and dallied the more difficult speech became, the pretense of not having noticed the doctor's peculiar behavior more and more impossible.

"Well, doctor, I suppose—" He did begin at last.

The doctor came forward into the room. He folded his arms and leant against the end of the table. He stared first at Annesley, then at Corrie, who sat hunched up in one arm-chair, and then at Elizabeth, who sat shivering in the other. "You know, I think you'd better tell me all about it. What happened exactly?"

"We found her in the yard underneath her bedroom window. That's all we know. We don't know how it happened," Annesley replied.

The doctor shrugged his shoulders.

"You've rung up the police, I suppose?"

"No. Of course we knew there'd have to be an inquest, but we thought that we'd better have you out to see her first, and that the police could wait until to-morrow."

The doctor shrugged his shoulders again. They were expressive and he used them well. "In cases of this sort," he said slowly, "in murder or manslaughter cases they generally like to be—"

They all interrupted him. Elizabeth ejaculated, "Oh!" Corrie uttered a weak, "Oh, I say!" and Annesley a more emphatic, "What!" but they were all a little late with it, and Annesley, at any rate, felt like a third-rate actor.

"Yes, murder. Murder or manslaughter. And as I was saying, the police like to be early on the spot in such cases. If you'll allow me to, I'll go and ring them up at once." He made for the door as he spoke.

"But how could it possibly be anything but an accident? What makes you think it is?" Annesley called after him, but the question went unheeded and soon they heard him at the telephone, and then they heard him go upstairs.

Annesley took the opportunity to remonstrate with his fellow conspirators.

"Look here, you two, can't you say a blinking thing?"

"You asked us to leave it to you," Corrie answered tersely.

"Yes, I did, but dash it all, when you're told that your sister's been murdered you must say something. To sit and say nothing's confessing your knowledge. Have a go at him when he comes downstairs. You're not usually so reticent. Ask him what the devil he means by it."

And when Dr. Butterworth came downstairs again Corrie made the attempt, but somehow his style seemed cramped and he used such words as "unwarrantable accusations" instead of those more forceful words which, had the situation been what they tried to make it out to be, would have come spontaneously to him. A producer, just told that what he thought was an early rehearsal, was in fact a first night, could not have been more depressed than Annesley.

13
A PUZZLED INSPECTOR

To expect a funeral furnisher to experience grief on the occasions of his undertakings would be unreasonable; reason demands a decently solemn face; decency expects a suit of black, and no man could ask for more. But a doctor! Birth, disease, recovery, relapse and death—he flits from one to the other between his meals. However keen on his profession and kind hearted he may be, the fact remains that the sicknesses of others are the succulent roots of his prosperity. There is no black uniform for him to don and do no more. Not only must he have patience with people suffering from complaints, as far apart as pimples are from pleurisy, but he must go over it all again with relatives able or crass, and always he must be pleasant and produce the proper remarks. No wonder if once in a thousand times he is found to be lacking in tact.

Dr. Butterworth was quite as tactful as most. But he had had a trying day. It was his second broken night that week and he was feeling rather seedy. He was dead tired. The circumstances in which he found himself were not exactly easy, and in trying to lessen the tension for the others, he palpably overdid it.

When he came back from the telephone he went and stood with his back to the empty fireplace, whence he let loose a dull rain of futile but well-meant remarks that somehow seemed to aggravate their grief.

"You know I've always thought this house the most prettily situated of any in the county!"

"Yes, it's very pretty," from Elizabeth, between sobs.

"Do you get trout upstream?"

No response.

"I thought that perhaps they might try to get up from the Priory lake to your ponds."

"I've never seen them," from Annesley.

A long anecdote about trout and their migratory habits from the doctor.

"It must be very nice having the golf links so near you."

"Yes," from Elizabeth. She could have shattered his head with a niblick.

"Do you play much, Mr. Corrie?"

Corrie made a fresh-air shot of his reply. He glared, inarticulate.

An anecdote of a hole halved in one from the doctor.

"Do you get any shooting?"

Then something seemed to snap in Corrie's brain and lightning lit the scene. He leapt to his feet, his face flushing hotly, and he vilified the doctor in one barbed and vivid streak of blasphemous vituperation. He thundered; he shouted; he waved his arms wildly.

Elizabeth, beyond bearing it, pressed her fingers in her ears.

Dr. Butterworth stood up, angrily astonished. But Bernard's blood-curdling cries went echoing through the house—cries that were loud enough to crack deaf eardrums or waken recent dead. "Marion! Marion! Mar-i-on!" he yelled.

Then suddenly he ceased—stood pointing with a shaking hand towards the open door. Yes, he could see her quite clearly. There she was, standing quietly, in the open doorway. She spoke to him. He could hear her quite plainly. "There—you mustn't—now, you know that you mustn't—you'll be in bed for a week, old boy"—the low familiar tones.

"Christ! Oh, Christ, she's there!" he cried, and then collapsed.

They got him on the settee, where he groaned and lay still, with his eyes shut. Dr. Butterworth felt his racing pulse. "You'd better be still. Here, stick your feet up for a time. I must remind you, too, that I did not come here uninvited."

"That's all right, doctor," Annesley answered. "You'll have to excuse us, you know. Mr. Corrie has these nervous storms. Mr. Corrie and Miss Corrie, all of us, we've had a trying experience. I'm sorry, but you can't expect Mr. Corrie to be feeling excessively polite after what you—after your, I think, unpardonable accusations. It may be no business of mine, but it seems to me that you might well have left such suggestions alone."

"Yes. Yes, I dare say I might. I can understand your feelings. Whichever way you look at it, it's not exactly pleasant."

"How do you mean—whichever way you look at it?"

"Some one, Mr. Annesley, some one strangled, or nearly strangled Miss Corrie. Either it was the result of a violent quarrel in which the poor girl was accidentally—a very unlikely accident if I may say so—pitched out of the open window. That may be manslaughter. Or it was just cold-blooded murder, and as I said before, whichever way you look at it, it isn't very pleasant."

"Death is never very pleasant."

"No. But sometimes it's comparatively pleasant."

"Well, I can only tell you again that we found her in the yard below the window. There was no one to do what you suggest has been done. Miss Corrie found the bedroom empty. I suppose you're not taking on yourself to suggest that she did it? Mrs. Glegg, the housekeeper, came down next. They woke Mr. Corrie, then me. I found her in the yard. We none of us knew a single thing about it until after she was dead."

Dr. Butterworth looked puzzled.

"Well, that's not my business. I'm thankful that it isn't. Who carried her upstairs?"

"I did. Miss Corrie, I mean Elizabeth, was with me."

"And you noticed nothing?"

"No. There was no light though, at first—a small lamp only. A fuse had blown, we thought."

Dr. Butterworth glanced at the dining-room lights. They were burning brightly.

"You've put a new fuse in then?"

"No. At least, I haven't. I don't think any one has. The current comes from the colliery power-house. Perhaps the failure was there."

"Yes, perhaps so. Yes, I think perhaps it's only fair to you. Come along upstairs for a moment with me, Mr. Annesley."

Dr. Butterworth had the key of the bedroom in his pocket. He unlocked the door and switched on the light.

"Now, do you see anything?" he asked.

"Yes."

"And neither you nor Miss Corrie saw it before?"

"No. As I've just told you, we only had a candle and a lamp. Later, when the lights came on again—we—well, we didn't look. There was nothing to be done—here. My friend and his daughter were upset. We were all upset."

"That you'll no doubt be able to explain to the police, but I think you'll agree that my statement, which has caused you so much natural annoyance, was justified. I shall have to wait until the police come. If you'll take my advice you'll have Mrs. Glegg in the dining-room and you'll all of you stay there with me until Inspector Jacobs arrives. I can't insist on it, but if I were in your place I should insist on it."

They had locked the bedroom door again and were standing on the landing.

"Yes—yes, I suppose you're right, doctor. It would be best," Annesley agreed after a moment. "But what about the others—ought we to wake them up?"

"What others—I didn't know there was any one else in the house."

"There's James, an old manservant who sleeps in a little room at the end of the upstairs passage, and a maid, who sleeps just across the passage from Mrs. Glegg. They've neither of them wakened through it all."

"How do you know?"

"I looked myself in James's room; Elizabeth looked in Katie's. They neither of them stirred."

Dr. Butterworth stood in thought for a moment, then he told Annesley that he would like to look for himself, and when Annesley showed him the bedrooms, without switching on the lights, or making sure whether the sleep of the occupants was feigned or real, he quietly opened the doors, put his hand inside, took out the keys, locked the doors from the outside, and then put the keys in his pocket.

"That will be best, I think."

And when they got downstairs Mrs. Glegg was called, and Dr. Butterworth went back into the kitchen with her while she made some tea. They drank it and waited for the police, the doctor, having learnt his lesson, silent at last, Corrie lying on the settee with his eyes shut, Elizabeth huddled in her arm-chair pretending an attempt at sleep, Mrs. Glegg seated respectfully on the edge of a chair near the wall, Annesley sitting on a corner of the table, one leg swinging, smoking his pipe, and all of them thinking of

the marks on Marion's neck, the doctor wondering if the
others could really have missed seeing them, the others
wondering whose hand had made them, going over their
story, wondering what they had missed, where they might
fail, and what the consequences would be if they did fail.

They arrived soon after three in a car—Inspector
Jacobs, the police surgeon and two constables.

The police surgeon and Dr. Butterworth made another
examination together whilst one of the constables sat in
the dining-room with the family and their guest. Then
Dr. Butterworth held a long private conversation with
Inspector Jacobs, gave him the keys of the bedrooms and
returned to Millingham, taking the police surgeon with
him. Inspector Jacobs made a careful examination of the
bedroom; he found nothing—no sign of struggle, no buttons or pieces of cloth, no finger-prints on the woodwork
of the window either. It took him more than half an hour,
and it took him as long again to search the yard after
Annesley had shown him where Marion was found. And in
the early hours, just before dawn, he wakened James and
Katie and questioned them. Then he had Corrie, Elizabeth, Mrs. Glegg and Annesley brought to him in turn
and he questioned them at length. He took very good care
that they had no opportunity of communicating with each
other either before or after the interrogation. Throughout
it all he was polite, considerate—even obliging. He neither blustered nor bullied, but looked and behaved like an
ordinary human being who knew his job, and wanted to
find out what there was to find out with the minimum of
annoyance and fuss.

When he left, a puzzled man, it was after six o clock,
and the morning sun was making diamonds of dew-drops
in the grass at the edge of the drive. Throughout the day
it blazed down on Cherry Hay where alternately Annesley

thanked high heaven for the inspiration that had made him wipe the woodwork and the window sill with a wet cloth, and booked himself a berth in baser regions for having been so asinine about the clock. It blazed down on the stream that tinkled prettily through the garden all day, as it had tinkled every day since the house was built and the garden made, and it blazed too, full on the dark-green blinds that were drawn in Corrie's bedroom where Marion lay on the bed. Elizabeth went in once. The room was stifling and she opened the window. She sat on the side of the bed and laid her hand on Marion's forehead. Beautiful she looked—calm—as though spirit departed left body refined—cold chiseled loveliness—it calmed Elizabeth to look at her.

Almost for the first time in her young life death's mystery gripped her. How did Marion die? Who killed Marion? How futile and silly! Where was Marion now—her unknown mother—all these millions of dead? How urgently important! How extraordinary that year by year she got nearer to the answer and hardly ever asked the question. It was like reading a book and not bothering about the end. It was like doing an exercise that never had an end—and then it did end—suddenly—infinity's unexpected edge. Full of it, she walked up by the ponds.

"Fore, fore!"—a man's voice.

"Oh, beauty!—you'll go and get your handicap reduced"—a girl's.

She could hear them across the water.

God! but how silly!

Later in the day she talked, rather shyly, with George on the same subject. He was not very helpful.

"After all, you must die—you can't help yourself, you know," he told her healthfully.

George had his limits.

But he was good—amazingly good. He made all arrangements about the funeral; Marion was to be buried in Millingham; up the drive and round by the road, it was very
nearly as far to Little Plenders as it was to Millingham.
Her father spent the day in bed recovering, and George
Annesley sat and talked with him, breaking the waves of
his temper much as a well-designed breakwater breaks real
waves, sideways, without sudden impact. Elizabeth could
not have done without him. He seemed so safe and sure.

Inspector Jacobs, however, over in Millingham, was not
at all sure. He seemed to be sure of nothing. He spent a
good part of the morning dictating a report and he made
heavy going. To begin with the constable clerk who took
down the shorthand notes in what was really long hand,
abbreviated, gapped and guessed at, had a heavy hand,
and it seemed to react on the report much as suet does on
dumplings. Altogether it was a dull, heavy affair with no
apple in it. There wasn't even a motive. Inspector Jacobs
had only dealt with two murder cases in his life—simple colliery village tragedies of jealousy and drink—but
he knew enough to know that murder minus motive was
mostly a game of blindman's buff.

The sun shone on the police station at Millingham just
as it shone on Cherry Hay, and it shone through the police
station window straight on to Inspector Jacobs as he sat
in his shirt sleeves comparing the typed report with the
rough notes in his book.

He turned over the pages to make sure that he had
missed nothing. There really did seem very little to go on.
Katie had been the only member of the household to hint
at possibilities. She had told him that Corrie and his sister
had frequent quarrels—often violent quarrels. On more
than one occasion she had overheard an actual threat.

"Yes, she ses something to him that I didn't hear and
he ses to her, 'I could kill you for that,' and I ses to Mrs.
Glegg, 'That's a nice thing for him to say to her.'"

Too, Katie had told him that Mr. Annesley, who was now engaged to Elizabeth Corrie, had previously been in love with Marion Corrie. Every one else had contradicted the suggestion, Annesley rather vehemently, and Inspector Jacobs was himself inclined to the belief that this earlier romance had been created by Katie herself. He remembered her round red face and big, brown, round eyes, and shook his head. He could place no reliance on Katie. There was altogether too much, "I ses to her and she ses to me" about her. But for all that, unreliable as he felt her to be, she was the only one to give him information that held even the germ of a motive. Corrie's threats, a violent outburst of temper, he half-strangles his sister and throws her out of the window, the others shielding him. Or if it was Annesley—love—what entanglements and dangerous disentanglements did the word not stand for sometimes?

The only thing the inspector did feel sure about was that there was some collusion somewhere. There must be, though he certainly could not prove it on the information that he had. All he had to go on was that Dr. Butterworth thought their behavior unnatural, and that he himself had similar feelings. Also they were all too cocksure about such unusually unsure things as time.

For Annesley he had laid a trap and Annesley, obligingly, had tumbled into it. He had questioned them each separately in the drawing-room whilst the others remained in the dining-room. Then those he had questioned were passed on to the kitchen. Annesley, like the others, told him that he thought the time when Miss Elizabeth Corrie had wakened was between 1.45 and two o'clock. When asked how he knew he had said, "By the dining-room clock. We looked in the room before searching outside and I noticed it then. It was just before two."

And the inspector had chuckled inwardly because he had already noticed that the clock had stopped at half-past one. When every one was out of the dining-room, he had gone in and moved the hands to half-past three; then, standing in front of it so that the time could not be seen, he had called Annesley to him again. He had seen to it that one of the constables was present as well. I wanted to ask you again about the time, Mr. Annesley."

"Oh, yes."

"You're sure it was somewhere between 1.45 and two o'clock?"

"Yes. I saw the time by the clock in here."

"You're sure you didn't make any mistake. You say you only had a candle."

"Yes, I'm pretty sure about it—I saw the clock."

"Would you be prepared to swear to it?"

A pause. Annesley beginning to wonder what there was behind it all.

"Yes. Yes, I think I could."

The inspector stood away from the clock.

"You see the clock has stopped—that's what made me so inquisitive."

Annesley relieved and rather triumphantly, "Yes, it's stopped since—at 3.30. It was going when I saw it—I remember hearing it tick." What fools these policemen were.

"Did you though? It stopped at 1.30. I've just moved the hands to 3.30."

At Cherry Hay, in the cool early hours, Inspector Jacobs had thought it dramatic—it had been dramatic—but now, in his plainly-furnished police-station office, he doubted if he had gained much advantage by it. After all, defending counsel would make short work of it. Every one agreed about the time of the accident, Mr. Annesley thought he saw the time by the dining-room clock, thought he heard it tick, when all the time the clock had stopped, but that did not necessarily implicate Mr. Annesley. In such circumstances any one might be excused a certain haziness about how they learnt the time. Indeed, it might be held damaging to his collusion theory. It was all rather unsatisfactory. He was afraid it might mean having some one down from Scotland Yard.

He closed his note-book slowly, pulling out its elastic band and letting it go with a snap. He would stop mooning over it and get to work on the verification of those statements that lent themselves to verification.

First he went to Plenders Pit where he was fortunate in finding Mr. Primrose. The inspector asked whether they supplied the current for the Cherry Hay lights.

"Yes, we do. It was a condition attached to our lease that we should supply electric light and power to the estate."

"Could you tell me if there was any failure in the supply last night?"

"I dare say we could." The big man bellowed for the office boy and sent for the engineer, and the engineer sent for the switchboard attendant, and ultimately the switchboard attendant returned with some weird-looking charts. "That's from the recording voltmeter, sir, and that's from the ammeter," he said, handing them to Mr. Primrose. "There's nothing about any stoppage in the night attendant's log."

The big man frowned at the long strips of paper. "No, no. There wasn't any stoppage."

"They say that there was at Cherry Hay."

"The fuse there perhaps."

"No, they say not. But, tell me, would these be bound to show a stoppage? They're automatic, are they?"

"Yes, yes, they're automatic. This shows the voltage—what the pressure was throughout the night—and this shows the current taken. As you'll see, there wasn't any stoppage."

"These bumps and wiggles in the lines—?"

"Ordinary variations."

"Well, couldn't one of the variations mean a failure in the supply to the estate? I don't quite understand."

After a quarter of an hour he understood that he would never understand. It seemed that electricity was far more complicated than he thought it was. Mr. Primrose endeavored to explain it to him in simple, non-technical language, interspersed with frequent appeals to the switchboard attendant. "Correct me if I'm wrong, Joe;" and then, when the attendant, who used astonishingly long words, did make a suggestion, he flew into a temper and went red in the face and loud in the voice.

Finally, the inspector gave it up. No, he would never understand it. He doubted if they did either. He would have to take their word for it that there had been no breakdown, and that if the night attendant had pulled out the switch on the estate circuit, he would have entered it in the log-book.

If you walk down one of the little side streets in Little Plenders—yes, the colliery part of Little Plenders has side streets—any late afternoon, you will be greeted with the surprising smell of frying bacon. The men, on the night-shift, like true Britons, are beginning their belated day with bacon for breakfast. The night-shift attendant in the power house at the colliery was having his when the inspector called. His wife gave the inspector a cup of poisonous tea, and it was the only asset attained by the visit. No, he had not pulled the switch out, he had not left his duty, he had not had forty winks, and no one else came monkeying about with his switches when he was in charge of the station. "So that's that, mister—what's oop?"

His wife defended him. "Why, Bob plays t' floot in t' pit band."

Later still the inspector called at the Priory. The lighting there was on the same circuit as Cherry Hay. If anything at the pit affected the lights at Cherry Hay, then the Priory would be bound to suffer too. He interviewed Professor Taverner and his two servants, Mrs. Primrose and a whole bevy of servants, Mr. Lobley and another bevy of servants, and just as he was giving it up, Miss Lobley came back from a walk—she had been over to Cherry Hay—and she told him that she had been reading in bed from one o'clock until well after two o'clock, she had had toothache, and the lamp above her bed had not so much as flickered.

14
A GRUESOME TEST

Marion died on a Sunday night. The inquest, held in a room at the back of the little town hall in Millingham and adjourned for a week at the request of the police, fell on the Monday afternoon, and on the following day Marion was buried in Millingham's beautiful cemetery. The fatal accident having taken place, the inquest and the burial followed just as thunder follows lightning—they were anticipated events, which Elizabeth, her father, and Annesley, each in his own way, braced himself to face. They knew the road ahead to be mountainous, rugged, difficult, but these were peaks they were prepared for. For the pitiless publicity and terrors of the time that followed, however, they were none of them prepared.

At the inquest, the county coroner, Dr. Chappel, had charge of the proceedings, and to Corrie's disgust he failed to hide the fact that an inquest for him was merely a matter of business. Indeed, he was almost off-hand, and a dentist deciding which tooth to extract could not have displayed more detachment. First he fussed about the ink—the pot was too full for his liking—and then he had the poor taste to exchange a jocular remark with Inspector Jacobs whilst Elizabeth sat nervously twisting her handkerchief until it resembled a piece of string, and her father fumed within. Annesley, on the other hand, quite undisturbed, glanced calmly round the room. The little court was crowded. He recognized one of the servants from the Priory. To him the coroner was merely a rather annoying person. On Corrie, however, he reacted like acid, which, poured on metal, produced poisonous vapors. Indeed it seemed to Corrie that the whole of the proceedings had been arranged to cause the maximum of annoyance to those most nearly concerned. During the laborious long-hand writing down of names, ages, occupations and addresses—facts which could all have been set down in advance and could none of them be disputed—he seethed inwardly. He drummed with irritable fingers against his trembling knee.

But once the preliminaries were over matters moved more quickly. Elizabeth, Mrs. Glegg, Corrie, then Annesley gave evidence in turn, just as, according to their story, they came on the fatal scene in turn; described the doings of the night—the finding of the body. If the opening had been tedious, now all was brief, abrupt, their statements unquestioned, unprobed, the coroner making no comments, and when Inspector Jacobs applied for a week's adjournment they felt that queer complex of relief and disappointment that comes to a nervous patient when a long-dreaded but imminent operation is unexpectedly postponed.

After tea on the day of the inquest, Elizabeth and George Annesley sat in deck-chairs on the lawn, where, a few yards away, rippling over the stones, the little stream made gurgling noises, and overhead the berries on the thorn tree were showing first autumn red.

"And next week we must go through it all again then," Elizabeth sighed, her eyes on the stream, her thoughts on the inquest.

"Yes—and worse. I'm afraid very much worse," Annesley answered her, thinking how pale she looked, how unnatural in black, and wondering if she understood one half of what lay before her.

"Did you expect it—the adjournment?" She turned to face him.

"Why, yes, of course. You see, if the jury returned a verdict of accidental death the police—well, their future investigations might be hampered a little. But if it's a verdict of murder—even against a person unknown—why, then—well, it's up to them to find out who the murderer was."

"Do you really think they'll find out all about—er"— she hesitated over and rejected the word "mother"—"about Daddy's wife?"

"You can bet your life they will—and a great many more things too. Where is he now, by the way?"

In addition to the bridge of red brick that carries the drive across the stream, there is a small foot-bridge in the garden itself; two heavy slabs of stones on a center stone up-ended. Elizabeth pointed to it. "He went over there just before you came out. There's a path across the fields round to the golf links."

"He'll come back by the ponds then perhaps," Annesley ventured.

They looked at each other in silence. As it happens sometimes, the same thought came to them both at once.

"Do you think—I don't think it's good for him to be too much alone," she faltered. "Shall we walk the other way round and meet him?"

So they went round to the end of the house, through the yard at the back with its big outhouse buildings, through the gate against which Mr. Primrose had leant when Corrie threw the piston at him, up the lane and to the ponds. But they did not meet Corrie. They could find him nowhere, though they crossed the field that lies between the ponds and looked up and down the golf links.

"I wonder where he's gone," Elizabeth said, worried.

"Oh, no doubt he turned back to the house. You're not fussing now, are you?"

"Yes, a little."

"Goose—but why on earth?"

"It—well, it just came to me, you know." She clung to his arm.

He laughed at her. He teased her. He called her pet names. He said, "Of course he never would," without mentioning what it was "he never would," and feeling reassured, she walked back arm-in-arm with him towards the house.

"I wonder how well you think you know your father, Elizabeth?" he asked her, as they neared it.

"Quite well, thank you—much better than I know my future husband."

"I doubt it. You should have seen him in France. Shaking like a leaf—green with fright—and then, when the time came and he once got going—"

"Ah, yes, but this—this is different."

They were nearing the house again. The sun was down behind the trees towards the Priory. A Morris saloon stood unattended in the yard, and from one of the sheds came Corrie's voice uplifted in angry protest; he was saying he was damned if he would do it.

They moved over to see what the matter was, but when they were only a few yards away from the outhouse door, Inspector Jacobs looked out, and seeing them, hurried to them.

"Excuse me a moment, Miss Corrie, but would you mind waiting where you are for a moment?" he asked, beckoning Annesley to one side.

She stood watching them talk together, wondering what the subject of their secret conversation was. She overheard the inspector say something about "wanting to spare her"—saw Annesley frown, but whatever the matter was, it was quickly dealt with, for in less than a minute Annesley nodded his head and came back to her where she was waiting.

"It's nothing. Just—just something they want us to do. Go indoors, will you, and I'll be with you soon and tell you all about it."

Elizabeth glanced at the car.

"They aren't going to take him away?"

"No, no. Nothing of the kind. Go in, there's a dear. There's nothing whatever to worry about."

She went slowly into the house, and Annesley and the inspector went into the outhouse building which once had been used as a cow-shed. On an old door, supported across two trestles, a number of plaster casts had been placed, and at the far side of it the police surgeon stood in argument with Corrie, who was obviously much disturbed.

There must have been half a dozen of the casts, and on the floor was a box of straw in which they had been packed. For a moment Annesley failed to comprehend their purpose. They looked just like shaped lumps of white plaster, models of little logs with irregular ends, all in a row on the dusty old door.

The inspector explained.

"I'm very sorry, Mr. Annesley, it's rather unpleasant, but it can't be helped—can't be avoided. They're models of Miss Corrie's neck. These marks outlined here in pencil show the exact positions of the bruises, and we want you and Mr. Corrie and James to take hold of them so that we can judge exactly where your grips come."

Annesley glanced at Corrie, who stood frowning theatrically with folded arms. There was a pause in the proceedings.

"Mr. Corrie refuses to make the test, Mr. Annesley, but we hope that you'll be more reasonable and that you'll help us to overpersuade him. It will look very odd, you know, if he doesn't."

Annesley nodded. There was no getting away from it so far as he could see.

"I think we shall have to do what they ask, you know, Corrie."

"Well, I'm going to—well, show you that we shan't."

Annesley shrugged his shoulders and tried again.

"Oh, come along, man, of course we must. I'll have first go. You do understand, inspector, that it's not a very pleasant job—particularly for Mr. Corrie. I should have thought that measurements would have done," he added, attempting to excuse Corrie's unfortunate attitude.

The police surgeon took one of the casts and placed it in front of Annesley instructing him by example. "There, see, your thumb on this side over this mark here, then grip and try to make your fingers fit with these marks here."

Annesley's hands were of the wide-palmed, rather stubby-fingered sort. He gripped, and as far as could be seen he covered the pencil marks exactly.

"That's bad," he said pleasantly.

Corrie became interested. "It's ghastly. I don't believe you've any right to ask us to do it either. You're assuming murder before the inquest's over and the jury may yet agree on accidental death. Besides, it isn't a test at all. A living neck would—would give, you know, and you can't see the contact marks either."

"But, Mr. Corrie, you really mustn't consider us in that antagonistic manner," the inspector replied; "we're not antagonistic. At least, I hope we're not. We're merely trying to find out. Surely you want us to find out. Surely it hasn't anything to do with where our rights begin and end when it's a question of finding out who it was who murdered your own sister?"

"Corrie, Corrie, he's right, and you know he is. But, inspector, there is something in what Mr. Corrie says about not knowing how nearly our fingers coincide with the marks—and about the model not yielding."

"And if either of our finger-marks do seem to fit are we to be suspected of murder because of it? Why, damn it all, man, hundreds of grips might fit it. It's an insult," Corrie added angrily.

Inspector Jacobs protested.

"No, of course you're not to be suspected of murder because of it. At present you're one of quite a number of people who might just conceivably have committed what may be a murder. To that extent any one who was in the house at the time is obviously suspected. Your own common sense ought to tell you, too, that it's in your interest to do what we want you to. People who put difficulties in the way of detectives become suspected, you know, Mr. Corrie."

"Look here now, inspector, I will not have you talking to me in that way about suspicion and guilt. You—well, wait until the—"

"Corrie, don't be an ass," Annesley interrupted. "The inspector here could get a warrant for your arrest to-night if he wanted to. Of course we'll do what you ask us willingly. Do you want me to try it again?" he asked, turning to the doctor.

"Yes, but just hold out your hand first."

He took a little tin from one of his waistcoat pockets. It contained a bright red paste, and he smeared some of it lightly on Annesley's thumb and fingers.

"Now try," he said. "Go carefully and try to keep your fingers on the marks."

Annesley spread his stubby fingers carefully and gripped.

The doctor scribbled "Annesley" in pencil across the end of the plaster cast.

"Now, Mr. Corrie, please," the inspector urged.

Sulkily, like a small boy having jam removed with a sponge, Corrie held out his hand—held it out stiffly in a vain attempt to hide its tendency to tremble.

"Now you'll do."

Corrie gripped. The plaster cast split into pieces beneath his hand. One bit shot off surprisingly and hitting a pile of empty petrol tins sent them clattering to the floor. Unstable and badly stacked, the small piece of plaster had been sufficient to send them flying. And in much the same way, the little incident, unexpected, yet inexplicably disturbing, snapped Corrie's nerves already frayed and taut.

"I can't! I can't! I won't!" he yelled like one who, tortured, breaks at last. He turned yellow-green and nearly fell.

The doctor made him sit down on an upturned tub at the side of the shed, and after a time when he became more calm, they persuaded him to make another attempt. This time there was no calamity, and the doctor scribbled Corrie's name across the model end.

"Is that all—can I go?" Corrie asked.

"Yes. And we want the manservant, James. Could you send him?"

Annesley made a move towards the shed door. "I'll go and find him for you," he said helpfully.

"No. I want you again, Mr. Annesley, if you don't mind."

Corrie departed.

"What is it this time?" Annesley queried as soon as Corrie had gone.

The doctor took yet another plaster cast from the box on the floor—a more weighty affair this time, the model of a man's neck.

"We want you to do the same with this, Mr. Annesley. This is a replica of poor Robson's neck. You'll remember holding his head in the water butt a few days ago. You printed your finger-marks nicely. Now, again please, right hand from the back."

Without the flicker of an eye, without sign of emotion or distress, Annesley did as he was bid. He smiled reminiscently. What pleasure it had given him to feel the big neck bending. This dummy neck, however, did not yield. It flashed across his mind to try and split it as Corrie had done, then he remembered that even if the inspector had no duplicate with him the police would be sure to have the mold from which the cast was made. He felt a little concerned, but Inspector Jacobs certainly should not see it. He handed it over to him.

"And now, what's the result of it all?" he asked quietly.

Inspector Jacobs handed the model to the surgeon who took it over to a little window at the back of the shed. He examined it and then the other cast as well.

"As nearly as I can judge without making exact measurements, Mr. Annesley's finger-prints come nearly half an inch short of the ends of the bruise marks in the case of Miss Corrie, and say an eighth of an inch short in the case of Robson."

"In your opinion then, doctor—"

"In my opinion, inspector, the man who gripped Robson by the neck may have gripped Miss Corrie."

"But by what you said just now, the two grips seem to differ by getting on for half an inch," Annesley said, with a note of protest.

"A man's neck—a girl's," the doctor murmured.

"Yes," Inspector Jacobs agreed, "and in one case the hand at the back and in the other, on the throat. Yes, there would be a difference."

The inspector paused and then continued:—

"Mr. Annesley, it seems to me that putting it at its lowest, you are going to be very much concerned in getting this mystery cleared up. As you pointed out a few minutes ago, I've no doubt that if I wanted to, I could get a warrant for your arrest. But I don't want to—"

"No. I should say there might be some risk attached to it," Annesley interrupted.

"Risk of what?"

"Well, of ridicule—and censure."

The inspector laughed. "Come, Mr. Annesley, I imagined that you were going to behave more sensibly."

"I am going to be sensible. Come now, what more do you want*?"

"Well, I may as well tell you that it will be my duty to keep an eye on you—have you watched, you know. Do you think now—could you arrange to stay here at Cherry Hay until after the inquest on Tuesday?"

"I am staying here until after the inquest."

"Good, that's that, then. Now, where's that manservant I won—"

"Here I am, sir."

They turned to see James James standing with a puzzled expression before the row of models on the door.

"How long have you been standing there?"

"Standing here, sir? Oh, a matter of a minute or two, I should say, sir."

"You ought to have knocked."

"Knocked, sir. Knock on a cow-shed door, sir! I beg pardon, sir, but I was told to come to you here, sir, by Mr. Corrie."

"Did you hear what I was saying to Mr. Annesley just now?"

The old man hesitated.

"In a manner of speaking, yes, sir."

"How do you mean 'in a manner of speaking'?"

"Well, sir, I mean that what I heard, I heard in my capacity as—er—butler, sir, late butler perhaps I should say, sir, and that it doesn't therefore signify."

Annesley laughed pleasantly, and the inspector beckoned him into the yard, leaving the police surgeon to continue his gruesome game of grip with James.

"I say, I'm sorry, Mr. Annesley. I had no idea he was there. I wouldn't have dreamed of saying what I did say had I known."

Annesley assured him that it was "quite all right."

"By the way, it isn't my business, but I was wondering whether you realized exactly what you were up against, and whether you've thought of getting some one to look after your interests—a solicitor?"

Annesley thanked him. The thought had occurred to him. It had come to him five minutes earlier whilst they were in the cow-shed. None the less, it was sporting of the inspector to remind him of it—typical of the fair-play British police force. They shook hands as boxers do before a bout.

There are two front doors to Cherry Hay, one, the one more generally used giving on to the yard near the drive, the other, stone porched, with side seats, on to the garden path. Annesley went through the small gate that divides the garden from the yard and the drive, and sat on one of the seats on the porch. He lit his pipe. He had plenty to think about. Could Corrie have done it in his sleep? It certainly didn't seem likely. He tried to picture how it could have happened—Marion getting out of bed to look out of the window—dark, yes, but perhaps she had heard a noise, or perhaps she merely wanted to feel the wind against her face—he had felt that desire himself; then Corrie, walking in his sleep, goes back naturally to his own room, sees a figure at the window—can you see though when you walk in your sleep?—he must ask some one—no, not Taverner—he made a noise perhaps, perhaps he was half-awake, and Marion, startled, turned round, and he, suddenly frightened, gripped her by the throat and pushed her out. Yes, that was just conceivable. Remembering Corrie, quite conceivable. But the bedclothes! Why on earth the bedclothes? There wasn't even a madman's reason for that. He ought to have asked the inspector if the bedclothes being there threw any light on the matter. Decent of him to remind him about a solicitor. He would get Corrie to go into Millingham or Blatchford to-morrow.

He sat there smoking for a good ten minutes, and was just getting up to go indoors when the inspector's car came round the corner from the yard. It was getting rather dark, but he could see the box containing the tell-tale models in the dicky. He watched the rear lamp vanish through the trees.

15
ANNESLEY IS LED TO A POOR CONCEIT OF HIMSELF

Suspicion! The Devil must chuckle when he sees how that sin thrives. Let it but get well hold and it spreads like the plague itself. How it began exactly, it is difficult to say, but it caught them all in its toils at Cherry Hay and trebled the terrors of the week between the first and second inquests on Marion Corrie. Perhaps Jack Girling brought the first germ with him, when he brought Annesley the letters from the French Horn, and Elizabeth overheard their conversation. But Corrie himself was the root source of most of their troubles. Elizabeth, Mrs. Glegg, and Annesley had taken enormous risks on his behalf. They were doing their best to get him ashore in safety, and now, with the tide topping the sides of their frail craft, "Perjury," instead of sitting still and being saved, he must needs take his erratic oar and spoil the rhythm of the rowing. Never in all his experience of him had Annesley found it so difficult to remember that, on his good days, Corrie was one of the best on earth, and that allowances should be made for those whose inner arrangements departed from the normal.

Marion was buried in Millingham the day after the inquest. But instead of their common grief uniting them, they quarreled before they got home.

There is a tendency in Millingham to criticize the town, its public hall, its entrances and exits, its market square—even its intellectual status—but should it be in fact as undesirable a setting for the activities of life as the inhabitants pretend, they have compensation in the knowledge that, once having ceased to live, they can decompose at peace in a cemetery as stately and suitable for the purpose as any in the country; a last haven of wooded hill and sheltered dale where wide asphalted pavements wind between giant oaks and firs—pavements along which the living may walk lovingly among the tablets of their dead—until they die too and are buried there.

Marion was buried there on Tuesday.

The soil is of sand.

"Dust to dust—"

The sexton dropped sand on the coffin.

Annesley squared his shoulders, his eyes prickly, his simple, orthodox soul disturbed—impressed.

They were standing on the hill-side just above the grave, Elizabeth beyond all caring, Corrie with his bowler hat held before his face to hide the streaming tears, hating and despising himself—hating it all. Just beyond lay a second open grave—a heap of new-turned sand—planks and slings—and in an hour perhaps this same sexton would be dropping sand in that, and then in others—in countless graves with just this same solemnity . . . one ghastly hired parade of organized grief—grief that every nerve in his body urged him to hide and keep to himself. Unaccountably he hated it.

Below the grave stood another group—Joyce, Mrs. Primrose. . . . And a little further along the path, others.

"That's 'im, hiding 'is face."

"Aye, 'e may well! Fancy facing it out like that . . . one of 'em did it."

"Daresen't stay away."

"T'gurl's bonny . . . but that ain't nowt to go by."

The inquest had been reported in the Blatchford daily papers.

That young man over there leaning against the oak-tree is on the staff of the *Millingham Mail,* and these are the first Peeping Toms a cheap press breeds and lives on—the advance guard of that vast array who, in a week, will take the tale of the Corries' agonies like mustard with their morning bacon.

The last look taken, they all went back to Cherry Hay together in the car, Corrie at the wheel, Annesley in the front seat beside him with Elizabeth perched on his knee, James, Mrs. Glegg and Katie in the back seat. And, as though they had not troubles enough already, Corrie must talk openly of suicide so that the servants behind him could hear. Then when Annesley touched him on the arm as a gentle reminder that they were not by themselves, Corrie, quite unnecessarily, jerked the steering wheel and made the car swerve until it nearly mounted a grassy bank at the edge of the road. He went as white as a sheet but finally pulled up in safety.

"Look here, am I driving this bloody bus or are you driving it?" he yelled, embellishing his speech with more than the bad word written.

Elizabeth pinched Annesley's leg, and, taking the hint, he swallowed his retort. They made the remaining mile along the main road in a highly explosive silence, and when they reached the gates Corrie jammed on the brakes and got out.

"If you must always be interfering, take her yourself. I'm going to walk," he said angrily, and banging the door, he made off along a footpath that ran through the wood by the boundary wall.

Elizabeth jumped from Annesley's knee, and out of the door on the other side, but by the time she had run round

the front of the car Corrie was yards away and pretended
not to hear when she called after him, suggesting that she
should walk as well.

"You heard what he said?" she said, turning to Annesley, distressed. Annesley knew his Corrie though, and tried
to persuade her to return to the car.

Mrs. Glegg agreed with him.

"He'll be all right, dearie. He didna' mean what he
said. The walk'll do him a world of good." And James said,
"Aye, that it will."

Elizabeth's eyes blazed with anger, or perhaps the near
tears made them bright. "You mean you just don't want to
take the trouble," she said unreasonably, and ran after her
father into the wood.

Annesley moved over into the driver's seat.

"I'd wait awhile if I were you, sir," Mrs. Glegg suggested.

They did wait. She was back in five minutes. Without
speaking a word she got into the car and they drove all the
way home in silence. Looking at her sideways, Annesley
saw a tear fall.

When they got home she went straight to her room and
it was tea time before they spoke again. By six they had
discussed Corrie's continued absence and decided to ring
up the Priory. They learnt that he had been there for tea
and he came home at seven seething with pent-up passion.
What on earth had they rung up the Priory for? Did they
want to make a — of him before all and sundry? Could he
not even walk from the gates without every one running
after him?

At the time they were in the drawing-room and Annesley, in response to a glance from Elizabeth, retired. He left
them to it, but he could hear Corrie ranting and raving for
a good ten minutes.

At dinner, Corrie hardly ate a mouthful, but sat with
his eyes glued on a book propped up against the water

jug. When the others spoke he frowned. Annesley itched to smack him and was thankful when, the miserable meal ended, he announced his intention of going to bed. But even that was not the end of it, and until nine o'clock, Elizabeth was constantly running up and down in answer to his bell.

"I'm sorry, George, but he really can't help it. We've got to make the best of it. It's a thousand times worse for him," she said, when at last he seemed to have settled down, and she was able to join Annesley in the dining-room.

"I know he can't," he said readily enough, though he was not too sure in his heart of hearts.

"Marion! Marion! Marion!" His shouts made the house ring. There was a crash of falling furniture.

They dashed upstairs to his bedroom. They found him on the floor beside the bed. A tray with a jug and glass had been set on a bedside table. The table had overturned, the jug was broken, the glass was in the middle of the room. His pyjama jacket was soaked.

"You're not hurt, Daddy, are you?"

Corrie rose carefully. He seemed remarkably calm and wide awake.

"No—no. No bones have been broken, I fancy. Get me another pyjama jacket. They're in the middle drawer."

He climbed back into bed and sitting there he changed.

He turned to Annesley with a wry little smile. "I'm sorry, but if you're going to join the family you'll get used to it—won't he, Elizabeth? Did I call out?"

"You certainly did," George assured him.

"I was afraid that I might. I generally know when I'm going to do it. George looks quite scared, Elizabeth. There's nothing to worry about, is there? Run and fetch me a fresh glass of water, there's a darling, and then you ought to go to bed yourself."

Elizabeth disappeared to fetch the glass.

"I say—er—would you like me to come and sleep in here?" Annesley asked with some hesitation.

Corrie laughed at the suggestion. "George, you're priceless!" he cried. "You haven't got a nerve in your whole hulk and some of the brain-cells are missing. When a child could see that I'm all on edge you treat me as though I were Bulldog Drummond. And now, when I'm feeling cucumber calm you offer to come and cuddle. Go to bed, laddie, and thank God that you've got good guts."

Astonished, in spite of his knowledge that Corrie could never be accounted for, Annesley said goodnight to Elizabeth on the landing and returned downstairs to the dining-room where he consumed much smoke and attempted consecutive thought. The night was chilly. There was a fire and he sat smoking in front of it. The kitchen folk went to bed. The house became quiet. Feeling the air to be stuffy, he got up and opened one of the casement windows at the end of the room furthest away from the fire and returning to his chair, he plunged into thought again.

It had occurred to him before how odd it was that he had had no word from Sir Victor Grahame, and now it struck him afresh. His uncle knew that he was staying at Cherry Hay. His uncle suspected Corrie. The newspaper reports had implied, clearly enough, that Marion's death was more than mere accident. The postponement of the inquest confirmed the implication and yet his uncle never wrote. Annesley was very glad that he did not. He knew well enough that their correspondence would be opened and a letter from his uncle referring to missing papers would call for explanations that would do his queer friend no good.

As he sat smoking his pipe and staring at the fire, Annesley had to admit that he had not been very successful as a sleuth. Probably, as Corrie said, some of the brain-cells were missing. At the time when first he had suggested to his uncle that they should collect Corrie, who had so surprisingly written his suspiciously pertinent paper on the subject of steel erosion, and Lobley, who was so obviously interested in the paper Corrie had penned, together on his unprofitable estate, it had struck him as being an inspired proposition. Then, when he first made the suggestion, Annesley had imagined that his uncle had been impressed. "George," he had said, "you'll get brain fever." And, foot-on-the-bottom-rung-at-last sort of thoughts rising in Annesley's brain, had skipped through promotion to knighthood. But now it all seemed different. Now he began to wonder whether, after all, he was more than the dull dole-spared nephew of a benevolent uncle. For the first time it struck him that perhaps the missing papers were not really as important as his uncle pretended. Two years or more had elapsed since they were taken from Hendon, and certainly no resulting epoch-making invention had startled an angry nation. The nation was no longer angry and had forgotten all about it. There could be no real urgency about the recovery of the papers, either, for, had they any value, they would surely have been duplicated. Now it was merely a matter of catching a thief, a thief whose capture Scotland Yard proper had given up when they handed the whole affair over to his uncle's less active department. The more he dwelt on it, the more convinced he became that he was merely his uncle's nephew, and the less he relished the relationship.

He picked up the poker and stirred the fire. A big lump of coal, dead, apparently incombustible, broke at his touch, burst into life and lit the grate with yellow leaping flames. It suggested synonymous fancies. That was the way a detective's brain should pierce dead ends and light them. But his brain! It neither pierced nor lit, but worked in circles breeding doubts. Never once had he really suspected

Corrie in the matter of the papers. True, Corrie was much of a crank but not of the kind that stole things. Now he began to doubt if Lobley had had anything to do with the papers either. He had reasons for doubting. On the Saturday before Marion died, Corrie, Lobley and he had played a round of golf together and whilst they stood chatting on one of the tees, with truly Machiavellian cunning, he had made an unexpected reference to Corrie's erosion paper just as Lobley prepared to drive, and Lobley, undisturbed, had smitten a beauty worthy of Braid.

"Know Corrie's paper*? Of course I know it. I bought half a dozen reprints to give to some of my staff. But it's one thing to write a paper about doing"—here, casually, in the middle of his sentence, he had driven the ball plump down the middle of the fairway—"things and quite another thing to do 'em," he concluded, gazing into distance, with club aloft, as Corrie sometimes did in dreams.

Corrie had attempted emulation.

"I should think it blinking well—" he began, but fluffing his ball to the ladies' tee, the rest of the sentence was lost in the rough.

No, Annesley thought, smiling as he remembered it, it had all been too natural. But if his uncle was wrong, and he was wrong, who did kill Marion—and why? Corrie, walking into his sister's bedroom in his sleep, waking up suddenly to see her standing near him in the dark, and pushing her through the open casement window in a panic of unreasoned terror. That was the probable answer.

Annesley's pipe had gone out. He rose, and kicking the dying embers with his foot, he told himself he was in a deucedly awkward position. But not because of any suspicions the police seemed to hold about him. The test with the plaster models and Inspector Jacobs's subsequent remarks did not really worry him, though it was certainly a pity that old James had heard what the inspector had said.

No, the awkward part of it all was his unknown connection with Scotland Yard. When it had merely been a question of missing papers that did not matter so much. Then he felt certain that Corrie could be cleared. But now murder was concerned. Now he was not certain that Corrie could be cleared. What would Elizabeth think of him now if she knew of his connection? Solemnly he had sworn himself to secrecy and now he dare not write to ask for his release.

He had just made up his mind to go to bed when he heard a sound of rapping. He glanced hurriedly round the room and as he looked a dirty hand appeared inside the open window, rapped on it gently, and then withdrew.

16
AND JACK GIRLING MAKES IT POORER STILL

Elizabeth, obeying her father's suggestion, went to bed but not to sleep. Neither did he, although as a rule, as soon as he had shouted, he settled down to sleep. She could hear him walking about his room. She pictured him tigering up and down in his dressing-gown. Then she heard him lock his door, and, knowing how he had always hated it when Marion locked his bedroom door at night, the sound of the key as it turned in the lock aroused in her a sense of uneasy fear.

She put on her dressing-gown and knocked gently at his door. To her surprise, he opened it at once and beckoned her into the room. He had his dressing-gown on as she expected. His thin, red hair was ruffled. She knew he had been running his fingers through it. He looked nearly fifty instead of more than ten years less.

"Can't Daddy-man go teep?" she asked lightly.

Towering above her, he frowned at her frivolity.

"Elizabeth," he said, in a hoarse stage whisper, "you'd better lock your door to-night."

"But, Daddy—"

"You heard me lock mine?"

"Yes, that was why I came."

"Well, do as I tell you."

"But, Daddy—"

"Don't argue. Go to bed. And lock your door."

"But why?"

He paced the room again, muttering theatrically, "Shall I tell her? Must I tell her?" and, seeing his growing excitement, attempting to keep him from tragedy, she said, "Come, Daddy, out with it."

"Very well, then." He stared at her solemnly.

She waited with what patience she could.

"Old James met me on my way back from the Priory to-night. He told me something."

Elizabeth waited.

"He told me something that I think I ought to tell you."

"Well, go on, Daddy."

"He says that he overheard Inspector Jacobs talking to George. From what he heard, Jacobs has definite reasons to suspect George of killing Marion—he told George that he was having him watched."

"How absolutely ridiculous!"

"You didn't think it so absolutely ridiculous when George suggested that I did it."

"No, I was angry with him. But that was different. George thought you might have done it somehow in your sleep."

"And that is more than absolutely ridiculous. It's—" He swore in. a hushed, hoarse voice.

"You didn't think it ridiculous yourself at the time."

"No, but I've been thinking—thinking things over since. You know, there may have been something in Jacobs's suggestion that George was once in love with Marion. You—you never know with love. And—and—well, some one killed Marion, you know. I should advise you to lock your door."

And to all Elizabeth's arguments he would only reply: "Some one killed Marion." At last she left him. She left him without one suspicious thought of Annesley. She settled herself in bed and attempted to go to sleep. "I'll give you a note. And I've no doubt that *you* can persuade him." She repeated it over and over again. She remembered how Marion had stressed the "you," remembered her thoughts as she walked to Little Plenders with the note. She had sung to herself on the way. Now she felt she would never sing again. As her father said, some one had killed poor Marion. Marion had been lying in the dark, just as she was then, and some one had come into her room, strangled her, and thrown her out of the window into the yard below. And the only people in the house were old James and George, her father, and Katie and Mrs. Glegg. It was *reductio ad absurdum* with no sane remainder left.

Then, after lying awake for what seemed like half-eternity, she thought she heard her father moving in his room again and opened the door to listen. To her astonishment she heard voices downstairs in the hall—Annesley's and another. Putting on her dressing-gown, fearing that it was Jacobs come to report some discovery, she crept downstairs. Half-way down the bottom flight she stopped. The hall light was on. A beam that supported the landing above hid half her view, and George, who was standing with his back to her, had neither head nor shoulders. In the quiet house she could hear what they said quite plainly. The first words to reach her were spoken by George.

"But what on earth makes them think so?" he said.

"They says it's a sex crime, sir." The voice was a gruff one.

"What the devil do you mean by that, Jack?"

"Well, you know, sir, Bill Larkin's cousin's a slop and 'e says 'ow all the force is certain you done it. And Katie Bollard, what's here, sir, she lives in t' village, and she says as 'ow you were sweet on t'murdered lady."

There was a pause. Annesley's anger was too great for speech.

"It ain't wot I thinks, you know, sir. Nor t'owd lady neither for all that."

Elizabeth crept softly up the stairs and back to bed. No, she did not believe a word of it, but she had heard enough. Marion *had* stressed the "you" when she said it.

When the hand appeared, Annesley had walked quickly to the window. Cautiously he put his head out.

"Oh, it's you, sir. I hope I didn't startle you, sir. It's me, Jack Girling."

Annesley recognized the gruff voice of old Mrs. Girling's enormous son.

"What is it, Jack?"

"Why, Mother wanted me to bring you these 'ere letters, sir. The police have been up at the Horn."

"But why didn't you come to the door. You might have—"

"The house is being watched, I fancy, sir. I'm not sure, but I thought I saw some one on t'little bridge as I climbed down into the garden by the pond. They've been asking for letters, sir. The old lady said there weren't none. I don't want to get her in trouble."

"Asking for my letters! Look here, you give me the letters through the window. Then I'll open the front door—you know where it is. I won't show a light. I want you to tell me about it."

The dining-room windows at Cherry Hay are high in the outside wall. Standing in the garden border below, a big man can barely reach them. Jack Girling was a giant. He handed them up to Annesley. One was addressed in his uncle's writing and had a foreign stamp on. He put them on the dining-room table, switched off the light in the hall, and opened the door just a crack and waited. Five minutes passed, and he was just beginning to wonder whether something might not have happened, when the door was pushed open and Girling came inside. As soon as he heard the door close, Annesley switched on the light again.

"Well, this is a sorry do, sir," Girling began, with a pleasant grin.

"Tell me all about it, Jack."

"Why, they come up this morning from Millingham, and asked to have a look at your rooms, sir. They was there a good hour—*and* busy."

"What did they do. Jack?"

"I weren't in. But Mother says as how they made a pretty upset. Searchin', they called it. Gave everything you'd got the once over. Drawers and desk and trunk an' all, so t'old lady says."

"But the letters, Jack?"

"She'd got 'em."

"Had she though—?"

"Aye, she 'ad an' all. They was in t'kitchen when they come, and she slipped 'em in 'er pocket."

There was a pause in the conversation, then, after a moment's hesitation, Girling continued. "They thinks as you done it, sir"—and the reader knows the rest.

And when Jack Girling had departed, Annesley locked the front door after him and returned to the dining-room, where he read his letters. They were none of them important except the one that came from Sir Victor. From that he learnt that his uncle was on the continent, that he would not be back for ten days or more. He had written from an hotel in Brussels, which he was leaving that day, and he gave no addresses. Annesley burnt it in the fire, which had so died down that he had to light the letter with a match. Then he fastened the window and went upstairs to bed.

Cherry Hay slept at last. The water in the stream tinkled steadily outside it. Inside, the water in the pipes plunked steadily through the night. The downstairs rooms were empty; upstairs, each room had its own recumbent figure. Sleep had enfolded them. Who killed Marion? It had been the last thought of each. Who killed Marion? Plunk, plunk, plunk. Thank God for sleep.

17

THE VERDICT

Next morning they all felt rather ashamed of themselves. Somehow, things seemed different in the morning. Bernard was at his very best. He was genial almost. He was down in time for breakfast. He inquired whether Elizabeth had had a good night.

"George," he said, helping Annesley to the most palatable pieces of bacon on the dish and reserving some rather unprepossessing rashers for himself, "I don't know what on earth we should have done without you."

George felt almost embarrassed. He had noticed the discrepancy between the remaining rashers. He felt certain which were his. And then, Corrie had helped him to the others after all. Not just by accident, either—there had been a hesitation. It was ridiculous of course, but it seemed to Annesley that if he could come to such incorrect conclusions about Corrie in relation to bacon rashers, his conclusion might be equally incorrect regarding more important matters.

Before they finished breakfast, the telephone bell rang and Corrie rose to answer it. They heard him making refusals in a pleasant, tolerant voice. "No. No, I'm sorry, but I can't. . . . No. No, I won't. I've nothing whatever to say. . . . No."

"It was only a reporter ringing up from Blatchford. They must make a living, I suppose," he said, rejoining the others.

He was astonishing. There was a letter for him from the managing director of the Magnet Company, asking him some questions about a patent. He was obviously pleased that the matter had been referred to him. He actually discussed it with Annesley. Did Annesley think he could be spared? He did not want to seem to be leaving everything to Annesley, but he ought to go to the works at Derby to look through some papers and drawings.

Annesley thought he could be spared, and feeling time and temper to be favorable, he raised the question of a solicitor.

"Oh, Ambrose Auty of Millingham's the man we want," Corrie replied at once.

"We ought to have the very best man we can get—and I don't think he's likely to be in practice in Millingham," Annesley said, opposing his friend with some trepidation, and thinking to himself that Corrie had probably only suggested Mr. Auty because his name was the first solicitor's in the telephone directory or for some other equally irrelevant reason.

"But, my dear fellow, why on earth not? Most of the most promising solicitors are entirely unknown, and a young unknown man is more likely to take a keen interest in our fate than Sir Somebody or other who's already made his name and dibs."

"It's a risk. There are plenty about already and we know nothing whatever about him."

"But, my dear fellow, I do know something about him. I heard Mr. Primrose praising him only the other day at the golf club."

But Annesley was unconvinced. "Look here, I'll tell you what I'll do. I'll ring up Inspector Jacobs and ask his advice."

"Ring up Jacobs! Well, that's good, that is. Did you hear that, Elizabeth? My sainted aunt. He'll ring up Jacobs!"

And having finished his breakfast, Corrie got up and left them at the table. As he went out of the door they could him speaking pleasantly to himself, "Well, well! Ring up Jacobs. That's funny, that is," like some plump, pleasant uncle talking to children.

Elizabeth and Annesley stared at each other.

"What on earth are you smiling at, George?"

"Well!"

"Daddy's feeling well. That's all."

"Then here's to his very good health."

Annesley raised his coffee cup. Elizabeth did the same. They clinked them together.

In spite of the appalling circumstances Elizabeth felt that it was the most pleasant meal she had eaten since they came to Cherry Hay. Looking at George Annesley she felt quite sure that she was right in feeling quite sure that he could not possibly have had anything to do with . . . Of course he couldn't. She was engaged to him.

And when she went into the kitchen she felt equally certain that James James could never have committed a harmful act in his whole existence. He was in a green apron cleaning boots. Mrs. Glegg was washing up. Katie came in with a tray. They were just ordinary people doing everyday things. It was impossible to believe that any of them could have murdered Marion. But it was impossible to forget that they might have done. As the week moved on and the inquest drew near, it became increasingly impossible to forget it. The police, the reporters, their own solicitor, the newspapers, they all suggested it every hour.

Professor Taverner and Joyce called on them during the morning. For a moment Elizabeth thought that Joyce was going to kiss her. "My dear," she said, "we are so dreadfully sorry for you all. You'll—you'll be sure to let us know if we can do anything."

It was nicely done.

Annesley could never make out why Marion and Elizabeth objected to Joyce. He turned to the professor.

"Taverner, I'm dying to look over the stables and see what alterations you've made. Corrie tells me that he hears most mysterious whirring sounds going on, and I think he's suspecting black magic."

"Oh. How is he, by the way?" From Joyce.

"He's standing it remarkably well. He's gone to Derby on business." From Elizabeth.

"It's the noise from the electric furnaces he hears, I expect," the professor said, turning to Annesley. "Come and look by all means. Come along with us now. Miss Lobley has the car."

From the outset Annesley felt quite certain that he might just as well have stayed at home. The agreement to his request had been too ready. Joyce drove, and he sat with the professor in the back seat. The car was a new one Lobley had recently bought. It was one of the big new Blicks, and it skimmed along the bumpy drive like a feather bed on velvet. At the stables they got out and Joyce drove on alone to the Priory. The professor took a small leather case of keys out of his trouser pocket, picked out a small one, and opened the heavy oak doors.

Annesley glanced round him with interest. Again, he wondered why the stables always gave him such a queer sensation—frequently he felt it when passing the building; now, it was more pronounced than he had ever known it. He felt as one who vainly attempts to recall a name; it is there in his brain, he knows it begins with a "b," his tongue curls on it—but it will not come. Only with Annesley it was not a name. It was a missing sensation. At some time or other. . . .

"Yes, that's Lobley's idea—though I doubt if we shall make anything of it."

Lost in thought, eyes inwards for once, Annesley had apparently been staring at a shed that stood in the middle of the stable yard. Outside it were two of Lobley's Little Giant motor bicycles, and now that the professor had broken in on his unaccustomed reverie he noticed that the saddles were missing and that the machines had been fitted with triangular tubular frames connecting the saddle-pins to the handle-bars.

Professor Taverner led him towards them.

"What's the great idea?" Annesley asked.

"Why, he's always trying to out-maneuver his competitors—you mustn't tell friend Corrie about this—and he wants me to devise a means of registering the starting torque of his machines. He says it's the psychology of the thing that counts. What he really wants to find is the draw-bar pull at starting, but he's seen the word torque somewhere and he will have it, though it's quite incorrect. Says it's a good talking point. But come and have a look at the lab."

The horse boxes had been bricked up half-way and fitted with factory windows. Half-way down the length of the main building, at one side of the yard, there were big sliding doors. The professor explained that they had to have them put there on account of the size of one of the rotary kilns. Inside it was beautifully light; the walls were well white-washed. There was a faint, sickly smell of escaping gas and creosote, and down the middle of the lab. there stood what looked to Annesley like a small cement kiln. The professor explained it to him. Explained too how the oils were collected and distilled. He talked at great length about calories and flash points, and whilst Annesley said "yes" and "I understand" in the proper pauses, he looked round him for any signs of engineering activities. He saw nothing to rouse his suspicions. He hardly expected to. The professor had been too ready with his invitation.

He walked thoughtfully back to Cherry Hay. It seemed as though he had been entirely mistaken in his theory that Lobley and Primrose had been even remotely connected with the missing Hendon papers. It was a theory based on the fact that he had found a copy of Corrie's erosion paper in a magazine that Lobley had been reading; on that, and on the fact that they were looking for a house with out-buildings or other accommodation for a laboratory. Now, Lobley had openly admitted his interest in Corrie's pa-per—he had purchased copies. And he, Annesley, had seen all over the laboratory. So far as the missing papers were concerned, he seemed to be back exactly where he was at the very beginning. And if that was the case, then the papers could have nothing to do with Marion's death, and Corrie must have pushed her out of the bedroom window. And having done it, he must have thrown the bedclothes on top of her. And that was the act of a madman.

When Annesley got back he rang up the District Facto-ry Inspector's office, and arranged with Mr. Humber that he should absent himself from duty until the unfortunate affair was cleared up. He gathered from Mr. Humber's manner that the police had already seen him. In the after-noon he went into Millingham and interviewed Inspector Jacobs, who, to his surprise, confirmed Corrie's opinion that they could get no one more capable than Ambrose Auty.

Corrie's reception of the information was characteris-tic. He returned from Derby about six o'clock in a high-ly irritable, nervous condition. He had come through a shower of rain and had skidded in the car.

"You don't mean to say that you've really been ass enough to consult Jacobs about it?" he asked angrily when Annesley told him where he had been.

"Yes, I have. Who should know who the best man is better than friend Jacobs?"

"But damn and blast it all, George, it's too — silly. Why don't you tell him we're all committing perjury and ask his advice on that."

Then, when Annesley told him that Inspector Jacobs had said that they could go to no one better than Ambrose Auty, Corrie astonishingly came out with, "There, I told you he was a bright young man, all the time." He was right again and nothing else mattered. The fact that only one minute before he had called George all kinds of an ass for mentioning the matter to Inspector Jacobs didn't matter. Nothing mattered so long as Corrie was proved right. Even the fact that "the bright young man" turned out to be well over sixty did not diminish his satisfaction.

Then, unfortunately, at dinner, there arose a discussion as to how much of the truth they should tell Mr. Auty. It was surprising what a little they knew about it. Did the guilty confide their guilt to the man who was defending their case and endeavoring to minimize the consequences? Did they say, "Look here, I was really going forty miles an hour, but I told the policeman eight," or did they say, "Honestly, I wasn't doing more than eight?" They decided eventually to maintain their official attitude with Mr. Auty, but there was much argument, and arguments with Corrie rapidly passed through disputes to quarrels.

The following day he went to Derby again in the morning, and the afternoon he spent at the Priory, although Mr. Auty drove out to Cherry Hay on purpose to see him. Twice during the week Mr. Auty threatened to drop their case, and by the time the deferred inquest came, he harbored feelings similar to those which had arisen in the minds of Inspector Jacobs and Dr. Butterworth.

The second inquest was again held in the room at the back of the Millingham town hall, and this time the

coroner, Dr. Chappel, certainly could not be accused of
abbreviating the proceedings.

To Elizabeth, who had read the newspaper reports of a
recent poisoning case, and who had imagined that these
contained the whole of the matter, it came as a shock when
she found that, in fact, two hours' close cross-examina-
tion of a witness cannot be compressed within the limits
of a single newspaper column. It seemed to her that there
was no limit to what the solicitor acting on behalf of the
police might, or might not, be allowed to ask them.

Throughout the long ordeal, however, the four chief
witnesses who were awake in the house on the night of
the fatality, maintained a reasonable amount of similarity
between their stories, and as Inspector Jacobs anticipated,
Mr. Ambrose Auty was quite capable of dispelling the
unfavorable impression initially created by Annesley's
unfortunate error with regard to the dining-room clock.

From the police standpoint, Katie was undoubtedly
their most telling witness. She was a nice, if rather emo-
tional, country girl and her natural hesitation in making statements which might be held to incriminate her
employer, was impressive. It was with evident reluctance
that she confirmed the story she had told Inspector Jacobs
with regard to the threats she had overheard. It was with
reluctance again that she admitted that her master was of
an irritable and volatile temperament. She stated, after
being pressed, that it was common knowledge that George
Annesley had been in love with Marion before his engage-
ment to Elizabeth, but she was not sufficiently robust to
withstand the onslaught of Mr. Ambrose Auty, who quickly succeeded in producing first, glaring contradictions,
and then tears.

There was a little sensation in the court when the
plaster casts of Marion's and the man Robson's necks were
produced and placed on the coroner's table. Inspector

Jacobs explained the tests that had been made in the cow-shed at Cherry Hay, and the gruesome replicas were solemnly handed over one by one for the jury's examination.

Mr. Ambrose Auty was, however, equal to the situation. He had been warned, and was able to prove that of the jury themselves at least five were possessors of finger-spans which—if the test were any test at all—might imply that they themselves were capable of murder. He ridiculed the attempt to calculate the different amount of yield between a girl's throat and a man's neck. Quite successfully he ridiculed the whole affair. The verdict was murder. Murder by person or persons unknown.

18
JAMES JAMES GETS A RISE

"Murder by some person or persons unknown." That was the verdict, and no one was more dissatisfied with it than Dr. Chappel, the County Coroner. He would have liked to probe further into things; to have located and labeled the unknown person. He would have liked to repeat the inquest in an attempt to attain finality. But the police brought pressure to bear. During the previous six months, coroners had been making themselves unpopular. There had been comments in the press about it. So Dr. Chappel received a letter from a certain important personage in the Home Office, Inspector Jacobs received a visit from Chief Inspector Bensham of the C.I.D.; there were only two inquests instead of twenty, and the verdict was open murder.

Chief Inspector Bensham and Inspector Jacobs discussed the whole matter on the evening of the inquest in the latter's office, and Annesley at any rate would have been interested could he have overheard their conversation.

"I can't help thinking I've seen him somewhere before," the Scotland Yard man said, fingering his dead-black tooth-brush mustache.

"Mr. Corrie?"

"No, the other, Annesley. I know I've seen him before."

"He doesn't strike me as belonging to the criminal classes."

"I've seen you before and you don't belong to the criminal classes," Jacobs laughed good-naturedly.

The man from London filled his pipe. "The coroner didn't like it," he said, as soon as he got it going; "but it's far and away the best. Now we can make a start."

Inspector Jacobs noted the "we." He had been afraid it would come to that. He thought of Elizabeth Corrie. He thought of some of the things that did not come out at a recent inquiry on police methods with witnesses, and he was sorry for Elizabeth Corrie. He was sorry they had sent down Bensham, who had a certain reputation. But he gave no expression to his thoughts, and merely asked, "You'll be staying at the Swan?"

"No, I'm going back to town to-night. I've got another case on."

Inspector Jacobs's relief was short lived.

"I shall be back again on Thursday. Then—then we'll go through it together. They'll break down in time. Dear me, now, where have I seen Annesley?"

"You haven't formed any opinion, I suppose?" Jacobs asked.

"It doesn't need any forming. One of them did it."

"Yes, yes, but which?"

"Ask me another. I should guess Corrie though. But I wish I could remember—"

"Now, I'm rather inclined to think it was Annesley," Jacobs interrupted.

"I wish I could remember where I'd seen Annesley—but no, I think Corrie. Going on general probabilities, I rather think Corrie. As far as I could make out, Corrie was quite fond of his sister. He might kill her under provocation in a violent fit of temper. He might throw the bed clothes out on top of her in a fit of temper. The bed clothes imply a fit of temper. But if Annesley killed her, then I don't see Corrie committing perjury to defend the man who murdered his sister. On the other hand, if Corrie killed her, Annesley might commit perjury. So might the daughter and the old servant."

"But Corrie was the last to be wakened."

"No, he wasn't. Annesley was. At least so they say—at present." Inspector Bensham smiled grimly.

"Well, I'm still inclined to—er—favor—Annesley." Jacobs paused over the inappropriate word. "I don't think the plaster casts can be ignored and Annesley's marks were nearest. And then, there was the mistake about the time."

"It's not enough to charge a man with murder on, anyhow. As Auty said—a smart man that—bruises aren't such definite hard-edged affairs as the marks that were drawn on the plaster cast. I don't know whose idea it was, but I don't think much of it. And the mistake about the clock. The fixing of the time didn't depend on it. Elizabeth Corrie looked at her watch. Too, there was the telephone call to the doctor. I don't know whose idea it was, but I think it was silly. I wish I'd been there. You're sure there were no finger-marks. No sign of outside entry?"

Both the criticized ideas had been Inspector Jacobs's, and he did not relish their disparagement. He could see difficult times ahead, but he had sense enough not to anticipate them. Aloud he said, "No, not a sign—no footprints or finger-prints or anything—not a ladder on the place." And, to himself, other things.

Inspector Bensham, however, often took very little notice of what people said to him. He took no notice at all of people's unspoken but often obvious thoughts. He spent a great part of his existence in making people say exactly what he wanted them to say, and in ignoring the rest. The fact that the local inspector was feeling a little sore did not bother him at all. All the way back to London he sat staring in front of him in the dining-car. The girl on the opposite side of the table found it so embarrassing that

she changed her seat. Inspector Bensham did not know
that she was there. He did not even notice the amusement of the diners at the table opposite when he struck a
match and tried to light a pencil he was sucking. He noticed nothing. He waded steadily through the album of his
memory and when he got to bed at night he startled his
wife by suddenly sitting up and saying, "Got it—the man
in Sir Victor Grahame's room!"

The recognition had been mutual. Annesley, however,
had remembered him at once. His uncle had told him things
of Inspector Bensham. Directly he saw Bensham's wooden,
expressionless face at the inquest, he knew that secrets
were secrets no longer, and that letters being dangerous in
the circumstances, he would have to hurry post-haste to
Scotland Yard in the hope that Sir Victor Grahame had returned from the continent. Like Inspector Jacobs, he saw
difficulties ahead. Did he know his uncle well enough to
admit perjury? He felt that he did not.

When they got back to Cherry Hay, he told Elizabeth
and Corrie about Inspector Bensham. They had stood the
strain of the whole ordeal better than he thought they
would. Elizabeth had been wonderful. Corrie had been
amazing. His erratic temperament had saved him. He was
like mercury, at one moment an oxidized, inert, dull gray
blob, at the next, a hundred elusive brilliant balls; you
never knew where you had him, what he would do or what
he would say, whether he would scintillate or sulk. At a
crisis that might have broken the heart of a Robot and
tested the nerves of the most robust, he, shell-shocked,
nerve-shattered and unstable, had played with his patents
and dallied with love.

They were having tea when he broke the news. Elizabeth had just put her cup down. "Well, that's that," she
said, referring to the inquest and fondly imagining that
the worst of their troubles were over.

"Yes, that's that. And now we're for it," Annesley echoed.

"You don't mean to say they'll go on?" There was a catch in her voice.

"Come and sit here by me, Elizabeth." He made room for her on the settee. He encircled her with a protecting arm. "You noticed the man with the long face, like a blacking brush with all but one row of bristles missing? He was sitting next to Jacobs."

Elizabeth nodded.

"Do you know who he was?"

She shook her head.

"It was Inspector Bensham of Scotland Yard."

"How on earth do you know?"

"I do know. Never mind how, but I do know. I'm afraid that our real difficulties have only just begun. And I can't help feeling that in the circumstances, you know, it might be better if I went back to the French Horn. Now that the inquest's over, I shall have to go back to work. Anyhow, I've got to go up to London to-morrow. When I return, don't you really think it would be better if I stayed in Little Plenders? You could always get me there if you wanted me. You know what it's been like this last week. You know what I think of it all, and your father knows, and keeps out of my way as much as he can. It isn't quite fair to him. It's wretched for you."

"But, my dear, you've been dear to me. A thousand times—no! We shall both want you here. I'm sure Daddy doesn't feel like that. As a matter of fact, he's worried on your account because he thinks the police think you did it. But he isn't staying away because of that. You know how he is—he just can't settle down—and there's Joyce."

On that they went for a walk together, Annesley trying to give her some idea of what they were faced with now that Scotland Yard were taking part. He repeated all his

earlier fears about the safety of her father if once it were
known that he had been in Marion's room on the fatal
night. He assured her that if they all stuck together and
maintained the attitude that had succeeded so well at the
inquest they would be able to save him. She did feel assured. She felt safer than she had done at any time since
Dr. Butterworth came into the dining-room unannounced
on the night when Marion died. And then, after dinner,
to which her father, who had spent the evening with the
Lobleys at the Priory, returned, James James asked for an
increase in wages.

It was devastating; a bombshell.

As a rule Mrs. Glegg brought in the after-dinner coffee,
but that evening, to their surprise, James James appeared
with the tray.

"Is anything the matter with Mrs. Glegg, James?" Elizabeth asked.

"No, Miss."

James set down the coffee on the sideboard. He turned
round and coughed.

"I should like to make so bold as to ask for a rise of
wages, sir," he said with exaggerated deference.

"Then you can blinking well make off and be bold
enough to ask somebody else," Corrie answered tersely.

"I think not, sir."

Corrie jumped to his feet. "You infernal old scoundrel—"

James stood still till the flow had ceased.

"I think, sir, it would be a very suitable opportunity
for increased remuneration. I was thinking, sir, of, say, an
extra thirty shillings a week, if I may be so bold."

They stared at him in open amazement, a scrutiny he
withstood with calm indifference.

"I was thinking, sir, it might be extremely awkward for
the family if I were to leave at this juncture, and that it

might at any rate be worth thirty shillings a week to you, sir, if my services were retained."

"You infernal scoundrel! Do you realize this is nothing short of blackmail?" Corrie shouted.

"Oh, dear me, no, sir, not blackmail. It's a very nasty word, very nasty, sir. I should never have dreamed of mentioning the word 'blackmail,' sir. I am merely suggesting, sir, that it might be convenient if my services were retained at the present juncture, and that I should like a rise of an extra thirty shillings."

And it was in vain that they pressed the old man for reasons or explanations. Whatever he had learned he kept it a secret. They could neither find out what he knew nor how he came to know it. To all questions he replied monotonously that it would be a pity if he left the family's service at the present time, that his request had no connection whatever with the misfortune that had befallen them, and that he thought he was worth what he asked for. He even had the impudence to ask for an immediate decision, and when they protested, with an effrontery that disturbed them, he gave them till breakfast-time to-morrow. It was an ultimatum. When he closed the door you could have heard the proverbial pin drop. Corrie crept to the door. For some reason or other he found it necessary to crouch as he crept. When he flung the door open, however, there was no one there, and, looking rather foolish, he resumed his seat.

"Well, now we're in a fix," Elizabeth whispered.

"If you'd taken my advice and had told Auty everything, this wouldn't have happened," Corrie said unreasonably.

Annesley stirred his coffee, deep in thought. What amazed him most was the amount that had been mentioned. Thirty shillings a week! Why not five hundred pounds? Did the old man really know anything, or did he just vaguely feel that something was wrong, that advantage might be gained by it, and fix a low amount, for the sake of safety? Supposing they refused to pay it. Supposing they did pay it and it became known that they'd paid it, would it be held as evidence of guilt? Fifty questions filled his brain.

"I think we shall have to pay it," he said, looking up from his coffee cup at last and across at Corrie, whom he expected to burst into flames.

"Yes, I think so too," Corrie said quietly.

"You see, if he asks for more, we can always consider it again. If it was a big sum that was quite obviously blackmail it would be a different matter. It was a threat but not just in so many words. Even if it should eventually come out that we gave him a rise I don't think it would be incriminating. We could tell the exact truth about it. We were not sure what to do. We knew that the police must attach a certain amount of suspicion to every one in the house, we thought that any story he might tell would damage our position whether it was true or not, and that on the whole we had better pay it. Yes, I do really. I think we had better pay it."

"I agree with you, George—absolutely. I'll go and tell him now. Then you two clear out. I want the table and I want quiet. Go for a walk. I had a brainwave in bed last night. Pneumatic shoes, George! Put that in your pipe and smoke it. There's thousands in it. Separate bladders for heel and sole, with a little connecting tube between. A valve on the tube. 'Mrs. Glegg, please blow up my Corrie shoes.' There's thousands in it. Who'd dream of motoring on solid tires? Yet we walk on solid leather."

His eyes were positively shining. He looked handsome almost, and muttering something about Duralumin retaining rings and the balance of pressure, he left the astonished lovers.

The following morning, Elizabeth drove Annesley into Blatchford, and he was not at all surprised to find an innocent-looking individual leaning against the wall that divided the Plenders Priory land from the Blatchford road. He noticed the motor bicycle too, but said nothing to Elizabeth about it.

At Blatchford he booked to London. His train arrived at one. He lunched, and then he spent a quiet hour on the Underground. He changed at a surprising number of stations. Returning at last to Westminster, instead of using the escalator, he used the emergency stairs, where he spent a further five minutes in the stooping attitude of one who deals with an undone shoe lace.

It was a lonely five minutes. Nobody passed him. He had the staircase entirely to himself. Emerging, he hurried to Scotland Yard and just before three—the commissionaire happened to be away from duty—he walked unannounced into his uncle's office.

His uncle was seated at his desk, and on another chair at the side of the desk there sat Inspector Bensham.

"Well, this is extraordinary; extraordinary," he said in an unpleasant, rasping voice. "This very moment, Mr. Annesley, I was showing your photograph to your uncle."

Sir Victor's healthy-looking face took on a deeper hue. He frowned. Then, leaning back in his chair, the frown gradually disappeared.

"We shall have to tell him, George, it's no good." He laughed.

Bensham, unbending, said he was sure it would be better.

Then Sir Victor Grahame briefly related the history of the missing papers, of Dr. Beresford's suspicions, of Bernard Corrie, of the chance friendship between Annesley and Corrie, of Annesley's activities as a factory inspector, of Annesley's succession to the Plenders Priory estates, of

the Magnet Motor Cycle Co., of Norman Lobley's suspicious possession of Corrie's paper on "Special Steels and
Their Erosive Properties," told the wooden-faced Bensham—who never spoke a word or moved a muscle throughout the narrative—the whole of the story.

Annesley, who knew the detective's reputation, had little time for thought, but during the narration of the facts
he came to the decision that whilst his uncle might of
necessity tell the story of the missing papers, he would
have nothing to gain and everything to lose if he admitted
the true facts concerning Marion's death. At any rate, he
would let the matter rest until he returned to Cherry Hay
and discussed it with the others. Of one thing he was glad.
He decided that his uncle having told Inspector Bensham
the whole of the story, it could not longer be incumbent
on him to keep the matter from Corrie and Elizabeth. It
was a weight off his mind.

"And now, about the murder. I've not been in touch
with George here, and only have the newspaper reports,"
Sir Victor concluded. "Tell me, what is the real view of the
matter held by the police?"

Bensham paused, then, quietly fixing Annesley with his
pale-blue eyes, he said, "Perjury, murder, and—and perjury to hide it."

"We have already gathered that"—Annesley laughed
pleasantly—"but at any rate you will admit, Inspector,
that it has been remarkably consistent perjury—in the
past, and if it's perjury as you suggest, it's going to be
consistent in the future."

"We'll have a little talk when the Inspector's gone,
George," Sir Victor stated.

"Certainly, uncle, but even if we're quite sure that the key-
hole's sound-proof, you won't get more from me than that."

"Well, that's where we stand," Inspector Bensham said
stiffly. "You asked me a question and I answered it—and

now, Mr. Annesley, I take it you won't object to my returning the compliment and asking some questions of you?"

Four o'clock came and went, tea came and went—five
o'clock, and the Inspector was still asking questions, questions to which Annesley constantly gave the answer, "As
I stated at the inquest," or "As my friend Corrie stated at
the second inquest," etc., etc.

And when the detective had at length finished, Annesley had a yet more difficult half-hour with his uncle, Sir
Victor Grahame, but he stuck to his story and refused to
state the facts.

19

WHAT THE MOON SHOWED

Mild misstatements and exaggerations, income tax returns and terminological inexactitudes, white lies, the kind of lies you tell yourself, lies told to liars, gray lies, business lies, just plain unvarnished lies, lies that others tell, damned dirty lies and—perjury; all divisions on a sort of graded Judas scale, each with its own practitioners and devotees—from that pretty girl we all know who likes to sound so lively and bright, at one end, through the poor wretched "general" who's broken a cup which "slipped of itself"; the business man who, seeking his profits, forgets his honor, and the white-livered skunk who shirks what is owing—right up to the very top of the scale where we have that double-dyed villain, George Annesley, who has stood solemnly, Bible in hand, and has said, "So help me God" and then gone and lied without lifting an eyelid.

Look at him! Just look at the bare-faced way in which he takes all the digestive biscuits out of the tin of "Best Assorted" without even waiting until the car attendant's back is turned! Look at those two big pieces of cheese lying naked and unashamed on his plate! Note his disgustingly appreciative manner of mastication. See the pleasure he gets from his pipe, and then admit that sometimes sin sits lightly.

He is in the dining-car on the 6.20 express out of Marylebone which will get into Blatchford soon after nine o'clock, where, having wired to Cherry Hay asking to be met, he is expecting Elizabeth in the Morris. As a matter of fact, he wired to Corrie. He said, "Please meet me Blatchford Central 9.7," but, all the same, he is expecting Elizabeth in the Morris. He is perfectly certain that Corrie, who hates driving in the dark, will have been feeling too frightfully ill to move—in fact, on receiving the wire, he will probably have retired to bed.

Before he had his dinner, Annesley himself was feeling almost depressed. In all his days he had never met any one quite so pertinacious and difficult as Bensham. Pertinacious! Annesley imagined that he had already been asked and had answered every possible question on the subject of Marion's death and the Corries' affairs. But Bensham's questions! They seemed to suck at the truth like so many leeches—leeches disguised as intended misstatements that one unwisely contradicted, leeches screened by sudden threats, leeches that branched out like octopuses and bred like rabbits before you could pull them off, that first sucked your blood dry and then sucked you again, devitalized and unresisting. And the conceit of the man! "Oh, I'll soon straighten matters out." "It's a great pity they didn't send for me before." "My opinion is that the local men have missed some clew." "Perjury is a very dangerous game, Mr. Annesley—very dangerous now that you have brains against you." It had been "I," "me" and "my" for nearly two hours and Annesley, when he got to his train, felt frayed and fagged out, but now, having fed, he felt better.

For, after all, there were compensations. Bensham, he had to admit, had the whole of the facts tucked away and indexed behind his wooden-looking face in a manner which gave them an entirely new significance. Compared

with Bensham, Jacobs was of no more use than an office
boy, and if Marion's death really had some mysterious connection with the missing papers, then it might yet be a
good thing that they had him for an ally. On the other
hand, if it were not quickly proved that the murder had
some connection with the missing papers, then they would
all have to be very much more careful than they had been
with Jacobs. Not because of any risk they ran as perjur-
ers—that thought never even occurred to Annesley—no,
it was because of Corrie that they would have to be more
careful.

The whole of the way north Annesley sat solemnly gaz-
ing out of the window. He wondered for the thousandth
time whether he had missed anything when Professor
Taverner had shown him over the stables. What would
Bensham, for instance, have seen that he had failed to see.
But it was not the detective's keenness of observation that
Annesley feared. It was these perpetual questions. When
Jacobs asked a question you answered him and felt that
you had finished—it was all as simple as a straight line.
But with Bensham it was different. His questions were
as simple as straight lines too, but straight lines crossing
create points, and after an hour there were so many points
the line of one question met the line of another, such a
tangle of cross connections, that conversation became a
net in which you floundered like some unfortunate fish.

Only once during the whole of the journey did the
frown vanish from Annesley's pleasant face, and that was
when he suddenly remembered the hour he had spent
dashing up and down escalators whilst Bensham sat at ease
conversing with his uncle.

As he had anticipated, Elizabeth and the Morris were
waiting for him at Blatchford: Elizabeth, whose eyes greeted him from between the points of her turned-up coat
collar, looking fresh and bright, the Morris, standing

between a Daimler and a Rolls-Royce, looking unbeliev-
ably *passé* and old.

"Been waiting long?" he asked her.

"Hours and hours. You're late, and I was early."

"Tutt, but tutt, and it's chilly too. Shall I drive her
back then?"

She gave up her seat to him, and after the Morris had
grunted and gnashed its gears for a few seconds, they set
out along the Millingham road. A good three miles of tram
lines and sundry traffic has to be negotiated before open
country is reached, and until they had crawled up the steep
ascent on the far side of the village of Redhill they hardly
spoke a word.

There Annesley changed into top gear again, and conversation became just possible.

"I've had a busy day, Elizabeth," he stated, in the manner of one angling for questions and comments.

"Tell me," she said satisfactorily.

"You'll be surprised. I've been to see my uncle who's
the chief of the department I work for at Scotland Yard."

The remark produced the desired effect.

"You! at Scotland Yard! I thought mechanical defects
were your job, not moral ones."

They crawled down the three-mile gradient past the
water works, and they crawled along the three miles that
separates the water works from the Plenders Priory gates,
and Annesley was still explaining, Elizabeth still asking
questions, as they turned into the drive between the rhododendrons.

"Look here, pull up, George. I must understand it better before we get back."

Annesley applied the squeaky brake and stopped the
car. They were half-way down the valley beyond the point
where the drive emerges from the wood into more open
park-land. When he switched his headlights off, the valley

lay like fairyland below them in the unreal light of the moon which hung low in the sky above the stable buildings.

"And you say Bensham does definitely suspect us of putting up a story?"

"That was not exactly the way he put it. He did mention the word perjury."

"I think he may be right."

"Seeing that you know he's right, it's very sporting of you."

"No. No, I don't mean that. I mean about what happened to Marion having some connection with everything you've just been telling me now. I'm quite sure that it has. But, oh, George, I wish you'd told me before. Why didn't you tell me before'?"

"I couldn't tell you. I'd promised not to tell."

"And now you've broken your promise. You might just as well have broken it at once."

"I haven't broken my promise. Now that Bensham knows all about it it's a different matter. He told my uncle that he couldn't ignore the possible connection; he refused point-blank to be hampered by any promise to keep it a secret, so I consider myself absolved."

"Yes, I see. But you, don't you think that there might be some connection?"

"I don't know. Really, I don't know. Anyhow, it isn't very obvious. All we do know for certain is that Dr. Beresford of the B.P.L. wrote to my uncle about your father's paper, that my uncle did suspect and may still suspect that your father had access to them, that both Lobley and your father have interests in motor-cycle companies, and that Lobley was undoubtedly intrigued by your father's paper. Those are the main outstanding facts. But I've been pretty well all over the stables—Professor Taverner took me—and they seemed to be doing nothing more than they say they are doing, carrying on experimental work on the low temperature carburization of coal. Too, even if they are really vitally interested in turbines, I fail to see why they should have killed poor Marion. It beats me *how* they could have killed her."

"Well, that's a detail."

"Oh, a mere trifle!"

"I don't care, it is. It doesn't matter how they did it. But they did do it. All that you've told makes a tremendous difference. And, George, you will tell Daddy everything, won't you? Yes, you'll have to, and, oh, he won't like it because of Joyce. He's most awfully fond of—"

Her sentence trailed off into silence. She gripped him by the arm.

"George! . . . Joyce!"

"I don't see how Joyce is involved even if the others—" he began stupidly.

"No. No. No! But don't you see! I've often wondered . . . Joyce, twenty, pretty, and Daddy . . . don't you understand?"

"You mean—"

"Yes. She was set on to him. To find out."

"But how beastly. Besides. . . . You, prettier still, not even twenty, and me, I'm only five years younger than your father, you know. No. It doesn't follow."

"You, why, you're twenty years younger than Daddy at least . . . poor Daddy. Besides, I'm not Joyce. It's different. You know it is."

Annesley had to admit to himself that there was a difference, but still he was unconvinced.

"But even so, I—"

"It fits anyhow," she interrupted. "Just to please me now, agree that it fits and let's see where it lands us. I'm going to start right from the very beginning. Listen!"

Annesley lit his pipe.

"First, Lobley stole the papers."

"We don't know that he did."

"No, but we're assuming that he did."

"How?"

"Oh, never mind. Never mind how. He stole them or bought them. He tells Primrose and they agree to experiment with it; then, just when they're estab—"

"But why should he tell Primrose? Why shouldn't he carry on his experiments at the Little Giant works where he has laboratories and everything?" Annesley protested.

"We're assuming things. We've got to sketch in a plan first and then see how the facts fit in with it. Perhaps Primrose got hold of the papers and told Lobley. Perhaps it was that way round."

"It's the very worst of detective practice. I've always been taught that in detective work you should build up theory on fact and not the other way round."

"I'm not a detective. I don't believe you're much of one either. But all the same, I do believe there's something in it."

"I told you I wasn't. It's only just because I'm my uncle's nephew and happened to know a little engineering and a lot of German that I'm even pretending to be one. Go on though, I won't interrupt you again."

"But I want you to help—make suggestions."

"Right. One of them stole or acted as receiver for the papers then. For some reason or other, they couldn't or daren't make any experiments at the Little Giant works; the low temperature carburization is all camouflage, and they're frightfully busy trying to build a turbine."

"Yes. That's it. I'm sure that's it. And isn't it obvious that they wouldn't make experiments at the works? You said yourself it would be worth an awful lot. How much would it be worth, George?"

"Oh, I don't know, but heaps and heaps—millions probably. Think what it might mean if only you could invent a really successful petrol turbine and get it on to the market, complete, and tried, and protected by patents before any one else got going. Yes, it might mean millions if it were handled in a big enough way. Too, I think they might take the risk of leaving it unprotected until they got it nearly complete."

"Well then, let's go on. They come here, it's exactly the place for it—they know all about Daddy's paper, they take the trouble of getting a copy. If they had stolen Dr. Beresford's memoranda they'd be worried about it too, and then they find Daddy as their next-door neighbor."

"Yes, I think that's right so far as it goes. It was the plan I arranged with my uncle, you know. But I still fail to connect it up with Marion's death."

"We're assuming that they did murder Marion. Now don't interrupt, George. What would they do in those circumstances. First, they would try to find out whether Daddy was working on the same lines, and that's where Joyce comes in. And, George, James James! He left the Priory to come to Cherry Hay!" Elizabeth felt a rising excitement.

"Yes, I have thought of that too. Until last night I felt sure in my own mind that he left the Priory for the reason that he gave us—because he couldn't get on with Primrose. I can sympathize with him—I don't like Primrose myself. Now"—George hesitated—"now I'm not so sure."

"I can't understand it all. If he was at Cherry Play on their behalf, why should he go and blackmail us? I can't understand it at all."

"Excepting that as he did blackmail us it proves that he's a rogue, and if he's a rogue, then his sudden inability to get on with Primrose becomes—er—er—what's the word I want?"

"Suggestive." Elizabeth supplied the word he wanted. "Yes, that fits too. They wanted to find out. Now, listen.

Suppose they did find out the truth, that Daddy had for-gotten all about his wretched paper and had no interest in turbines at all. In that case they would want him away from Cherry Hay. They would still try to frighten him away. Professor Taverner was always making out that Daddy is worse that he really is—always talking to Marion about his brother's private nursing home."

"Yes, that fits too. I had thought of that, Elizabeth. But why kill Marion? And who did kill her?"

"I believe that James killed her. He came downstairs to kill Daddy and she found him out. Saw him going into Daddy's room in the middle of the night, say, and he saw that he'd been found out and gripped her by the throat—perhaps he didn't mean to kill her."

"And then, having killed her by mistake, he threw her out of her bedroom window—and then, threw all the bed clothes out on top of her. You know, Elizabeth, I've always been worried about those bed clothes. I believe that if we could once understand the reason for the bed clothes be-ing there, we should know everything. For myself, I don't think James had anything whatever to do with it. Not with the murder. His grip didn't fit the bruises. I'd swear, too, that he was fast asleep when I went into his bedroom. Be-sides, if he had a hand in it he wouldn't increase his risks by blackmailing, if it was blackmailing. He'd want to stay quietly with us until it had all blown over."

"Well then, let's assume that it wasn't James. Let's go back. We've agreed that they wanted to get him away from the house or murder him. If James didn't do it, no one in the house did it. And if no one in the house did it, then whoever did do it must have got into the house either through one of the doors or the windows."

"Perhaps James made them a key. Perhaps that was what he was there for."

"All the doors were locked when we tried to find Marion, but still. . . . Too, remember what Daddy said about seeing her outside the window. You can't ignore that."

"I don't know, Elizabeth. I really don't know. Corrie admits that he'd been seeing all sorts of impossible things. Hands and faces."

"George! George! Supposing he did really see the things he thought he saw. They were trying to frighten him. They knew he was a nervous wreck."

"Well, in that case we've got to be logical. If we say he really saw hands and things outside the window, then we mustn't say he didn't see Marion slip from the bed clothes in mid-air outside the window."

"Yes, it's always the bed clothes," Elizabeth agreed. "Marion was hanging in mid-air outside her bedroom window. She was wrapped up in all the top bed clothes and slipped. Then the bed clothes dropped on top of her. Some one tried to strangle her. She was sleeping—"

Elizabeth clutched at Annesley's arm.

"George! She was sleeping in Daddy's room. It was *Daddy* they were trying to strangle."

"By Jove, yes! And that fits too. It means that it was done by some one outside the house. Some one who didn't know. It wasn't James James."

"The lights were off and they couldn't see."

"And the lights come from the colliery powerhouse."

"And Joyce again! It was Joyce who said she was awake at two o'clock with toothache—said that her bedroom light never went out at all. It was a lie—arranged. We're getting on."

Elizabeth felt a sudden excitement. It seemed to her that they were on the very brink of the solution, that the next step forward would bring their eyes above the hill and open out the view. But they took no step forward. The desired inspiration simply would not come. They sat quite still in the old Morris, whose side-lamps made two feeble blobs of yellow light on the moonlit drive ahead. The night wind through the trees of the dark wood behind them made music like the music of a shell, which, held to ear, sings of the distant sea—soft, elusive music—which, held in hand, is yet a thousand miles away. Deep in thought, they neither of them spoke. Five minutes passed. Ten. Then Elizabeth felt Annesley stiffen suddenly. She turned to him expectantly. In the light of the moon he looked pale beside her.

He was staring ahead.

"What is it?" she asked.

"The moon. Elizabeth, look at the moon," he whispered excitedly in reply.

The queen of night at her fullest beauty rolled slowly above the clump of trees that grew by the stable buildings, and at the level of the lady's eyes, across the calm round face, as though masked for the harvest ball, was a bar of black.

They gazed at it astonished.

The black band suddenly slipped to hide the lady's mouth; now it was a chord across the lower arc. There it stayed stationary for, say, a count of ten, then dropped like a stone from the face of the moon.

"Helicopter?" Annesley murmured.

"An aeroplane?" Elizabeth asked.

"Yes, and engined with turbines or I'm a Dutchman. There wasn't a sound. The wind's this way and there wasn't a sound. And think of the size of it! We're not half a mile from the stables and it didn't span the moon. That settles it."

"You mean they did have the papers?"

"Yes. I mean that and more. They murdered Marion. Corrie did see her outside the bedroom window. She was hanging from that aeroplane or from another like it. It makes everything possible."

"Do you mean. . . . Could it be done?"

"Why, yes, easily. I should think quite easily. It looked as though they could stay put exactly where they liked. And think of what they do with ordinary planes. . . . Re-fueling. . . . Turbines! Why! Unlimited, almost weightless power. All of us flopping about like butterflies and land-ing in our own back yards! Oh, yes, it could be done right enough."

"What are you going to do, George?"

"Go to bed and think. It cuts out our perjury risk though. We must get hold of Bensham."

Free-wheeling excepted, and the lie of the land was wrong for that, there was nothing secret about the prog-ress of Annesley's elderly Morris, so they switched on the headlights and chugged noisily round by the stables to Cherry Hay.

All seemed quiet at the stables—there was no move-ment, no light in the windows, nothing to indicate that an aeroplane had landed.

"Elizabeth, I'm an awful ass. I've just this minute re-membered something," Annesley whispered as they passed beneath the beeches.

"Tell me."

"Wait till we get in."

At Cherry Hay all was quiet too. Corrie had gone to bed and Mrs. Glegg was sitting up for them. She made them some coffee and they sent her to bed. And then, when they were alone, Annesley told Elizabeth what had caused him to make the remark as they passed the stables.

"You know I knew all the time that there was some real reason for my feelings about the stables. It isn't that I've actually been feeling afraid of them—that would be too ridiculous—but all along I've known that at some time or other something happened to me there. And it came to me quite suddenly as we motored through the trees. It

was when I was a boy. I was staying at the Priory in old
Colonel Annesley's time and there was a bully of a groom
who used to frighten me. I was rather a little terror, I
think, and one afternoon I crawled up an old brick culvert
that takes the water from the stable yard into the lake. It
takes you right into the foundations where you can stand
upright and walk about, at least I could then, and I remember I had poked a stick up one of the gratings right
underneath the colonel's favorite hunter, frightening it so
much that in prancing about it strained a tendon. Unfortunately, I left the stick poking out of the grating and the
groom, who was furious, and recognized it as one I had
been playing about with, was waiting for me at the other
end of the culvert when after a happy half-hour I crawled
out of it again. He made a grab at me. I escaped, and he
caught me again among the beeches. He gave me a thor-
ough trouncing and complained to the colonel, who gave
me another. For weeks I was terrified, and it all came back
to me just now as we motored through the trees."

"But still, I don't quite see—" Elizabeth began.

"Well, the culvert's still there, I expect, and though I'm
not so thin as I was at twelve, I imagine I can still wriggle
up it. Perhaps they keep their aeroplanes below ground."

"But could they?"

"I think they might. Just imagine it, Elizabeth, what a
difference a turbine engine would make to aeroplane design. Think of the difference between a thousand-kilowatt
steam engine set and a turbine set!"

"Dear George, please stop. I haven't the foggiest idea
what a whatawhat is?"

But they sat up and discussed it for half the night,
Annesley rhapsodizing at intervals over the epoch-making
possibilities of a petrol turbine, Elizabeth more concerned
with their immediate plans and how they would affect her
father.

20
BENEATH THE STABLES

In the morning over breakfast, Annesley disclosed his connection with Scotland Yard to Corrie, who, unfortunately for all of them, had risen in one of his most irritable morning tempers. As he ate his egg, he listened to George's difficult and round-about explanations in an attempted stony but obviously fragile silence.

"So you see it seemed to me the only sensible thing to do," George finished, rather lamely.

Apparently too pained for speech, Corrie continued to dislike his egg, which had not been long enough boiled.

Then, when Elizabeth told him what they had seen on their way in from Blatchford the night before, he ridiculed the aeroplane theory and every suggestion involving either the Lobleys or the others at the Priory. It was all full-blooded nonsense.

And when, after skirting gingerly round the subject, Annesley did eventually hint at the part they suspected Joyce might be playing, he told them both to shut up with such vigor that they shirked the full issue and left him only half-informed of what their real opinions were.

"You're mad, I think, and you've probably both been seeing bats," he spluttered, unable to contain himself longer, and pushing his unfinished breakfast from him, he stamped out of the room, banging the door behind him.

Through the rest of the day he moped about in an irritable state of hurt, high dudgeon, refusing to take any part in the many discussions that occupied much of Elizabeth and George's time.

They both agreed that Inspector Bensham should be told of their previous night's experience, but when Annesley rang up the station at Millingham, he learnt that the detective had not yet returned from town.

Annesley was not altogether sorry. Inspector Jacobs asked if there were any developments and if there was anything he could do, but Annesley told him nothing; so far as the missing papers were concerned it was a matter that lay in his own province, and quite suddenly, even as he spoke into the telephone, he was seized with an irresistible desire to crawl once again up the old brick culvert just as he had done when a little boy of twelve.

For all three of them the day passed slowly. For Elizabeth and for Annesley, who had decided to make the venture immediately after dinner, the seconds in the later hours took on the length of minutes.

Then, when the gong sounded, Corrie was nowhere to be found, and after waiting for a quarter of an hour, they decided to go on without him. Except for the single dinner they hurriedly ate together in a crowded restaurant when they went to Kew and then to the theater after, Annesley and Elizabeth had never dined alone. It was an occasion. The yellow sunset, wide-spread to the north, shone for once through the window of the dining-room, lighting up the old oak paneling along the wall, till it glowed below the contending electric light, like burnished bronze. Annesley had never noticed it before. He thought it gave the room a rich—luxurious—almost Eastern air. Elizabeth, remembering, and nothing loth to remember, Marion's hatred of mourning, was wearing a pale-green frock. A red silk shade adorned the electric table standard, and she was catching its reflection in the hollow of her spoon, where, with size diminished but brilliance enhanced, it glowed like some rare red ruby. He sat at the table end, she just round the corner, and whether this simple ordinary arrangement, or some hidden enchantment that the evening held, was the cause of it, it gave old Mrs. Glegg quite a fluttery kind of feeling through the breast when she came in with the soup.

For the long married, meals alone may prove bearable, distressing, or pleasant, according to cooking and temper. For the very recently married, delight may be added to dinner by mere possession of plates. But for lovers, there is a glamour about a dinner eaten alone, and be their imaginations of the least excitable order, it will be spiced with sweet suggestion. Later on perhaps their association will not be determined by dinner; then the savory at the end of the feast will be the hors d'oeuvre to further happy hours. It was an occasion.

Twice during the meal Annesley rose from his chair and switched off the electric light, to learn from the uncurtained window how the daylight dallied. "It'll be dark enough in half an hour," he said the second time.

"I wish we knew where Daddy was," Elizabeth replied.

"But we do know where he is—or as good as. He's gone to the Priory. He's gone to see Joyce."

"We don't know that he has."

"No. But, come now, we're almost sure. After what we told him this morning, he'd feel that he wanted to see her. I did think of asking him not to go, but I knew it would be no good. Risky, rather, though."

"Do you think he's in any danger?" Elizabeth asked, leaning earnestly towards him.

"Yes. Yes, I'm afraid I do."

"Don't you think we ought to run over in the car then and find out? Or ring them up on the telephone?"

"No. It wouldn't be any good. If he isn't in any danger they would only be able to tell us that he stayed for dinner there, or something silly of that sort. If he is, then they'd tell us they hadn't seen him whether they had or not. Whether we called or telephoned it would all amount to the same thing. It wouldn't be any good."

"But, George, can't we really do anything?"

"We're going to do something. In half an hour I'm going to spoil a suit of clothes in trying to crawl up the culvert between the stables and the lake. Policemen could do no more. Even if they could get a search warrant, which I doubt on the information they've got, they couldn't do better than that. If your father's really in danger and they searched the Priory and the stables too, I doubt if their searching would save him. But perhaps he isn't in any real danger after all. You see it's nearly a month since poor Marion was killed, and if our suspicions are correct they've had their aeroplane all the time. They've had countless chances too. Often and often he's been to the Priory alone before."

"Y-e-s."

For a little period silence fell between them. The window, the closed half, which when they sat down showed daylight, was now a mirror backed by night. And through the other, the open half, they could hear the liquid music of the stream and see a few faint stars which were winning a weak existence against the waning light.

"Y-e-s." Elizabeth, who was playing with a little pile of bread crumbs on her plate, repeated, with a hesitation so pronounced that "Yes" was almost "No."

"Y-e-s, but I don't like it all the same."

She flicked with her fingers and scattered the slowly collected crumbs.

"Before," she continued, "when Daddy's been to the Priory he really hasn't known what he pretends he doesn't know now, and it seems to me it makes a difference. He may say something. No, I don't like it. It seems to me that we ought to ring Inspector Jacobs up. Do, George. Ring him up now. Ask him to send us some men out here. Tell him you want them but won't tell him why, then if Daddy does come in you can say you've made a mistake and send them back again. If he doesn't come back—well, it might be rather comforting to have them ready here on tap. You can still do your crawl up the culvert."

Annesley agreed, agreed without annoyance, and Elizabeth, accustomed to her father's acrimonious arguments, adored his acquiescence. And having proved him once she tested him again, for when, after arranging matters satisfactorily with a puzzled and rather unwilling Inspector Jacobs he returned from the telephone, she greeted him with a pleasant, mock-determined "I'm coming culvert-crawling too."

He looked amused.

"You may come if you like—but not up my culvert. You can wait in the copse by the lake."

She nodded, satisfied again that now he refused to give way to her entirely.

"Then you'd better get busy and change," he said.

"Change?"

"Well, you can't go girl-guiding in a pale-green frock and pink silk stockings."

"Would a mackintosh and black ones do?"

"The stockings would. But, if you're coming, you've got to change your frock. The mackintosh might come unstuck and give the show away."

She made a face and disappeared.

And when she had gone Annesley hurried to his bedroom, where he donned a pair of old gray flannels. As he pulled them on he debated the merits of braces or belt, but having private doubts about the diameter of the culvert and the change in his own circumference between the ages of twelve and thirty-six, the braces won. He tested the buttons. He discarded his collar. Then putting on a pair of old tennis shoes he amused Mrs. Glegg in the kitchen, where he rendered them inconspicuous by smearing them thickly with blacking. It took him ten minutes, and by the time he was ready Elizabeth was ready too, and waiting in the hall.

"Will that do?" she asked, opening her mackintosh and showing him gray sweater, gray stockings and shorts.

It was after half-past eight when they left Cherry Hay. The air was cool, and a spider web across the gate felt wet and cold against Elizabeth's forehead; she was glad that in addition to changing her clothes she was wearing the mackintosh. Arm in arm they crossed the little bridge above the stream, followed the drive up the hill through the trees, and hurried on towards the stables. Even at first, quite unnecessarily, they talked in undertones.

"I hope I shall find it all right," he said.

"How long do you think you'll take?"

"Oh, twenty minutes, say, at the outside. It can't be very far up the culvert itself—a couple of hundred feet—and then I shall want a few minutes for a good sniff round. I've got a jolly good flashlight with me. If I find anything, we'll get in touch with Jacobs right away when we get back. He told me he's coming himself. And if your father's not back when we get back we'll tell him about that too."

"Yes, and I'm glad I came as well. If you aren't back in twenty minutes, I shall run like a hare to the house."

About three hundred yards from the stables they left the drive, branching off to the right, where a streamlet ran down a gulley to the lake.

"Have you got a watch?" he whispered.

"Yes. Radiolite."

"Good. Well, look here, give me half an hour. The culvert might be blocked or something. I forget just how much room there was."

She whispered, "Yes." It was still by the lake; no ripple, ruffled the surface. No breath of wind disturbed the air. He put one strong hand behind her neck and kissed her. "Won't I be dirty when I get back?" he chuckled like a small boy, and added, "Now, not another whisper. We've got to go nearer to the cottages than I like. There may be dogs. There's no great hurry."

Indeed it seemed to Elizabeth that apparently Annesley thought that there was no hurry whatever, and that if they reached the culvert by dawn it would meet the requirements of the situation. Every few yards he stood still for a few minutes, and wherever the bank of the lake, along which they were working their way, was low, he crouched. She followed his example. He never turned round once and it seemed almost that had she twisted her ankle or broken her leg, he would have gone on alone without her.

Looking back on the evening, it stood out more clearly than anything else—that first slow crawl, that, and the way the time behaved in jerks, the minutes, now each an endless age, eternity extended, then, when she would willingly have forfeited a finger for a fraction of one, flashing by like the individual photographs that merge to make a moving picture.

Between the stables and the margin of the lake, dwarfed by the shadow of more vigorous trees, there stands a grove of sycamores—a stunted, somehow sinister assembly with twisted stems and sticky, blighted leaves, which now in late September fell among nettles that grew beneath them—a wicked little wood in which witches well might mumble and walk at night among bleaching bones. Here Annesley stopped, held up his hand in a gesture of farewell which

was just apparent to Elizabeth against the night sky in the
lake, crawled on hands and knees along the water's edge,
and, just as she wondered whether he had mistaken the
place, disappeared.

Leaning against the trunk of one of the little sycamores, Elizabeth marked the time by the luminous dial of
her watch and prepared to wait. For a short time she heard
faint splashings—then there was silence.

There was more splashing than Annesley had bargained
for. The water ran right up the culvert, which, to his astonishment, was no bigger than a good-sized pipe; apparently,
not only had his own circumference increased, but the culvert itself had shrunk. He had to kneel in a good foot of
water at the edge of the lake before he could get his robust
shoulders in. He felt like a cork in the neck of a bottle.

However, after scraping his shins on the edge of the
brickwork, after much painful, but forceful, wriggling
about, he found himself at last lying full length on his
belly in six inches of water, with his arms stretched out
helplessly before him. To keep his chin clear of the water
he lay in, he had to strain his neck back. In one hand,
above the water, he held his precious flashlight, which
caution forbade him to use. Carefully, he humped up his
middle; there was room for a movement of just six inches.
He did it again, drew up his knees, and pushed himself
forward. The wear-resisting properties of the skin on his
elbows were entirely unsatisfactory. They were agonizingly
non-existent. He made another attempt. This time he
kept his weight on one elbow, moved the other elbow forward a couple of inches, transferred his weight to that,
then moved the first. It was slow, but possible. His flashlight hampered him surprisingly, but he did make steady
progress, excruciating progress, bringing unaccustomed,
quickly aching muscles into play. Fifty feet or so along the
little tunnel, the water thickened to a none too sweetly

scented slime through which he slithered, contracting and extending like some inept, worn-out worm that jerks its last underground journey. Then, gradually, foot by foot, the slime turned first to mud and dried to dust; it gave his tennis shoes a better grip, and his movements improving with practice, he made easier and more rapid headway. Now, at any moment, on humping up his back, there would be no constricting brickwork above him. Encouraged by the thought, he made an extra spurt of speed and sprained his hand against a root that stuck through the side of the culvert. For a moment it hurt atrociously. But that was not the worst of it. There were other roots as well. Groping about he counted six, with tangles of smaller stuff between. The way was blocked.

The little tunnel was black as ink. What was, initially, merely an escapade, cramp, trivial accident, constriction and lack of light, had turned to high adventure. He would not have thought it possible that crawling up a culvert in the dark could have tried him so profoundly. He longed to know how near he was to the end of it—whether further tree roots barred the way. He hesitated with his finger on the button of his flashlight, but common sense prevailed. It was purchase for pushing he wanted rather than light for looking. He managed to dislodge three of the more slender roots, but in the dark, unprotected by instinctive blinkings, when they broke, the dirt that came with them flew into his eyes. He clinched his teeth—he was damned if a few slender tree roots should foil him. But he struggled in vain, he could neither break them nor force his way through; it was a complete lesson in the equality of opposing forces. Each time he increased his efforts he did nothing but drag himself forwards. No matter how hard he pressed with aching back and smarting half-skinned knees against the brickwork of the culvert, he slipped before the roots gave way. In his efforts he dropped the flashlight.

Then, feeling about for it in the dark, he accidentally switched it on. Like lightning he dabbed his hand on the light, lay still for a time, listening, panting, exhausted.

All seemed quiet ahead. Temptation overcame him and he took his hand away. Expecting brickwork, he saw bright jewels. Immediately in front of him was a curtain of fibrous roots through which passed the stouter roots he had struggled with, three of them still firmly fixed, three he had broken hanging free, and through the screen, bright red and blue and brilliant green, there danced the eyes of angry rats. He hissed gently. "S-s-s." They scuttled away. There was nothing else for it, he would have to go back and come in again with a knife—then he remembered that he had left his knife in his other clothes. But he would have to go back. Elizabeth would be running for the police unless he returned within the half-hour and he calculated that his time was running short. It was shorter than he thought it was, for his worm-wriggle back again was more difficult even than his advance. But at length, with a gasp of relief, he felt his tennis shoes in water, and soon he was stretching his aching back.

He found Elizabeth where he left her.

"I was giving you another five minutes," she whispered. "I haven't seen a soul, though I thought I heard a movement in the trees on the other side of the wood."

"Which one was it? Do you know?"

He explained what had happened.

"I can't possibly break them. I don't think I could loosen them if I went in backwards and pushed with my feet. We shall have to go back to Cherry Hay for a knife. There's nothing else for it. Though I didn't hear anything I'm determined to have a look."

"Do you think we could get at the roots from the top? If you went in again and pulled at the roots, perhaps I could spot the tree. I'm certain I heard it moving."

"It's an idea. But, no, I really think I'd better go back. We shouldn't be sure. It would take nearly as long. These trees would take more uprooting than you imagine. We might make a noise. I shall have to go and fetch a knife. What an ass I was not to bring one."

She put her hand on his arm in the dark.

"Why, dear, you're wet through. But look here, couldn't I crawl past them? You could come along behind me for company, you know; then I could go on with the light."

"I don't like it somehow."

"But could I get by them?"

"Yes, I think you might. But supposing there's some one there."

"Not very likely at this time, is it?"

"More likely now than at any other—we know they were flying at night."

But Elizabeth, every bit as brave as he was, pressed to be allowed to go, though he told her of the rats, and after hesitating, after extracting a solemn promise that she would return at once if she heard any one moving about, he agreed to her suggestion.

She took off her mackintosh, and going on hands and knees, she followed him to where the culvert opened to the lake.

Elizabeth held the flashlight and he crawled in behind her. The extra room for movement given by her slimness made a world of difference. She easily outdistanced him. She made sudden little spurts of speed, waited impatiently until he touched her foot, then hurried on. She was through the tree roots before he reached them. Forgetting that Annesley couldn't see her when he came up, she waggled a foot by way of farewell and pressed forward alone into darkness.

Almost immediately the culvert opened out into something more nearly like a real tunnel. She guessed that she must be underneath the stable yard. Once she thought she heard the sound of voices, but she felt no fear. Once she managed to turn round sufficiently to flash her light back down the tunnel, where she could see Amnesley's white face between the roots of the trees. She signaled O.K. in dashes and dots.

A little further on the tunnel bent to the right, and she noticed a faint light ahead of her. It came from an open grating in the roof. She was in a little chamber about ten feet square. In each wall there was an opening, which, she guessed, led to other parts of the foundations, and she was just making up her mind which she should explore first, when there was a crash above her head like metal hitting metal, then sudden commotion and tramping of feet.

"Ugh—ugh—ugh—you devil." There was a heavy thud, the grating darkened, and something tinkled to the ground. She recognized Primrose's voice, imagined some one being shaken and flung to the floor. For a moment she nearly called out, but remembering her promise to Annesley, realizing that nothing could be done, she crept up to the grating and listened. Primrose was talking again angrily—she was sure that it was he.

"He shall damn well suffer for that! Has it damaged them, Dan?"

She gathered that they, whatever they were, were damaged. Dan said something cut short by a string of oaths terminating with the question, "And now what the hell are we going to do?"

"If you'll take my advice—hop it."

"Hop it? Hop it? Where the hell to? It's not so easy to hop it out of England with the police after you."

"Well, the police'll be before you if you don't do something quick." Elizabeth recognized Joyce's voice.

"But still—" Lobley, she thought, protesting weakly.

Then Primrose spoke again—she half heard a reference to the lake. Then he continued in a louder, exultant voice. "Listen! I know. I've got it. Take him to Plenders Pit—the trigger was only moved to the end of the bank this morning . . . three hundred feet . . . shove him in one of the skips."

"Yes . . . no one think of looking . . . later buckets bury—" She only caught half-heard snatches.

Waiting to hear no more, without further hesitation, Elizabeth made for the tunnel. Regardless of risk she switched on her light. Something flashed on the floor. Kneeling down, she found her father's pince-nez.

Reckless now, she swung her light on the grating above. She could hardly repress a little cry. Between the bars, half-hidden, but clear enough for certainty she saw her father's white face. A wisp of lank red hair hung down between the bars, and even as she looked she saw an eye-lid quiver. Thankful for the sign of life, but full of apprehension, she hurried back to Annesley.

She kept the flashlight on.

"Get back—quick—for all you're worth, get back. Don't wait for me. Get back," she whispered as she neared the tree roots.

He began to retreat.

But a crab in a crab pot was not more neatly caught than Elizabeth was when she tried to pass the roots again. They sloped at just the wrong angle. The devil himself could not have arranged them better. The harder she pushed the tighter they held. Annesley came back and they struggled and tore in the tight little tunnel.

"They've got him. George, do leave me."

"I'm damned if I will. Look here, try to turn sideways a bit, can't you?"

She made the attempt. A fork pierced her breast. She cried with the pain. She nearly broke down.

"They're going to kill him. They're taking him to the pit to kill him and bury him there. They're going to kill him. George, dear, do please leave me—go and tell Jacobs and then come back."

"No. Look here, make one more try. Can't you get hold of that one there? Now, see, I'll push this way. Now, both together. Ready. Go!"

Annesley thought his back would break. Sweat poured from him. But, at last, a mere wreck of her sweet brave self, with her sweater torn to shreds, she struggled through. Then the retreat began, and the retreat from Moscow itself, though more prolonged, could not have exceeded its agony. His knees and elbows raw from his double journey, every movement Annesley made brought torture with it. He was one big ache. At times he feared he might have to stop altogether. And always Elizabeth was pressing. They could feel each other's breath.

"I can't go any faster, dear."

"My poor!"

"You're sure that it was Corrie."

"Yes. I told you. I'm certain. I picked up his glasses. What are we to do?"

"We may be in time. I'm glad you didn't let them know you'd heard them. It gives us a chance. I hope Jacobs really came and that he brought some men."

Their faces a foot apart, they talked in broken jerks as slowly they wriggled their way back down the culvert. Annesley gave a little cry of pleasure when he felt his feet in the water at the bottom of it again. Soon he was helping her out. For a moment, tattered and torn, plastered with mud, regardless of bleeding knees and knuckles, they clung to each other, exhausted, on the edge of the lake.

Then, breath regained, Annesley took command again. As he backed along the culvert he had come to a decision, and, his decision made, he stuck to it, ignoring the attractions of alternatives. It seemed to him hopeless to attempt any offensive against the stables themselves. Already, probably, Lobley's big Blick was speeding towards the entrance gates through the rhododendrons. As they clung together he had half-imagined that he heard the drone of a distant engine—half-imagined, too, a noise like some one pounding against a door.

But he stuck to his decision. Taking Elizabeth by the hand, he scrambled up the gulley and they hurried, with what speed they could muster, back to Cherry Hay. There, to their relief, they saw the police car. Two constables stood talking in the yard and Mrs. Glegg was just letting the Inspector out of the front door as they arrived. They were just in time.

Inspector Jacobs was in no amiable frame of mind. It was all very well for Annesley to ring him up and tell him to come out to Cherry Hay without giving rhyme or reason for it. It had cost him a game of bridge and an evening out with his wife. She had tried to persuade him not to come. She had been rather bitter. But, however vague the message, he had not dared to risk a refusal. When he arrived at Cherry Hay and asked for Mr. Corrie, Mrs. Glegg could only tell him that he was out. She did not know where he was. She did not know where Mr. Annesley or Miss Corrie were either. She knew nothing. He waited for more than an hour, and by the end of it his grievance had grown not a little. He spent part of the time in rehearsing the conversation he would have with his wife when he got back home.

He was just telling Mrs. Glegg to ask whoever came in first to ring him up immediately, when he heard Annesley and Elizabeth running down the hill towards the house.

"Jacobs! Jacobs!" Annesley called.

They came into the light from the open door. The Inspector stared, as well he might. They were almost unrecognizable. He had never seen anything like it. There was blood all over Annesley's face. They were both in rags. Annesley's trousers had great gaps at both the knees. Elizabeth's stockings were down in folds about her ankles. They were wild-eyed and blood-smeared and panting for breath. Already full of suspicion regarding Annesley, in his angry frame of mind, their plight roused no feelings of pity.

"What on earth—" he began.

"Quick, they've got Corrie. Quick, to the colliery! They're going to—"

Annesley hurried forward and took the Inspector by the shoulders as he spoke. But the Inspector was not to be hustled. He drew back.

"Steady now. Steady. What's it all about? I've been waiting here for more than an hour. Who's got Mr. Corrie, and what have you been up to?"

"They've got Daddy," Elizabeth sobbed.

"Primrose and Lobley. They're taking him to the colliery to tip him out of the buckets on the ropeway. There's not a second to lose. Make for Plenders Pit as quickly as you can." Annesley spoke wildly.

"Mr. Primrose, the colliery manager, and Mr. Lobley, of the Priory, tip Mr. Corrie out of the ropeway! Come, sir, tell me another. Do you mean for a practical joke?"

Annesley stamped his foot. It was exasperating. The precious minutes were speeding by and the Inspector drawled on as though he was a coroner at an inquest. They simply could not make him understand it. He failed to see how they could have got into a state like that merely by crawling up a brick culvert. They looked to him as though they had been fighting. And what was all this about aeroplanes?

Elizabeth sat down and cried.

Then, foolishly, Annesley only made matters worse by divulging his connection with Scotland Yard and threatening to report the inspector's stupidity to his uncle. The Inspector knew that that must be wrong. To tell the truth, he was a little vague about Scotland Yard. Bensham would have known Annesley, had he anything to do with Scotland Yard though. He felt sure of that. So, instead of having the desired effect, Annesley found that his threats only made matters worse and landed them into a whole fresh series of slow-witted questions.

At last he gave it up.

"All right then, Inspector. If Mr. Corrie is murdered, don't expect pity from me when you lose your job. I think you must be the biggest fool in the police force. Come on, Elizabeth, we must do what we can by ourselves."

They disappeared into the night, leaving the puzzled Inspector standing in the doorway.

"We'll go across the golf links to the pit bank. We might do something there perhaps. Can you manage it?" Annesley took Elizabeth by the arm and they hurried to the gate that led to the ponds. They had just reached it when Jacobs called after them.

No sooner had they left him then the Inspector began to wonder whether he might not have made a mistake after all. Quite suddenly he realized what it would mean for him if by any chance the queer incoherent story he had listened to should be wholly or in part correct. He dashed into the yard.

"Mr. Annesley," he called, "I'm going to the colliery."

"Right. Hurry," came faintly back.

The Inspector heard the gate bang. He jumped into the car with his men.

Annesley and Elizabeth heard the engine running. They were thankful to have gained their end at last. It had taken them a precious quarter of an hour.

"My God, what an ass!" Annesley muttered, as they ran towards the ponds. The rest had done him good, though. He had got his second wind. Elizabeth began to lag behind him.

"You go on," she panted, "don't wait for me."

He hurried on. He heard her heavy breathing getting fainter and fainter behind him as he sped along the links. For the first time he began to hope that they might yet be in time. It would take some arranging. There would be men about the colliery. Primrose would have to get them out of the way. The devils, though! And they would have pulled it off too, if Elizabeth had not overheard them. He imagined the ropeway working steadily, piling up the grave, whilst the police vainly scoured the country for Corrie. They would think he had murdered Marion and had made his escape—either that, or suicide. They would drag the ponds. But who would dream of digging up a pit bank. Plenders Pit bank—in the moonlight it loomed up darkly ahead.

21
AT THE PIT BANK

Elizabeth, with Annesley the length of the long hole ahead, lurched, like some exhausted but determined second in a marathon, down Little Plenders golf links. She could hear Little Plenders church bells pealing. The moon, which had risen while they were wriggling down the culvert, was silvering the shale on the further side of the desolating dump to Plenders Pit. It was a Friday night, and back from almost unremembered times, on a Friday, the village campanologists have set Little Plenders church bells pealing. No one, not even the vicar himself, knew quite why they did it, but the same eight men had rung the same eight bells for the last eight years with a quite unnecessary hebdomadal persistence; had they not acquired that nicety of timing pertaining to the perfect peal, then now they would never attain it. Certainly it was not for practice that they rang them. That, like an agitated pedal cyclist, who tink-les feebly at some sudden-looming lorry, they rang the church bells on Fridays to remind the colliery company of the church's mere existence, and that their pit bank bade fair to bury it, might just as well explain it. It was just a habit and an institution. Mrs. Girling's gigantic son, Jack, who was forty-seven and "did" the vicarage garden, had not missed one single Friday in the whole of thirty years—and that was by no means a record. When

first young Jack was given a rope, there were no Little
Plenders golf links, and the shaft of the pit was just being
sunk in the wood, which then grew right to the churchyard
wall. In those days, the village maidens and young men
made love there, and in more than one mean cottage, the
notes as they burst from belfry, and died away on distant
air, brought back to mind some wooded glade and words
that once were whispered there—words which then had
stirred and throbbed like trumpet calls, but now, when
the bells stirred memory, came back like feeble evanescent
echoes across the intervening years of care. Yes, in those
peaceful days, faintly through trees, Plenders bells had
blessed many a maiden's whispered "yes," but later, when
the trees were cut, and laborers toiled where larches grew,
and the pit dump, like some creeping sore that eats into
fair white flesh, spread ever out towards the church, the
bells had to battle with less romantic sounds; with noises
made by tipping trucks that bucked at each other like
fighting rams, banged into buffers, and shot out sudden
cascades of shale—with noises made by little grimed green
engines—tankers that rattled their cranks, and clattered
about with trailing trucks, as they shrieked at the church
bells derisively with ear-splitting spews of steam.

But the bells won the bout for all that, for a time came
soon when the tip grew too steep for service by trucks on
rails, and the company, for that reason and for the sake of
economy as well, scrapped rails and trucks, and engines
too, and replaced them with the aerial ropeway, whose
buckets, or skips as they are called at the pit, came creeping along on wires, and Plenders bells could peal in peace
and quiet again. Yes, quiet and peace, and on Fridays and
Sundays—bells. And whilst the bells rang, and whilst they
were still, the buckets dropped filth on the growing hill,
day in, day out, and hour by hour, falling filth and shale
in showers, till the tall steel towers which had been erected

above the existing tip were submerged almost, and from down below, it looked as though the bucket bottoms must bump against the bank. Then they built towers taller still, away on the virgin earth, and the great dump grew and spread so fast that church, and bells, and golf links too, seemed likely to be buried.

Indeed, on a night when the wind shifted about in gusts, if you stood on the hill by the French Horn at the top of the village, you could almost imagine catastrophe already come, and that the bells, which rang one moment clear, were buried the next, and would ring no more. But this night was no blusterer. It was late September—calm and clear. The harvest moon, golden, perhaps through gazing on much ripe corn, or perhaps from the glory of the after-glow through which, beyond earth's rim, she smiled upon her lord the Sun, lit the pit bank to silver, then laced it with golden threads—the little cracks and crevices where rain ran. If on such a moonlight night as this—on this Friday night of all nights, say—you had stood by the wall at the end of the garden behind the French Horn, you would have seen the shadow of the bank thrown right across the fairway of the fifth. And had you clambered down and walked to where moonlight and shadow met, you would have seen a row of well-defined black dots above the line of demarcation. Annesley, breathless, well-nigh worn out, wet through with sweat and caked in mud, pelting with head down across the grass, noticed the black dots too— noticed with despair that the dots began to move. With bursting lungs he dashed ahead. He had just reached the final tower, a veritable Eiffel Tower, round which, on a wheel, the buckets turned to make their empty journey back for more, when he heard a click, and looking up, he saw great rocks come hurtling through the air. They crashed against the steel work of the tower, and following them came a cloud of shaly flakes that glittered like metal against the moon. Could he hope to catch Corrie and save him if he fell from such a height? Or should he scramble up the bank? Could he reach the buckets—could he hold them if he did? Could he tip poor Corrie out to safety, or were the buckets rigid and locked until the trigger tripped them? In an agony of apprehension he gazed at the steel work above him. A narrow inspection ladder zig-zagged from side to side—he had noticed it when playing golf—and, two flights high, where a strut and stays made junction, hanging like an anchor, he saw what he thought was a workman's pick.

After a moment's hesitation he rattled up the rungs, caught at the haft and hurried on. Perhaps he could force the point of the pick between the wire rope and the wheel and force it off, though what the consequences would be if he succeeded he did not stop to consider. He was half-way up. There was another shower of rocks and shale. Now he was breathing dust. He could hear Elizabeth racing up—hear how she gasped for breath.

Poor Elizabeth, when she got there, had to cling to a corner of the tower for support.

"Stand clear! Stand clear, Elizabeth!" he yelled. "Stand clear!"

She withdrew a dozen paces, and, standing there, still short of breath and faint, she suffered the torture of fear twofold—fear for her father—this next bucket coming, now creeping clear of the pit bank top, now approaching steadily, slow as a hearse, across silver-blue sky, would it fling her father, if still alive, to a dreadful death among the scattered rocks below?—fear for her lover who zig-zagged precariously up the sky, now leaning towards her, now leaning away, foreshortened and reckless and insecure.

He was nearing the top.

A bucket was tripped and rocks rained.

He had reached the last flight of the ladder now.

He seemed to hesitate and stop.

Another bucket neared the trip. She hardly dared look. She screamed. Click! It had tripped. She screamed again with useless arms upraised. Her father, who would scream no more, came somersaulting silently across the steel-blue sky.

Annesley who saw it, and heard it too, hurled away his useless pick, and risking two rungs at a time, hurried helter-skelter down the little ladder. Once, missing his footing, he scraped his shin to the very bone against one of the sharp steel bars. Looking down, he saw Elizabeth creeping forward; looking up, another bucket drawing near. He shouted another warning. Now the narrow ladder sloped the other way, and for a moment he could not see her. He prayed God that she did draw back. The ladder turned him towards her. She had. She was clear. She was standing there beneath him wringing her hands.

"Keep clear, Elizabeth, keep clear!"

At last he was on firm ground.

Another bucket crept clear of the pit bank top. There was a belch of dirt—a cloud of dust. He darted in, and catching hold he dragged the poor half-buried body out.

To Annesley, it seemed exactly like the night when Marion died, all over again; he on his knees leaning over the dead—Elizabeth there by his side. That other night had been dark and clouded. Then the wind had stirred, but he had maintained his habitual unruffled calm. Now the night was calm and he—? As he knelt over poor battered Corrie and brushed the dirt away, he felt distress that was altogether new to his experience. Strong as he was, the night's events had tried him; his unaccustomed cramped exertions in the culvert, his wrestle with the roots that barred his path, the shock of the news Elizabeth brought him when, distraught, she returned from her lonely search among the stable foundations, the agony of that second slow retreat on elbows and knees already raw, the race to Cherry Hay, the exasperation of the delay with the fat-headed Jacobs, the dash down the links, his climb up the tall steel tower, the sudden surges of apprehension that swept him as bucket after bucket neared the trip, the ghastly crack when Corrie fell, his own hurried descent, the pain of his bone-bare shin, all had exhausted physique, and played on steady nerves till they were tuned to a pitch as near to breakdown and hysteria as Annesley had ever known.

Then, as though shocks enough for one short night had not already been dealt him, Elizabeth suddenly flung her arms about his neck. "George! George!" she cried. "It isn't Daddy!"

He had been just on the point of bending closer over the body, and the sudden unexpected action bowled him over. It sent a pain down his leg like a knife. And when he fell over she fell with him. They both went together right on the top of the dead man's body.

It broke her. Racked with unreasoning terror, she shrieked and struggled. Annesley was shaken too. On their knees once again, they clung for a moment closely together.

"I—I'm—so so-sorry," she sobbed. "It was—awful—I'm all w-wound up."

"But, my blessed—my dear one—there, it's all right. I felt just the same myself. We're both played out."

His deep, dear voice was soothing. She shivered for a moment in his arms.

Then, putting her gently from him, he bent more closely over the dead man's body. Now that he came to examine it more carefully, Annesley found it difficult to understand how, covered in ashes and filth though he was, he could have mistaken this pale-faced, black-haired man for

Corrie. He was just wondering who on earth it could be when he felt Elizabeth touch him gently on the arm.

With one arm raised she was pointing above her.

Quiet before, the silence now was so intense that to Annesley it almost seemed to hold the attributes of petrification. Elizabeth in silhouette with her head thrown back and arm uplifted, the pit bank black like a sable wave that had set on the point of breaking, the cloudless steel-blue sky, the placid moon, the shining wires—no sound or movement stirred them. The squeaking of the ropes had ceased. And, clear in the bay that was cut in the sky by the tall steel tower and sloping bank, like some black deadly berry that hung there, a bucket had stopped almost touching the trip.

Elizabeth lowered her arm. They clung to each other again. They were alone in the world and it was theirs, and the moon shone calmly on them. He kissed her tear-stained face.

"George—is it—does it mean that he's safe?" she whispered.

"It looks as though Jacobs may have got 'em anyhow—we ought to go and see though. Can you—do you think you could possibly manage it?"

Annesley felt his vigor returning. He helped Elizabeth to her feet, and with courage renewed, staggering and stumbling over the rough, unequal ground, they set out along the bottom of the bank towards the pit.

22

"COME INTO MY PARLOR—"

For Corrie, it had been one of those days when decisions and the cancellation of decisions follow each other with such rapidity that the brain grows feverish and incapable. First, he would walk over to the Priory and have it out with Joyce at once. Then, no, that would look as though he took Elizabeth and Annesley seriously. He would ignore their slanderous suggestions, which he had very well understood, and wait until she called. On the one hand he remembered some of his conversations with Joyce, remembered how interested she had always been in his affairs, on the other hand he felt sure that she really cared for him. Yes, she did care for him. He could not be mistaken in that. And with every wobble, as the day dragged to its close, he became more afraid that there might be something in it.

Finally, towards evening, his hesitations took him slowly along the drive in the direction of the Priory. The beautiful outline of the old building stood out in black relief against the pale yellow of the evening sky. Not a breath stirred the air. The big beeches by the stables were still. And through the dusk, between the stables and the Priory, he met Joyce. She was dressed in white, and seeing her, he despised himself for doubting.

"But I was only just this minute thinking of you. How nice of you to come and see us," she greeted him merrily. "I was just taking a message from uncle to Professor Taverner in the lab. Do you mind waiting? I shan't be ten minutes."

He nodded. There was admiration in his eyes.

"Go round to the lawn, then, and I'll join you there."

The Lobleys lived in the middle section of the Priory. A sloping lawn, shrub bordered and velvet-smooth from more than a century's mowing, lies between the house and lake, and walking there, now more at peace, Corrie decided to put the matter to the test and disclose to Joyce what Annesley had told him.

Soon, she was calling him softly from the French window of the drawing-room that opened on to the lawn.

He went to her. His heart swelled within him. She was on the settee. In the dusk he thought she looked more beautiful than ever—ethereal. She made room for him by her side.

"Oh—er—Joyce, I wanted badly to have a talk with you," he began with some difficulty. "I was—er—having a talk with Annesley this morning and—er—

"And—er—was one of your sock suspenders down—er—then, as it is now?" She laughed, mimicking his pauses. He bent down to rectify the sartorial defect and the loose end of his tie fell out of his waistcoat.

Then, when he straightened his back, she must go and re-tie it for him, and the provocative approach of her face to his set his brain a-whirl, and almost before he realized it he was in the middle of a proposal.

She tucked the ends of the tie in. She raised her adorable eyebrows, and he looked just below them to learn his fate. Her pretty lips seemed to be framing "yes" and then, just as he stood on hope's high peak, she said she thought she heard a bell ring.

"It must be the telephone, I think," she said. "Wait here, dear, I won't be a minute."

And so, standing quietly by the open window, Corrie waited. She had not refused him. Before him the sloping lawn looked gray as his past unsatisfied existence, and, in the evening light, the shrubs like black bogeys standing round it; but beyond it, like the future of his hopes, free from these shadows, lay the lake—a sheet of gold that glorified the saffron sky. He heaved a contented sigh, looked at the scene, and looked again, his attention held. A shrub had surely strayed from the ranks. Was that a lantern moving—pale in the contending dusk?

Just for a moment Corrie, short-sighted, could not quite understand it, but then he saw that it was the white face of a man who came towards him across the lawn. The shadowy figure made straight for the window where he stood—gazed up at him—a squat little man with a dead white face.

The drawing-room floor was a foot above the level of the ground and Corrie peered down, waiting for him to speak.

"Well, Mr. Lobley, I've changed my mind and I want a thousand more," he said at last, in a not uneducated voice.

Corrie, suddenly interested, made no reply.

"Yes, I've changed my mind. I was here last night and I saw the little aeroplane, so I guessed you've pulled it off. It's worth another thousand surely now. Ask me in, and we'll talk it over."

Corrie glanced behind him. Joyce had left the door ajar. The room was in shadows, and remembering what Annesley had told him at breakfast time, he beckoned the man with the white face to come in through the window.

"And why do you think that you deserve another thousand?" he asked as soon as the man was inside. A good leading question he thought it.

"Oh, come, you know well enough. You'd never have done it, would you now, if your man hadn't had the notes about the special steel?"

"We might have done. We had other sources of information," Corrie said at a venture.

"May be—perhaps. That, however, is not the point. You've got your information and you're going to make money out of it. But I've got information and I'm going to do the same. I've all the necessary proofs. Too, the police might be a little more active over the affair at Cherry Hay if they knew all that I know, I'm thinking."

Corrie felt a sudden thrill. He stood in the window, wondering how to gain more information without giving himself away.

And Joyce, returning and hearing voices in the room where only five minutes before she had left Corrie alone, stood and listened outside the door. Then, taking off her shoes, she crept quietly out of the front door and round to the French window on the grass. The unexpected visitor was standing with his back to it, and springing forward she clutched at his neck with her strong, young fingers.

"Bernard? Help! Hold him!" she cried. "He's a rogue." Her voice had excitement in it.

Corrie did help. Helped so effectively, that in less than five minutes the white-faced visitor lay gasping on the floor where they bound him with a clothes line Joyce ran and fetched from the kitchen.

Together they lifted him on to the settee.

"You stay on guard for a moment, Bernard, and I'll run and telephone to uncle. He's staying late at the works, but he can be here in twenty minutes. I—I know this man. He's tried to blackmail uncle before."

She took a small pistol from a drawer in the writing desk and handed it to him. "Take this," she said, "it might be useful to you later on."

Mechanically Corrie took the little weapon, stood holding it half-surprised, but before he could question her she was gone.

Alone, he looked at their victim. It certainly seemed unnecessary that he should be armed with a lethal weapon, for in addition to binding his legs together—they looked like polonies in string—they had tied his arms behind his back. The squat little man lay helpless, making gurgling protests through a gag: a cushion-cover torn in strips, above which his furious eyes rolled wildly.

Corrie walked to the switch, and pulling it down flooded the room with the searching realism of electric light, that seemed at once to disperse the shadows of the room, draw a veil of black across the pale panel of twilight sky framed by the French window, and made a distant, doubtful, ill-lit dream of his romance. Five minutes earlier, in the kindly dusk, he had been on the very brink of an accepted proposal, now, pistol in hand, he stood in a blaze of hard light, guarding a neatly trussed villain. It was a change of scene—sudden—astonishing—disconcerting. He was wrong. Elizabeth and Annesley were right. It was evident that Lobley had really got hold of the papers Annesley had told him about at breakfast-time. The man lying on the settee had had a hand in it, and now he had come for a further fee. It was clear that the deal had not been a personal one or he, Corrie, would not have been mistaken for Lobley. Clear, too—and this was the shattering part of it—that Joyce must know something of it.

Glancing again at the captive, an idea occurred to him. He went over to the settee and felt in his pockets. In the side pockets there was nothing, but in the inside pockets there were papers. He took them out, putting the pistol down on a little table so that he could look them through. There was a receipted Blatchford hotel bill and several envelopes from which he gathered that his name was

Palmer. Then, just as he was on the point of extracting a letter from one of the envelopes, he heard footsteps in the hall, and a moment later Lobley and Primrose came in, followed by Joyce.

Lobley picked the little pistol up from the table and locked the door. Primrose closed the French window and stood with his back against it. Joyce sat down in an armchair. Like players in some dumb charade, not one of them spoke a word. Corrie looked up quickly. He had no more than a vague feeling of surprise—it hardly amounted to uneasiness. It was not only their silence that intrigued him, but Joyce had clearly indicated that they were alone. She had told him that she would telephone to her uncle at the works and that he would be here in twenty minutes. The window had been standing wide open until Primrose closed it, and certainly he would have heard a car arrive. No car had arrived and yet here was not only Lobley but Primrose as well; Lobley, pistol in hand, a frown on his common, intelligent face; Primrose, leaning against the French window, his hands deep in his trouser pockets, an expression at once truculent and satisfied lighting his porcine features.

Joyce was lighting a cigarette. She looked unhappy. Corrie half imagined that he saw Primrose scowl at her, and then she was the first to speak.

"Mr. Corrie *has* been so helpful, uncle. I really don't know what I should have done without him."

She blew thoughtful smoke from her cigarette.

Corrie, puzzled, but for once polite, said: "Oh, not at all." Or words to that effect.

"He's been altogether too helpful," Primrose grunted.

Corrie looked from one to the other. Suddenly he realized that he was in danger.

He saw Lobley and Primrose exchange glances and then Lobley spoke. "Corrie, we've got to know where we stand, what you know, and what you're up to."

"What the devil do you mean by 'up to'? I'd just proposed to Joyce when this fellow butted in, if you want to know."

Joyce turned her head away.

"I mean what do you know about our affairs? I wasn't referring to your amatory escapades."

"You swine! I'll knock your head off if you talk to me like that." Regardless of the odds against him Corrie was getting excited.

"We may be swine, Mr. Corrie, but we don't go to our friends' houses and then impersonate them," Lobley said coldly.

"It's a dashed dirty trick," Primrose grunted. "Damned awkward for you too."

Then Corrie went off the deep end. He would have been wiser to keep quiet, but he called them swine and swindlers and many things besides, ending his tirade with a definite accusation of Marion's murder. He told them, too, how they did it—helicopter and all.

And never was failure to restrain a red-haired temper more thoroughly well paid for. They closed in on him. Lobley with pointed pistol, Primrose with ham-like hands outstretched, and almost before he could resist, they had him bound with the remainder of the clothes line which Joyce, who kept her eyes from his, handed to them.

They sat him in a chair and tied him to the back. They took the improvised gag off Palmer and set him in another. Then they sat down themselves and held counsel.

Corrie was certainly no coward, but his blood ran cold at the opening sentence.

"Well, we must put them out of the way, that's certain—they both of them know too much." It was Primrose who spoke.

"Yes. It's a pity. I'm sorry, Corrie, but it really can't be helped. You shouldn't butt in on other folks' plans," Lobley said.

"We needn't waste time in discussing that. All we have to decide is how we are going to do it," Primrose said impatiently.

"Well, what about a nice little ride to Skegness, and then a few miles further east in the helicopters? That, I think, would be as sweet and safe a way as any," Lobley said. Then, turning to Corrie, "They're the cutest little machines," he continued, "they don't span nine feet and could lift a cow—turbine for the main propeller and two for the helicopters controlled by switches a child could use. The speed's rather high—about two hundred miles an hour—and there's not much room. There's only room for one in fact, and we'll have to hang you from the perch. You'll be cold, I'm afraid, but it will act as an anesthetic, and it won't take long. It'll soon be all over. We'll take you up say five thousand feet and I've no actual experience, but from what I've been told, you'll be dead before you reach the water."

Palmer whimpered, whined for mercy, made suggestions of self-incrimination that would put him for ever in their power, but they all of them went unheeded.

"No," Primrose thundered.

"No," Lobley repeated quietly.

Palmer turned to Joyce—Joyce turned away.

Corrie, his burst of passion having subsided, sat staring straight before him. Something, he thought, might perhaps be done at the stables. They would have to take them to the stables, where he felt certain the aeroplanes were housed, and either on the way there or at the stables themselves then something might be done. Here there seemed nothing to do. Palmer was obviously no good at all. Whimpering quietly, crying like a child, he evidently had no two opinions as to the serious nature of the threats that Lobley and Primrose had made—they meant business. Curiously, as Corrie sat helplessly in his chair, he was not

in the least dismayed. Just then he cared very little indeed
about what became of him. Joyce had not only betrayed
him, but she had made him look a fool. He would never
live it down as long as he lived and the attempt was not
worth making. It was only his naturally combative char-
acter that made him bother his brains over means of
escape. Death by drowning from a great height was, after
all, bound to be a speedy affair. Perhaps he would struggle
and yell when he felt himself being lifted out of the stable
yard at the end of a rope attached to the helicopter. At
two hundred miles an hour the rope would fly out like the
weighted tail of a kite—and he would be the weight at the
end of it. Yes, that was certainly an idea. If the rope holding him was short enough, then surely he would fly out
right under the tail. And supposing that his arms were not
still bound to his side he might perhaps manage to get a
hold on it. It was an idea, but there were certainly a lot of
ifs about it. Did helicopters have tails? Would they unlash
his arms? Was it not more likely that they would take both
Palmer and him down to the stables lashed to their chairs?
Was it not more likely still that even if his arms were free,
he would be paralyzed to incapacity by cold and fright?
He wondered whether they would let go at two hundred
miles an hour—in that case he and Palmer would describe
parabolas.

He wondered at what height they would be released and
at what angle they would strike the water. It was a nice
little problem. Or would they bring the little machines
to rest like hawks, five thousand feet up, and then, instead of swooping down on it, allow their prey to fall? Five
thousand feet! How long would it take to fall five thousand feet? Gravity! Thirty-two feet per second per second.
Thirty-two—sixty-four—ninety-six—an arithmetical pro-
gression to death. No, it would not take very long to do
five thousand. He would certainly not be able to count as

many as he counted after the doctor that day when he had
his appendix out. On that occasion, the doctor leading,
it had been, "One—one, two—two, three—three," right
up to "twenty-six—twenty-six, twenty-seven—you're not
to kick, Mr. Corrie—twenty, let me go, you fool"—he had
heard himself yell it—heard the yell go echoing through
vast empty halls till they were cut off with an explosive
crack by blank oblivion.

Yes, he would yell again like that when he took that last
wild dive, he was convinced that he would, though now
he sat quite calmly. Like some dead comet with a stifled
cry of terror for a tail he would hurtle through the dark
night air. And this time there would be no nurse at hand
to greet him. . . .

Primrose and Lobley had been talking together in low
voices in the French window and Corrie was roused from
his unpleasant reverie by hearing Primrose say in a louder
tone that he, for one, would take no risks.

Joyce sat quietly on the settee. She had picked up a
book, and with her eyes on Primrose and Lobley she was
scribbling something on the fly-leaf of it. Then catching
his attention, she carefully tore it out and crossed towards
him. With her back to the others for a second, she held it
out, and Corrie saw that across the sheet she had printed
in pencil, "Knock the Bicycles Over." He nodded. Hope
revived.

Lobley went out and fetched the car, and Corrie and
Palmer were released from their chairs, gagged securely,
and escorted to it, where they were placed on the back seat
with Primrose in between them. Lobley took the wheel,
and Joyce, to Corrie's surprise, the seat beside him.

23
IN THE STABLE YARD

Lobley's big Blick was a powerful luxurious affair. It was the sort of car you might expect to meet driven by an immaculate chauffeur, with a single, purple-faced passenger reading the *Financial Times* in the deep recesses of the back seat—in fact, it was a managing director's car. Indeed the Blick Company advertised it extensively as a managing director's car, and in their advertisements they gave a list of some of the managing directors who used it. Among the listed names was the name of Norman Lobley.

On one of Corrie's visits to the Priory, Lobley had shown the advertisement to him, not deliberately of course—no, it just seemed to happen in the most casual, natural way in the world. The advertisement appeared in the *Automobile Owner* among many other papers, and quite by chance a copy of the *Automobile Owner* happened to be lying on a table in the drawing-room at the time when Corrie called.

"Has it ever occurred to your people to advertise their bicycles in any of the motor-car papers?" Lobley had asked him.

"I don't know. I've nothing to do with it, but I hope they're not quite as abysmally asinine as all that," Corrie had replied.

"Oh, but you mustn't be so conservative, Corrie. The days of conservative unadventurous policies are dead. Now

I'm always telling my people that you can't stand still in business. That if you're not moving forward along with the times then you're going back. Fresh fields and pastures new, you know. Car owners sometimes have sons, and sons ride motor bicycles—Little Giants generally for choice. Hallo! What's this? . . . Well!"

He had been carelessly turning the pages of the *Automobile Owner* as he spoke. Now he chuckled in a manner that implied that he was just a little amused—just a little surprised, but that had surprise and amusement not predominated he might have been annoyed.

"Well, I'm bothered! What won't they do next now?"

He handed the paper, open at one of the advertisement pages, to Corrie. The sheet was headed "Another Important Managing Director Finds His Blick Essential to Big Business." Then came a photograph of a Blick, somehow touched up to look twice as large and glossy as life, with Lobley, glorified to match it, standing at the side. He stood with one foot on the running board, and quite obviously he was just off to the annual meeting to declare a record dividend. Below the picture was a note detailing briefly the merits of the Little Giant bicycles, the gilt-edged fullness of the company's finances, and the successful pushful importance of the company's managing director. The manufacturers, who knew what they were about, would be very pleased to hear from other successful managing directors. They would be pleased to arrange for demonstration drives, and presumably too, for photographs and puffs.

Corrie was not a managing director. He had ridden neither in Lobley's nor any other Blick before, and if he had written to the company telling them what he thought of the comfort of it on this his first demonstration drive, his letter would have been of no practical use whatever for purposes of propaganda. But then, it must be admitted that the conditions could hardly be considered favorable.

To begin with, the rope round Corrie's legs prevented his trousers from giving properly at the seat, which caused his braces to cut distressingly into his thinly covered shoulder-blades. Also, even a drive as short as the drive from the Priory to the stables—a matter of not much more than three hundred yards—can be three hundred yards too long if you sit with the biggest part of a cushion cover firmly rammed into your mouth, and have the sensation that you are not only going to swallow it but, ameba-like, all your own swallowing machinery along with it as well. Again, although the back seat of a Blick may have all the three-passenger capacity the makers claim for it in their advertisements, they quite obviously made no allowance for porcine people like Primrose, who sat with his legs wide apart and his elbows well akimbo, thereby locking his unfortunate fellow passengers, Corrie on one side and Palmer on the other, securely into their cramped and uncomfortable corners.

Corrie indeed was so acutely uncomfortable, that, when Joyce got out to unlock the big stable doors, although the light from the powerful head-lamps of the Blick lit her pretty hair to look like a halo, just as his own headlights had made a halo of it only a few weeks before, now it did not impress him at all. He failed to notice it even. He had other things to think about and other things to look for—subvertible motor bicycles for instance. Why, he wondered, should Joyce have suggested a cycle-overturning campaign? Not that it mattered very much. As far as Corrie could see, bound as he was, he was quite incapable of overturning anything, but why had she suggested it? Was it a trap? Or, relenting a little, was she helping his release?

The heavy doors pushed open, the car glided quickly into the cobbled courtyard, and to Corrie's satisfaction, there, right in the middle of it, was an open-sided shed in which, side by side, there stood two Little Giant machines. He had barely time to notice that they were painted a peculiar dead absorbent shade of leaden black, when Lobley swung the car round at right angles and brought it to rest with the headlights full on the door of the recently converted laboratory wing.

The engine stopped and Lobley and Joyce got out. Primrose, however, remained seated. He planked one big fat hand in front of Corrie's face and the other in front of Palmer's, pressing them both back yet more securely into the corners of the car. Corrie experienced all the preliminary symptoms of suffocation, but even so, through a chink between two fat fingers lit to blood pink by the light just ahead, he was able, vaguely, to see something of what then happened, and the door of the car being open, he was also able to hear.

First, Lobley hurried into the laboratory and came out again almost immediately with Professor Taverner, to whom he stood talking in front of the car, and Corrie guessed that although they stood there in a blaze of light, the brilliance and the dazzle of it must make the back seat of the Blick appear unoccupied. Taverner was blinking.

"Did you say it was Corrie?" he asked with annoyance.

"I'm sorry. Yes, he's waiting at the Priory now. We couldn't stay and we couldn't get rid of him either," Lobley replied, attempting to soothe him.

"Damn!" The professor made the nice little word sound quite unfriendly—then he shut his thin lips so tightly on it that you could not have got a piece of tissue paper in between them.

"We tried to get him to telephone across to you, but there's something wrong with the line. And, as you know, we couldn't very well send him across to see you here," Lobley continued.

"But what is it all about? I was just in the middle of a final distillation."

"He says it's something about a patent, but Joyce and I were just starting out for Millingham, and he said he wanted you."

"Well, it's excessively annoying. That clumsy fool, Robson's, not to be trusted alone, perhaps—" At this point, Corrie imagined that the professor glanced towards the car as though he were going to suggest that Lobley should run him across to the Priory in it, but Lobley forestalled him.

"But can't you lock Robson out of the lab while you're away? You needn't be long. We'd run you across, only we're dining in Millingham and we're late already. He's waiting in the upstairs study."

The professor shrugged his shoulders and gave in. Muttering something about a day's work spoilt and Lobley's lack of understanding, he went angrily back into the laboratory, to return a minute later followed by Robson (Corrie recognized him as the brute in overalls who, by the water-butt, had captured joy by cruelty to kittens), looking angry and disgruntled.

Taverner locked the sliding laboratory doors. Lobley went to the courtyard doors and got out his key to unlock it. He told Joyce to turn the car round just as though they were really going into Millingham to dine.

Then Primrose moved one fat finger a fraction and opened out the view, and Corrie, in the unlit back of the car might have been in the second row of the pit, his interest for a time sufficiently intense to deaden the tortures consequent on the discomforts of the seating. The floodlights were playing full on the big double doors in the middle of the back scene—an amazingly realistic piece of workmanship. Through the open door of the car, he could hear all that was said on the stage.

Lobley took out his keys to open the lock. He fumbled about. He looked at his key. He tried again.

"My key must be bent or something, I think," he said, turning to Taverner. "Lend me yours, will you?"

The professor took a little leather key-case out of his pocket, selected a small key, and then handed the lot over to Lobley. Then Lobley put the professor's key in the lock, gave it a sudden jerk that bent it, unlocked the door with his own key, and handed the borrowed key-case back to the professor, who, none the wiser, put it back in his pocket.

Then Corrie saw no more, for Primrose closed up the gap between his fingers. He heard Lobley tell Professor Taverner that he had no need to wait, as Robson would close the doors; then the big car lurched forward; Primrose took his hand away, and once more Corrie could breathe with comparative comfort through his nose. From the time they first entered the stable courtyard to the time they left it, not more than five minutes could have passed, and they were back again in less than that, for as soon as they had rounded the first bend in the drive, Lobley switched the lights off, headlights and sidelamps too, and Joyce, on his instruction, turned the big Blick cautiously round and drove it back to the stables in the dark.

Then, when the doors had been locked behind them, they switched the lights on once again and this time they all dismounted, Joyce, Lobley and Primrose in the manner ordinary, Corrie and Palmer pushed and pulled after the manner of unimportant merchandise in sacks that travel by train at rates described with a happy optimism by the companies as "owner's risk." There was an air of hurry; Corrie sensed shortage of time. Primrose whistled softly and the man Robson appeared from behind the shed in the middle of the yard.

"Where's Dan?" Primrose asked him sharply.

"He's in the cottage."

"Fetch him here at once, then—you've got to go up— both of you, and this time it won't matter if the passengers do slip so long as it's not too soon."

Robson disappeared, and Lobley and Primrose leaving their victims lying on the ground, wheeled the two motor bicycles out of the shed into the light from the car, where they set them both up on their rests.

Lying on the cold cobbled floor of the stable yard, Corrie suddenly felt that his nerves, which, up to this point had been numbed to normality by the sudden changes in his situation, were now beginning to give. It occurred to him again that unless the gag in his mouth was removed he would not be able to yell when he wanted to, and precarious as his position was, the knowledge seemed to make it worse. He began to make little convulsive movements, but just as he was on the very brink of breakdown, Primrose bent over him, took him roughly by one arm and jerked him to his feet, then remembering that, clothesline bound, he was incapable of walking, put big fat hands under his elbows and carried him across to where the two bicycles stood, as though he were a tailor's dummy.

"You'll be interested," Primrose laughed, as he set Corrie down on his feet.

Corrie, cramped, could barely stand unaided, but the bicycles were not much more than a couple of yards away, and remembering Joyce's injunction, he examined them with an interest keen enough to keep him from collapse. He felt that there was something strange about them. Though he could not immediately locate their peculiarity, he felt sure they were not just ordinary looking motor bicycles. Was it that the wheels were smaller than usual, he wondered, or did they only appear so because he felt a little dizzy and saw them in the horizontal beams of the Blick headlights? The engines, too, seemed queerly placed.

But before he could come to any decision his attention was attracted in another direction. Robson and another man, whom he guessed to be Dan, appeared from the laboratory pushing before them what looked like a complete section of one of the laboratory benches. It was complete

with sinks and taps, and with Bunsen burners and back-
rack, though the last had been emptied of bottles. It moved
forward silently as though mounted on rubber wheels, the
two men pushing it till they brought it to rest close to the
two machines.

And as if this alone was not sufficient to keep Corrie's attention from funk and fear, he could half overhear
the conversation of Primrose and Lobley and Joyce who
stood talking together a few yards from him. They took no
more notice of him than if he were truly a tailor's dummy,
though once he did imagine that Joyce tried to catch his
attention, and that then her glance moved quickly in the
direction of the bicycles.

Next minute Robson and Dan were hurriedly extracting
screws from the top of the laboratory bench, and it seemed
to Corrie that the screw-drivers they worked with revolved
like Catherine "wheels. Now he was feeling really dizzy—
almost light-headed.

Indeed he felt so sick and ill that it was a marvel that he
managed to stand at all, but, as minute followed minute,
some subconscious streak of obstinacy just managed to
maintain him. As a matter of fact the whole business was
over in less than twenty minutes, but so far as Corrie was
concerned it might have been twenty seconds or twenty
years, for the rapid and evidently well-practiced movements of the two men, such scattered fragments of conversation as he could catch between Primrose and the others
by the car, sudden sweat producing spasms of swamping
fear, noises in his own head, queer assorted piecemeal bits
of past and brief blessed interludes when he felt all the
bravery of some deliberate V.C., though collected and reg-
istered in orderly sequence by his senses, were jumbled by
his brain. His brain ran riot. He felt as though his head
had suddenly been equipped with a kaleidoscope in which
some epileptic Einstein in a frenzy took the attributes of

space, courage, sound, cowardice, memory and time, and made them pattern, repeat and change places among the multiplying mirrors at the bottom.

"Are you quite sure Taverner's safe?"

Robson is letting down one side of the bench.

". . . to follow him and lock the door on him as soon as he gets inside."

"You're sure that . . . to be trusted?"

"Besides, his key to the stable doors is useless. I tried it after I bent it."

"Yes, Lobley, I must admit you did that very nicely."

". . . back again here in less than an—"

Joyce and Lobley and Primrose—treble and tenor and base—thin attenuated tones that fade away and boom again, then lose themselves in tantalizing years of empty space.

Twenty-two—twenty-three. Corrie feels impelled to count. He counts the numbers slowly.

It is fitted with shelves and on the shelves are parts of machines painted a peculiar lead color like the bicycle frames themselves.

". . . but, Lobley, it's no use . . . millions . . . damn it . . . hang for them—"

Wings—slotted and shuttered—propellers, two tubular triangular affairs, cylinders that stupidly look like electrolux vacuum cleaners, the ends fitted with discs like the one he found when he buried the rabbit. No, I shall be better again in two ticks. It's the beastly car. One hundred and seven. How quickly Robson works. Poor you, why you're shaking! You'd better sit still for a minute. Lord! but how pretty she looked. I nearly went over that time. Two hundred and seventy-three. Or is it two thousand? You did it very well, darling. That was Primrose calling Joyce a pearl before swine. They're putting the propellers on above the triangular things. That round looking thing

will be a turbot. A thousand and twenty-six and you're not
to yell—you fool with a football in my mouth. A thousand
and twenty-seven. They must have got water in the anesthetic. Perhaps the dispenser knocked a bicycle—knocked
a bicycle—

Whilst Corrie swayed and rambled in a vain attempt
to keep the terror he felt at bay, Robson and Dan did
conjuring tricks with the motor bicycles. Evidently they
had been through it all many times before, and the inter-
locking frames which accommodated many of the parts in
an already completed state, self-locking nuts, and every
facility that dead accurate engineering can give to assembly, rendered the transformation from motor bicycle to
helicopter aeroplane possible in an astonishingly short
space of time. There were two rotary explosion chambers,
and these were suspended immediately below the triangular framework that locked the handle bars to a pin beneath
the saddle. The exhaust from the explosion chambers was
connected to the inlet sides of the turbines. Robson was
just bending down to tighten up one of the short connecting pipes before fixing the wings, which were placed in
position last of all, when Corrie, either by design or accident, fell forward on the top of him.

Robson pitched right into the machine, which went
over sideways off its stand, taking the other one with it.

And the next thing Corrie remembered was Primrose in
a purple passion holding him with both hands by the neck
and shaking him backwards and forwards like the piston of
a high-speed engine. He remembered that, and he remembered trying to yell with the gag in his mouth, and then he
was incapable of remembering or noticing anything whatever, until he found himself seated in a steel bucket that
creaked slowly forward in the moonlight above the top of
Plenders Pit bank.

24
A FLAT CONTRADICTION

Jack Girling may have remembered, indeed he did remember, the time when the shaft of Plenders Pit was sunk in
Plenders Wood, but one bed-ridden old villager remembered navvies lodging in Little Plenders at the time when
the branch railway line to Millingham was laid, and his
great-grandfather could have told of times when the forest stretched unbroken to the Blatchford road, which was
little more than a cart track then, and of the building
of Plenders Priory. And years before that, a bridle path
leaving the Blatchford road where now the Priory gates
are, skirted the ponds beyond Cherry Hay, which did not
exist, crossed the high ground that now accommodates the
colliery sidings and took you out on to the Derby road—
also no more than a cart track then—hard by the hamlet
of Lanby. In those days the moon must have shone on
Robin Hood and Little John, on men who would never see
a pit and rode through the forest on horseback, on out-
laws and friars and robber bands, on villains who carried
fair ladies off and on knights who came to their rescue.
At that time, perhaps on the very spot where the colliery
sidings stand to-day, she may have shone on some gallant
rescuing knight as he held back a silver birch-tree bough
to assist his exhausted skirt-encumbered lady. And time,
it is true, brings its changes, the forest has dwindled to

what is really little more than a collection of good-sized woods struggling for existence in a house-scabbed, pit-sore country; but a few centuries more or less, what odds does it make to the moon? Why, since she shone down on the knight and his lady she has added a fraction only to the total of her journeys round the earth, and now here is George Annesley holding up a coupling chain to enable his Elizabeth, in shorts, but exhausted too, to crawl between two railway trucks.

They had reached the colliery at last.

But they left the bottom of the pit bank sooner than they should have done, and found themselves cut off from the colliery offices and other buildings by acres of truck-filled sidings.

At a colliery, the persistent refusal of "orders," "output" and "trucks" to keep on a decently friendly footing grays managerial hairs, and as this was a period when orders were scarce and output some four shifts short, empties had gathered at Plenders Pit like so many hungry locusts. There were trucks labeled "Plenders" and "Sherwood," trucks labeled "Loco Coal Only," and with queer inappropriate names like "Rose Smith." Annesley and Elizabeth, worn out and silent, must have hobbled past fifty, and, casting shadows of wheels and shadows of chains, long lines of them still loomed ahead.

Annesley called a halt.

"Look here, Elizabeth, we're getting further away. Those are the offices over there. We'd better crawl through them, I think."

He held up one of the coupling chains whilst she stooped underneath it, and having repeated the process some half-dozen times they were relieved to see Inspector Jacobs's car standing in front of what was obviously the office building.

On Friday nights no shift was working. The yard seemed deserted; there was no one about. The office door was standing open, and entering, they found one of Inspector Jacobs's men. He stared at them, as well he might.

"You're in a pretty pickle if I may say so, sir. The inspector was only wondering a few moments ago where you might have got to."

"Where is he?" Annesley asked shortly.

"He's with the manager. Not half ratty too, he is. A nice little goose chase you've sent us all on if I may say so, sir, without offense."

"But haven't you got Mr. Corrie?"

"Mr. Corrie! But that was what I was only just telling you, sir. Mr. Lobley met Mr. Primrose here by appointment. Came straight here from Blatchford, he did, on his way home to go through some papers with Mr. Primrose, the manager. The man in the power house confirms that they were here at seven. Mr. Primrose took Mr. Lobley into the power house to show him something. And Mr. Lobley says as how he was sure that he heard his niece say that Mr. Corrie was going to call on her to-night, and when the inspector rings up the Priory, sure enough he was there all the time. He'd only that minute gone. The inspector's not half ratty and I must say as you've led us all a nice goose—"

"Man, if you don't tell me where they are, I'll see that your name's in all the newspapers to-morrow as the most fat-headed ass in a fat-headed police force. We've just seen one man killed on the pit bank. If they get Mr. Corrie, you'll be to blame. Come now, take me to them at once!"

The constable was impressed. He took them out into the moonlit yard. "They went that way—there—past the headstock. The Inspector asked to see the ropeway, so I expect that that's where they've gone."

They followed the constable's directions, Annesley calling, "Jacobs! Jacobs!" as they limped towards the headstock
down the yard. They passed close to the great straddling
headstock uprights, along the side of a low brick building—outside was a collection of truck wheels and queer
little rollers—and then, just ahead of them, at the side
of a taller building, they saw the back of Lobley's Blick.
Finding it unoccupied, Annesley called Jacobs loudly by
name once again.

"Hallo! Who's that?"

The voice seemed to come from nowhere. They looked
up and down the yard but there was no one to be seen.

"Is that you, Mr. Annesley?"

They spotted him at last. The building near which the
car stood was in the shadow of the moon and the inspector, high up above them, was leaning over the handrail of
a gallery that ran along outside it.

"I say, where's Corrie? We've just seen your man at the
office. It's all lies about his being at the Priory. Where are
Mr. Primrose and Mr. Lobley?"

"Primrose is here, anyhow."

Another head bent over the handrail, and even in the
shadow of the building his attitude looked so aggressive
that Elizabeth tightened her grasp on Annesley's arm.

"You slanderous young devil, I'll have the law on you!
Come along up here and explain what you mean by it."

"I'm not young enough to be put off by blustering of
that description, anyhow, Primrose. Proof is the answer to
slander charges. How do we get up there?"

"There's an outside staircase, twenty yards back, just
round the corner of the building, Mr. Annesley," the
inspector said; "but I'm afraid you've made some awful
blun—"

But Annesley, without waiting for the end of the sentence, Elizabeth still on his arm, limped away to find the

staircase that led to the gallery above them. The turn of events disturbed him. Where was Corrie all this time? Were Primrose and Lobley so sure of themselves that they dared to brazen it out? Or, horrible thought, was it just conceivable that Elizabeth had been mistaken? But the man who had been tipped out of the bucket on to the rocks below—there was no mistake about that. Elizabeth had been right—but it had been the wrong man. She was very quiet. He looked down at her as she hung quietly on his arm.

"Are you all right, dear?" he whispered, as they began to mount the stairs.

They were out of the shadow now. She looked up and he could see how pale she was.

"Y-e-s. Feeling perfectly topping," she answered, shivering against his arm.

Together they limped up the staircase, to find on gaining the gallery, that the Inspector and Primrose were neither of them, there. Voices came to them through an open door. They followed the sound and they were in a long room full of shadows; one side of it was open to the air and the moon cast shadows of steel uprights across the wooden floor; down the center was a row of hanging electric lights, and they made shadows too. It was more like a story-high railway platform than any ordinary room. Half-way down the open side of it there was a colossal funnel-shaped structure built of concrete. Near this, Primrose, Lobley, Inspector Jacobs, and two of his men and a fitter in blue overalls were talking together in a group. As they hurried, as quickly as they could, towards them Annesley recognized the distant hum of an electric motor and revolving gears. He could feel the platform tremble slightly.

Suddenly he realized that they were at the business end of the ropeway along the pit bank top. He was just wondering whether the noise of the motor meant that it was moving again, when a bucket—he had no idea that they

looked so big when you stood close to—came creeping
quietly along the edge of the platform. It passed under the
concrete structure, there was a rattle followed by a dull
rumble and the bucket with its contents slipped away into
the moonlight.

Annesley, too lame to run, almost beside himself with
pain and anger, limped towards the little group.

"Stop it, you devils," he cried, putting a hand roughly
on Primrose's shoulders.

Primrose pushed him angrily away. He stumbled and Lobley just saved him from falling. He winced with the pain
from his leg. He was completely played out, and as sometimes happens at such times, one single idea obsessed him.
Momentarily he forgot Corrie, he forgot Elizabeth, he forgot everything—everything except the buckets on the ropeway. At any cost he felt that the buckets must be stopped.

Elizabeth was by his side again. Lobley was speaking.

". . . seem a little beside yourself. Why, man, what a
state you're in. And Miss Corrie too. There's some silly
mistake somewhere, Miss Corrie. Now, please, both of you
be less melodramatic whilst we find out how it's happened.
Rest on these sacks for a time." He approached Elizabeth
intending to lead her to a pile of empty sacks a few paces
from where they stood.

Elizabeth shrank from him; clung closer to Annesley
who began to recover.

"If you don't give immediate instructions for these
buckets to be stopped, Inspector, I'll stop them myself.
I'll smash the motor. You . . . where's the switch?" Annesley turned to the fitter, who made no response.

"And if you don't immediately escort this young fool to
your car, Inspector, and take him off my colliery premises,
I shall be compelled to have him thrown off," Primrose
growled in a voice that shook with anger.

The inspector looked unhappily from one to the other.

"Really, you know, Mr. Annesley, you do seem to have been mistak—"

Another bucket appeared, crept along the platform edge, filled at the funnel, and passed out of sight. Annesley, full of fear for Corrie, interrupted the inspector.

"But look here, Inspector, Miss Corrie heard these men say that they were going to put her father in one of the buckets and bury him under the tip. She saw her father through the grating in the stable yard. She can't possibly have been mistaken—she found his glasses on the floor. And when you get here, here they both are. They're making a fool of you. If it were not for my damned leg I—"

"My dear Annesley." Lobley interrupted before the Inspector could speak. "I'm trying to make allowances, you're obviously overwrought, but you're talking arrant nonsense. We haven't been near the stables. Professor Taverner will be able to tell you so. We've both been here since seven. The man in the power house was there when we went in and he's told the Inspector as much. Corrie is at the Priory, or rather he was ten minutes ago, enjoying himself with my niece."

"Who says so?" Annesley asked.

"She did—on the telephone," Lobley answered.

"Who spoke to her?"

"I did."

"Oh, you—I thought as much."

"And so did Inspector Jacobs. You'll have to think a little more."

"Did you speak to Mr. Corrie himself, Inspector?"

"No, I did not. But Miss Lobley told me that he had just that minute left. And really, Mr. Annesley, you know, I think we had better close this unfortunate business. You'll find your father safe and sound at home I'm sure, miss," Inspector Jacobs concluded in a kindly voice, turning to Elizabeth.

Furtively, Elizabeth had been searching her scant garments for her father's glasses. She could find them nowhere.

"I should like to see the glasses Miss Corrie says she found when she saw her father through the grating," Primrose asked in his deep voice, noticing her growing discomfiture.

"I can't find them. I did pick them up, Mr. Annesley saw them, but I—I think I must have dropped them."

"I thought as much." Primrose laughed unpleasantly.

Another bucket slipped silently past them.

"Serious accusations of this kind, you know, Mr. Annesley, ought not to be made on conversations heard through gratings between people you couldn't even see. I must ask you to—"

"But I saw Daddy. I know it was Mr. Primrose and Mr. Lobley. Do you think I don't know Mr. Primrose's voice when I hear it?" Elizabeth half sobbed.

"And we actually saw a man tipped out of one of the buckets, and killed," Annesley interjected.

"What man?"

"We don't know who he is. We left him just at the foot of the end tower. It's scandalous that we should stand talking here. I beg you to have the ropeway stopped, Inspector. Why does Mr. Primrose object to having it stopped just for half an hour whilst we make sure? It must be stopped, I tell you. Where's the switch?"

The man in overalls turned inquiringly to Primrose.

"No," Primrose roared. "I'll have no one giving instructions on this plant while I'm here. Inspector, will you please have Mr. Annesley removed, or am I to do the job myself?"

The Inspector looked about him indecisively.

"Did you say you actually saw a man killed by falling out of one of the buckets?"

"*Yes,* I'm telling you," Annesley shouted.

"But why in the name of heaven didn't you say so at once?"

"He's dead. Corrie might still have been alive if you'd done what I asked you to at once. He may be alive yet. Have the motor stopped. Where is the motor? You—go and pull out the switch."

The man in overalls made a move.

"Come back," Primrose roared.

"Go on," Inspector Jacobs ordered sternly. Lobley had happened to take off his hat, and the moonlight shining on his forehead, had shown the Inspector little beads of moisture there. The Inspector waved one of his men to stand by the door that opened on to the gallery.

The man in overalls hesitated.

Inspector Jacobs pulled a pistol out.

The man in overalls obeyed, ran to the end of the platform, pulled out a switch, and the hum of the motor ceased. A bucket appeared at the end of the platform, slowed, and came to rest almost opposite where they were standing.

"You shall hear about this, Inspector," Primrose shouted.

"In my opinion, Primrose, you are entitled to see his search warrant," Lobley suggested quietly.

"You shall—perhaps to-morrow. In the meantime, tell me how many of these buckets there are on the rope."

"I've no idea," Primrose answered shortly.

"Twenty-six, sir." The man in overalls, who had come back from the switch, supplied the information.

The Inspector made a move towards the bucket. "We'll tie a handkerchief to this one and examine them one by one as they come round," he said.

"And kill Corrie in the process—what on earth is the good of doing that," Annesley said angrily.

"It's all no good if you ask me," Lobley said pleasantly. "You heard what my niece said on the telephone."

"And the man on the links—how did he get there?"

"We only have your word for it that he did get there."

They were standing in a little group again, Annesley irritated by the interminable argument but afraid to protest and make more delay. The Inspector only half-convinced—scared lest he should be making a mistake, alive to the importance of the people he was dealing with, Lobley persuasive and pleasant and sure.

Seeing that his words were having an effect on the Inspector, Lobley continued. "Come now, Inspector, don't you think it all rather absurd and far fetched. Mr. Primrose, who after all has the same claim to be believed as Mr. Annesley, has told you that we have never seen Mr. Corrie to-night. I tell you the same."

They were standing in a little excited group round the hesitating Inspector. There was a queer noise just behind them.

They turned as one man.

Corrie, pale as death, was standing in the swaying skip. He was leaning against one of the iron uprights for support.

"It's a bloody, blasted lie," he said, and fell back in the bucket.

25
JIG-SAW COMPLETE—BUT ONE BIT OVER

A fortnight had passed since Corrie's ride in a bucket along the top of Plenders Pit bank. At Cherry Hay there were two convalescent invalids—Corrie, still confined to his bed upstairs, and downstairs, Annesley on the settee in the drawing-room with his damaged leg sticking out stiffly before him.

It was eleven o'clock. Upstairs, the nurse was bathing Corrie.

"Now the body."

"No, nurse. Not the body. The body doesn't like it."

"Yes, the body. The back of the body first."

Corrie turned over with a groan and the nurse got to work on the back of the body. She was to leave them that morning, and he rejoiced in anticipation as she applied the soap.

"Gosh, I'll be glad when you're gone, nurse."

"Patients generally are. It means that they're getting better."

"It means they won't blinking well wash for a week."

"It's the last time I shall wash you at any rate, I'm glad to say."

She sponged the soap off.

"Nursie!"

"Well?"

"Do you notice anything peculiar about my backbone? I'm always meaning to ask the doctor about it, only doctors are all so damned callous."

"It looks all right to me. What's the matter with it?"

"Why, I was looking at it in the looking-glass the other day. You know the dodge—two looking-glasses—'Is the hair short enough at the back, sir?' sort of thing—and—well, it seemed to me, to be all in little pieces. It feels all wibbly too when I run my fingers up and down it. You don't think it's disintegrating, do you?"

The nurse had suffered. She had been "had" so often that now she had not the faintest idea whether she was being "had" or not. She answered him shortly.

"They're vertebrae."

"The devil they are! Is yours in bits like that, as well, nurse?"

"Of course it is."

"But Annesley's isn't. At least it isn't to the same extent. There's a back for you! I had a good look at it when I was beginning to feel worried about mine. To all intents and purposes it's a one-piece backbone. It was seeing his that set me wondering."

"He's got some flesh on him. Not a bag of bones like you are."

"Muscle, nurse, muscle. He wouldn't like you to call it flesh. Now, why don't you wash his back, nursie? He's still got his leg in bandages and so I'm sure you're quite entitled to. You could kneel on it. You could get a pail and floor cloth and one of those mat things with turned up edges maids kneel on, and have a really jolly half-hour."

"You're getting better. I think the doctor'll let you see Sir Victor."

And while, upstairs, the nurse performed her last ablutionary offices, downstairs, Annesley sat with his leg up. The paper had slipped to the floor. He was wondering

about the springs of the old Morris. He imagined it, with a
heavy list to one side, coming down the drive through the
rhododendrons. He hoped that Elizabeth would take the
corners carefully. She had gone into Blatchford to meet
his uncle.

Elizabeth did take the corners with care. The springs of
the Morris withstood the strain. George heard her blowing the horn as she came down the hill through the trees,
heard the front door open, heard her saying, "George is
in here, I'm going up to see Daddy," and then Sir Victor
Grahame stood before him.

"Well, uncle!"

"Well, George, my boy. How's the leg? I like your young
woman. Nice girl. Young, too. No fool. Make you a good
wife. Lucky chap. Congratulate you."

George returned appropriate thanks.

"Nice place this. Pretty. What are you going to do with
the Priory? If only this were Surrey now, you could turn it
into a golfing hotel."

They were still discussing the future of Plenders Priory
and its proprietor when Dr. Butterworth arrived. First he
dealt with Annesley's leg, and then he went upstairs. And
when he came down he told them that if Corrie slept between lunch and tea, Sir Victor could see him afterwards.

Corrie simulated sleep so successfully that at three
o'clock Elizabeth tip-toed out of the room to the sound of
his heavy breathing.

Then, after tea, when she had got him ready for the visit, and had called down the stairs, "Come along," uncle and
nephew went up to the bedroom, Sir Victor making the old
staircase creak, and Annesley having recourse to crutches.

They found Corrie, wearing a Jaeger jacket, propped
up against a pile of pillows. Elizabeth sat on the edge of
the bed. The fire flickered pleasantly. Corrie, who was
used to it, seemed set for convalescence.

"Congratulations on your lucky escape, Mr. Corrie," Sir Victor said, bending over the bed in a heavy attempt at a bedside manner; "and apologies for any share I may have had in the terrible times you've been through."

"If it's any one's fault, it's the fault of that great brainless hulk, Annesley, for letting the Priory to Lobley. I get nearly scuppered and he'll get compensation for the non-completion of his leases."

"I nearly got a broken leg, anyhow," Annesley growled good naturedly.

"Well, tell us all there is to tell us, anyhow, Sir Victor," Corrie continued. "Robson turned informer, I understand, but that—that, and a letter from Joyce is all the news I've had so far. That skew-eyed blasted nurse has—"

He was getting excited.

"This nurse'll send every one out of the room if you don't keep quiet," Elizabeth said, putting a hand over his mouth, and urging Sir Victor to get on with a just perceptible jerk of her well-shaped head.

Sir Victor took the hint.

"Well, Robson has turned informer. They're all being charged with the murder of Palmer as that's the more certain case. Primrose and Lobley will both be hanged without a doubt. Robson and the other chap, Dan, I should guess, will get life sentences. Your sister was undoubtedly murdered, Mr. Corrie, but it was murder by accident. As far as I can make out, Taverner really knew very little about it."

"I'm glad. I like the professor," Elizabeth interrupted; "but he did, you know, he did know something about it. He was always trying to make Marion believe that Daddy was worse than he was. I'm sure he wanted to get him out of the way."

"Yes, he did. He admits it. Lobley and Primrose told him that quite by accident they had hit on a certain steel alloy possessing remarkable qualities, in the laboratories at the Giant works. They gave Taverner the stolen notes which, of course, they had re-written, and they told him that now they had the special steel they were proposing to develop a small petrol turbine. Taverner says that the turbine design was nearly complete when he took over. He says that friend Lobley is a remarkably clever chap, and that he had not the very least suspicion of him. At the time when they approached him, Taverner had been doing some research on low temperature carbonization, and the suggestion was that he should continue with it as a cover for the other. They offered him terms that he couldn't ignore—good cash down and more to follow.

"At first he was inclined to think their secrecy absurd, but then, they showed him your paper, Mr. Corrie, and told him that you were living at Cherry Hay. They told him, too, of your connection with the Magnet people and all that they knew about you. He really did think you were there to filch their secrets. And to confirm his suspicions they found—at least, miss—"

Here Sir Victor looked awkwardly at Corrie and hesitated.

"It's all right, Sir Victor," Corrie said quietly. "I know that her name is Temple, and I know her relationship with Lobley. I've had a letter from her which these tyrannical women only allowed me to read yesterday."

"Yes—well, you see when she found a piece of one of their turbines in your car it naturally confirmed all they had said to the professor. He did want you out of the way. His brother's nursing home, in fact, was his idea. He jokingly suggested too, the holding of a hand covered with phosphorus paint at your window, though he never meant it, and did not know that they had carried his suggestion out. It was Primrose's idea to pull you out of bed in the middle of the night. They intended to leave you in one of the woods. They took both the aeroplanes up, with Robson slung from one of them and Dan from another. They hovered over the house and then let Robson down. Robson and Dan were both provided with shielded flashlights and they had signals to guide them all arranged. It was easy enough for Robson to put his hand in the half-open window, undo the hasp, and slip off his perch on to the window-sill. Then, when he saw Dan outside in his place, he went to your bed to gag you, but he fumbled and lost his head. In the struggle he got hold of you, as he thought, by the throat and rolled all the bedclothes round you to deaden any noise. He picked you up and handed you through the window to Dan, who hung suspended just outside it. Then he got hold of his own rope and flashed the signal to Primrose in the aeroplane above him telling him to rise. Then, Dan, in trying to flash his sign, let you slip. You wriggled just as he moved his arm, he says, and the bedclothes made you difficult to grip. You slipped and fell, and then he heard a door bang in the bedroom. And it wasn't until next morning that they knew it must have been Marion all the time."

There was a moment's silence, Annesley moved uneasily.

"Poor Marion—she always got the worst of everything," Corrie said quietly.

"Yes, but, uncle, surely after it had happened, knowing that they had the helicopters available and remembering that he had suggested frightening Corrie by tapping at the window himself, Taverner must have known that they had had a hand in the murder."

"No, he swears he didn't. He says he did tackle them with it at first. At first he thought they must have been responsible. Then after the inquest—well—he thought differently."

"And how was it that Palmer didn't know Corrie from Lobley?" Annesley asked.

"Palmer had worked in the laboratories at Hendon. Lobley, like a sportsman, has refused to implicate any one. Palmer is dead and we'll never know the facts. But it's easy to imagine them. A bribe to a bottle washer, say—or a charwoman perhaps, to leave a window unlatched. Palmer knew his way about. Probably he had friends on the metallurgical staff at the Little Giant works."

"Joyce—she'll be all right—she won't be sent to prison, will she?" Elizabeth asked.

"No. Neither she nor Taverner."

Corrie moved uneasily.

"She told me a good deal in her letter. She was to have had five thousand pounds if they pulled it off. They very nearly did. It meant more than five thousand to Joyce, though. In her letter she tells me she never dreamed of getting me into real danger—things all went wrong and piled up suddenly on her at the end. She did make assort of half-attempt to save me but she hadn't the pluck for the job. To incur Lobley and Primrose's displeasure meant— no, but I oughtn't to tell you of that. She fooled me properly though, and I swear before God I'll never speak to a girl again—excepting perhaps to Elizabeth here when I want a hot-water bottle filling."

He looked very tired. He patted Elizabeth's hand.

Annesley grunted. He knew his Corrie.

"But she did save you, Mr. Corrie," Sir Victor continued, "I think perhaps you're just a little hard on her. As soon as Lobley and Primrose had made off with you in the car, she ran to the Priory and released Taverner. They had got him safely locked away in an upstairs room. He telephoned to the police station and was told that Jacobs had already gone to Cherry Hay. He telephoned to Cherry Hay and there Mrs. Glegg told him that the Inspector had already set out for the colliery. Then he ran to the lab, broke a window, and short-circuited the main switch. They had got an unusually heavy cable from the power house at the colliery to the lab because of the furnaces and it threw out the overload release on the main panel and stopped the ropeway from working. Professor Taverner saved your life in my opinion."

Corrie shook his head enigmatically.

"You say Joyce saved my life. You say Taverner saved my life. But it was poor Marion who really saved it—yes, she saved me really—she saved me when she got me a job in the Patent Office."

They looked at him with interest. He had slipped a little down the bed. He had turned a little on his side. Elizabeth straightened the bed clothes.

"You see," he continued dreamily, "I remember Primrose trying to shake my head off after I pushed Robson against the helicopter, and the next thing I remember was staring at John Temple's patent skip trip in the moonlight. British patent number one seven nine nine something—dash the number—now I've forgotten it. There had been—objections. My job was looking into objections—" Poor Corrie, he was getting sleepier and sleepier. His head slipped on the pillow as he tried to finish his account. ". . . remember half—strugglin'—holding trigger—being rocked—that chap, Blodly, lying—so told him was a blobly liar—in—"

His sentence tailed off into incoherence. His eyes closed. Elizabeth held a finger up. He was fast asleep.

And after dinner, uncle and nephew went into it all once again. Sir Victor became inquisitive about the night when Marion died, and Annesley repeated the inquest version of events.

"Then what made Bensham so convinced you'd committed perjury, I wonder?" Sir Victor questioned when he had finished.

"I'm dashed if I know," Annesley answered innocently. "But our James James seemed to hold Bensham's opinion."

"Why, what d'you mean?"

"Well, just after the inquest, he demanded a rise in wages. Thirty bob a week he wanted—*and* he got it."

"You—you outrageous gang of abandoned liars," Sir Victor spluttered.

Annesley looked pained.

"I can only refer you to the evidence given on oath. Besides, friend James has suffered a reduction since."

"Do you mean to tell me they haven't sacked him?"

Annesley nodded.

"He's a very nice old man, and they've decided that— well, that he just wanted to better himself a bit."

Sir Victor looked puzzled.

The clock on the mantelpiece told them it was midnight.

"Well then, the only piece of jig-saw left has got James James's wages on it," Sir Victor said, struggling out of his chair. "If you didn't commit perjury, it doesn't fit anywhere. The picture's complete without it."

Annesley chuckled. He went to the door on his crutches. They passed out through it into the hall.

"It seems to me too dashed silly to keep on a servant after he's tried to blackmail you. I know they've dropped his wages again, but it does seem daft to me. I can't understand it. I'm quite in the dark. Don't you think it's a daft thing to do yourself, George?"

"James is marrying Mrs. Glegg," Annesley answered cryptically. He switched off the light as he said it, leaving Sir Victor still in the dark.

MURDER AT GLEN ATHOL

NORMAN LIPPINCOTT

A strange clan—a grotesque dinner party—and violent death in a little Pennsylvania town!

THE DESERT LAKE MYSTERY

KAY CLEAVER STRAHAN
Author of THE DESERT MOON MYSTERY

THE STUDIO MURDER MYSTERY
THE EDINGTONS

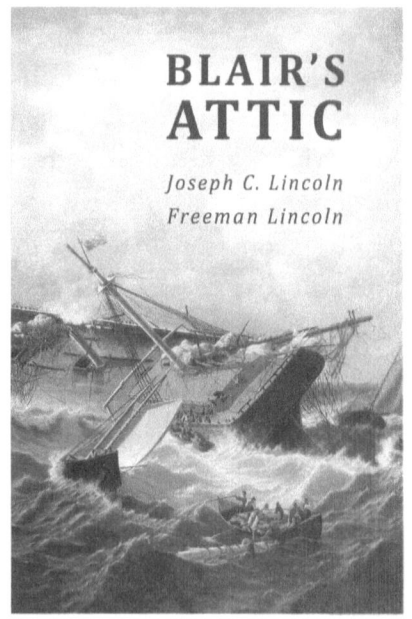

BLAIR'S ATTIC

Joseph C. Lincoln
Freeman Lincoln

COACHWHIP PUBLICATIONS

COACHWHIPBOOKS.COM

THE INCONSISTENT VILLAINS

N. A. TEMPLE-ELLIS

HENRY JAMES FORMAN
THE REMBRANDT
MURDER

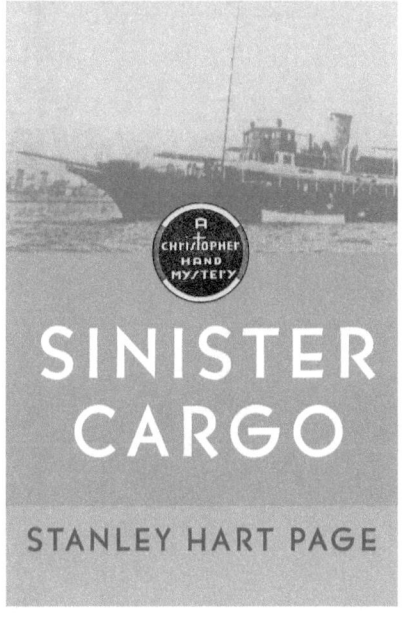

A CHRISTOPHER HAND MYSTERY

SINISTER
CARGO

STANLEY HART PAGE

A CHRISTOPHER HAND MYSTERY

THE
RESURRECTION
MURDER CASE

STANLEY HART PAGE

COACHWHIP PUBLICATIONS

COACHWHIPBOOKS.COM

CLUES OF THE CARIBBEES
being certain original narrations
of Henry Poggioli, Ph.D.
T. S. Stribling

MURDER
IN A WALLED TOWN
KATHERINE WOODS

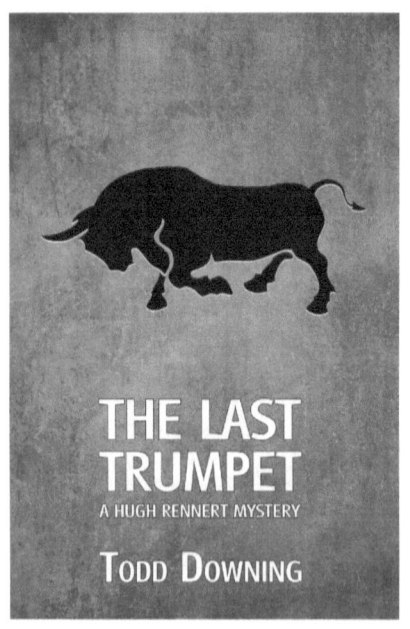

THE LAST
TRUMPET
A HUGH RENNERT MYSTERY

TODD DOWNING

LOUIS F. BOOTH
THE BANK VAULT MYSTERY
BROKERS' END

COACHWHIP PUBLICATIONS

COACHWHIPBOOKS.COM

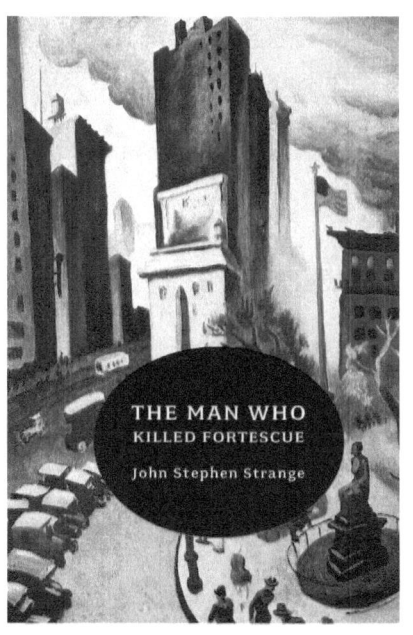

THE MAN WHO
KILLED FORTESCUE

John Stephen Strange

POISON CASE | MURDER CASE
NUMBER 10 | NUMBER 33

FROM THE FILES OF
THE MICHAEL JOYCE AGENCY

LOUIS CORNELL

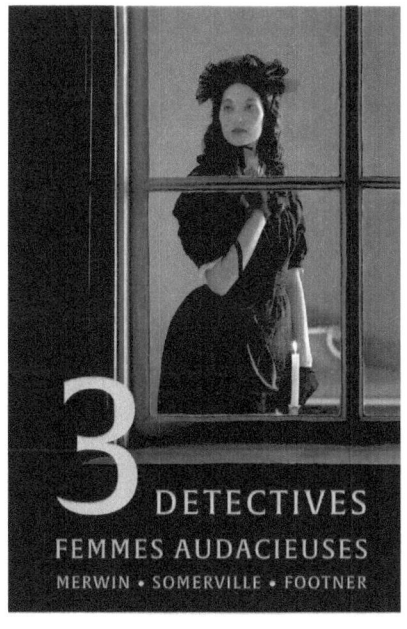

3 DETECTIVES
FEMMES AUDACIEUSES
MERWIN · SOMERVILLE · FOOTNER

MEDORA
FIELD

WHO KILLED
AUNT MAGGIE?

COACHWHIP PUBLICATIONS
COACHWHIPBOOKS.COM

GOLD BULLETS
CHARLES G. BOOTH

The
Jekyll-Hyde
Murder Case
MADELON ST. DENIS

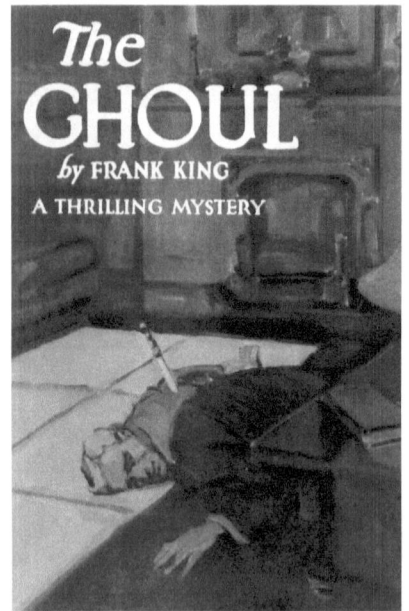

The
GHOUL
by FRANK KING
A THRILLING MYSTERY

THE 5.18
MYSTERY
J. Jefferson Farjeon

COACHWHIP PUBLICATIONS
COACHWHIPBOOKS.COM

MURDER AT SEA

RICHARD CONNELL

GRIMM DEATH

HELEN BURNHAM

THE MURDER OF
LALLA LEE
—
THE TELLTALE
TELEGRAM

THOMAS KINDON

MURDER
IN THE
MOOR

COACHWHIP PUBLICATIONS

COACHWHIPBOOKS.COM

THE SEVEN BLACK
CHESSMEN

John Huntingdon

MURDER
ON THE
BLUFF

ESTHER TYLER

THE 5.18
MYSTERY

J. Jefferson
Farjeon

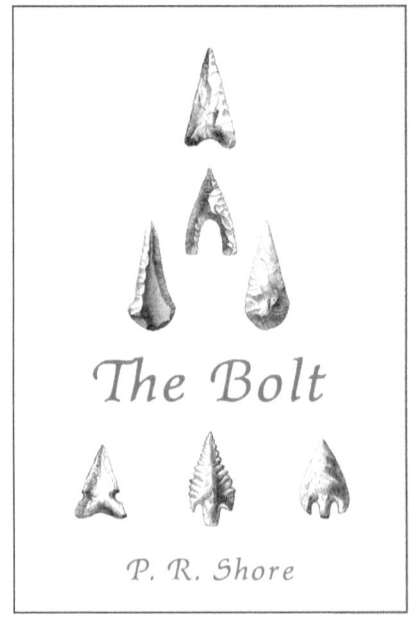

The Bolt

P. R. Shore

COACHWHIP PUBLICATIONS

COACHWHIPBOOKS.COM

HIDE AND GO SEEK
with, GOING TO ST. IVES

COLVER HARRIS

A JUDGE MASSIE MYSTERY

THE CORPSE IS INDIGNANT

DOUGLAS STAPLETON
and HELEN A. CAREY

ODDS-ON MURDER

DANCE

JACK DOLPH

THE MAY DAY MYSTERY

OCTAVUS ROY COHEN

COACHWHIP PUBLICATIONS

COACHWHIPBOOKS.COM

www.ingramcontent.com/pod-product-compliance
Lightning Source LLC
Chambersburg PA
CBHW050358260626
47156CB00003B/787